THE LOST DOOR

Marc Buhmann

To my beautiful wife, Francine. Thank you for all your love and support.

CONTENTS

acknowledgments

Thanks to the following people for their feedback and support: David Moore, Lisa Krause, Bruce Buhmann, Veronica Smith, and especially my wife Francine. I very much appreciate the time and energy you all have invested in reading early drafts of this novel.

prologue

Gray swirled around her. Dying! She had to get out of here, but how? There was no escape, nowhere to go. Was this it? Was this how it was going to end?

The gray grew dark and gloomy. Suffocating. She was scared. It wasn't time! Not yet. Not yet. Not...

And then all was still, and she felt herself starting to ascend. But to where? Would she return home, or would she end up in some vast ether of nothingness? She was in uncharted territory, incomplete. So many questions, so many unknowns. If she had a body she'd be trembling.

In hindsight it had been a mistake to falsify Claire's memory. She'd been only trying to help though, to try and protect her. Having suffered loss herself she didn't want Claire to deal with the pain.

And look where it got you, she told herself again for the—how many times? Too many. *Trapped. Unable to leave.*

That was neither here nor there now. It was done and she would suffer the consequences. She just hoped her judgment all those years ago wouldn't seal the fate of billions. *If you don't return with me life as we know it will cease to exist,* he'd said. She wondered, more now than ever, if that were true? Could her selfishness really have impacted so many?

Not by choice, she told herself. *Your hands were tied.*

Liar, another voice said. *You were scared.*

She recognized that it, too, was her voice, though more mature and knowledgeable with age.

There was nothing she could do but wait to see what would happen.

As she rose she felt Claire slip away. Poor Claire. It was never supposed to be like this. *I'm so sorry, Claire.*

She was ready for the inevitable, scared yet anxious, wondering what would happen.

In a faraway place she heard a tiny voice. She sought it out, searching the blackness. Everything echoed here. Where was it coming from?

She focused and felt a glimmer, like a twinkle from a distant star.

There! Could this be the answer? Would this buy her time?

She swam to it hoping—no, *praying*—that this would work. She needed just a little more time to find him. She needed him to come back, to make her whole.

She was almost to the glimmer, the voice growing in distress. It sounded like…

A thought occurred to her. Would she be damning her the same way she'd damned Claire? Did she want to take that chance?

Yes!

She floated toward the light—toward the voice—and hoped.

* * *

The first thing she heard was the slow rhythmic sounds of a heart rate monitor. *Must have dozed off during one of my shows again,* Claire thought. *Grey's Anatomy? Maybe one of the old ones: ER or Chicago Hope?* She struggled to open her eyes, the tired lids fighting, wanting to stay closed. A brightness pierced the thin opening and she pinched her eyes closed. What the hell? Why so bright? Again she tried, slower, compensating for the light, waiting for the brain splitting brightness to ease.

Her surroundings came into focus and Claire saw she wasn't in her living room. *Murray* was on the television hanging from the wall, the guests thankfully muted. Disinfectant seeped into her nostrils. Claire looked down and saw she was in a bed covered by white sheets. An IV drip fed a clear fluid into her arm. Next to her, sleeping in a chair, was her daughter Emily.

She was in the hospital and having a sense of deja vu. Claire pushed herself up with a grunt. How long had she been here? Her body ached, every muscle throbbing in anger. The last thing she remembered was drinking, something that had become a ritual pretty much every night as of late. It was the only way to help her sleep, to dull the abandonment. Why the memory of her husband running off had resurfaced was a mystery, but it had with a vengeance.

"Mom?" Emily stared at her with radiant blue eyes.

Just like her father's.

"What are you doing here?" Claire rasped. Her throat was raw and on fire.

"You don't remember?" Emily asked, concerned.

"If I did I wouldn't be asking." Claire massaged her throat. "Can I have some water?"

"Sure." Emily stood and took an empty Styrofoam cup with a straw to the sink and filled it, keeping an ever watchful eye on her mother.

"Stop it."

Emily's brow furrowed. "What?"

"Staring. I don't need to be scrutinized."

Emily returned to her mother, handing her the cup. Claire pinched the straw between her lips and sipped at the water, every swallow burning. Claire could tell Emily was holding back, that she wanted to lash out at her.

"How do you feel?" asked Emily.

"Hell. What do you think?" She tried to clear the rawness in her throat. "What happened?"

Tears sprang to the corner of Emily's eyes. "I found you… dead."

"Don't be so dramatic."

Emily lost it. "Don't be so dramatic? You *died!* Do you know how scared I was? If I hadn't found you when I did—" She looked incredulous and hurt. "I was so scared. What would I do if you died?"

Unsure how to respond Claire lifted her arms and Emily fell into them. "I'm alright, sweetie. I'm alright."

"Why, mom? Why?" Emily sobbed into her mother. But Claire didn't respond. Instead, she hugged her daughter, comforting her as she had when she was a child, stroking her hair. After a time Emily's crying subsided and she pulled away, wiping away the tears with the back of her hand. "I'm sorry."

"Don't be. So, what do I need to do to get out of here?"

"Let me go talk to the nurse."

Emily returned a few minutes later with a nurse in tow. She looked at the readings on the monitors and asked, "How are you feeling?"

"Sore."

"As expected."

"When can I leave?"

"The doctor will be in in a little bit to evaluate you."

"That's not an answer," Claire said with a hint of annoyance.

The nurse ignored it. "You can discuss that with him. Can I get you anything?"

"No. I'm fine."

The nurse gave a false pleasant smile and walked away.

Claire looked at Emily. "That wasn't helpful."

"Did you think they'd just let you leave because you asked?"

"Hoping."

"Wishful thinking more like it."

"Same thing." Claire sipped her water and it went down a little easier.

"Well, now that you're up I'm going to go home. The place needs to be cleaned up. But I'll be back in a little bit, okay?"

"It's really not neccess—"

"Yes. It is. I'll be back soon," Emily said and leaned in. There was something in her eyes, something Claire didn't recognize. It was defiant and daring, and it took her aback. It was a look she'd never seen in Emily, as if a stranger was hiding behind those eyes and it scared her.

"I love you," she whispered and wrapped her arms around her. The hug was warm, familiar, and strange.

I
present

one

David Rottingham drove his rented Ford Taurus along the two-lane Highway 49. The window was half down, and he inhaled the fresh pine morning air. He hadn't entered town yet, he could already sense the change. On the surface everything seemed as picturesque as always but beneath was a rot. He wondered if the locals could sense it too.

The last time he'd been in River Bend was twenty years ago at the tender age of sixty-two. His wife Lilly had died a year earlier, and between the time of her passing and his leaving River Bend he'd been lost. His life had revolved around her from the day they had met, only rarely separated more than a day. In many ways his life had ended when hers had, and with no children to help with the grief, for the first year he'd just gone through the motions.

During her final days she'd spoken nonsense, prattling on about shadows, someone named DeMarcus, and something called *turmoore*. He had no idea what that was, went so far as to look it up, but it was a mystery. He just assumed it was the ramblings of a sick woman on the verge of death.

For months he suffered from insomnia after she died. Then one night he'd had a dream. It had been a fall morning, much like this one, when David awoke feeling unburdened. The dream was still fresh in his mind and it was all about Lilly and her life. In it Lilly had encouraged him to move on, to live and learn what he could before his time was up. This is a gift, she had said. Enjoy it; treasure it. For the first time in more than a year he awoke with a purpose. Over the course of the next three months he packed up his belongings, sold his home, and went out in search of whatever it was he was supposed to find.

Now he was back home. The forest gave way to the town, which appeared to have changed little. The bus depot on 6th and Circle and Ed's Service across the street were still open, both desperately waiting for new coats of paint. He didn't see anyone, but he heard the torque wrench echoing out from the open garage door. Down the block was the Green Forest Inn. While he'd never stayed there he knew the woman who ran it, a lovely woman named Shelly Lynch, and had no doubt that the rooms would be quiet and comfortable.

It was still early and David decided to take a small tour of his old town. He had fond memories of the small creek that was the natural border of the town, or more specifically the willow tree that hugged its edge. It was only two blocks away, and assuming it wasn't flooded this year he could stand for a little exercise to stretch his legs.

The first thing he noticed when he got to Willow Creek was the cobblestone bridge. Even after all this time it hadn't been replaced. Seeing it was comforting; it was older than him, old even when he was a boy in the 40's. It looked to have been patched here and there but, overall, had stayed the same.

David parked the Ford, killed the engine, and stepped out. His joints popped as he stretched, a pleasurable feeling. He walked to the side of the bridge and looked down. The creek was at its normal depth and quietly meandered along its rocky bed. He was happy to see the familiar rutted path leading down the embankment. It didn't look slippery and he figured he'd give it a go. What the hell, right? He slid only once, caught himself, and made it safely to the edge of the creek.

David sat, brushed the dirt from his hands, enjoying the quiet. No traffic, no car horns, no one screaming or yelling. River Bend was indeed a little corner of paradise. But even paradise had its shadows, something he knew all too well. The layer outsiders saw was picture perfect but longtime residents—who lived beneath the fold—knew its secrets and were good at pretending they didn't exist.

That was every small community.

David looked along the creek to the willow tree in the distance. It glowed in the sunlight, its thin branches stretching to the ground. He fought the tears that sprang to his eyes but they fell anyway. A bright beautiful day, the wind and creek producing a ballad, birds chirping—

"You alright down there, sir?" said a gruff voice.

David looked up. A man in a wrinkly button-down shirt, sleeves rolled up, and khakis, leaned on the bridge with his hands.

He wiped the tears on his sleeve, waved up. "Fine, fine. Thank you."

"Curiosity got the best of me, I guess. Wanted to make sure you hadn't stalled. You alright to get back up?"

David glanced at the path and shrugged. "I think so."

"Alright then. Have a nice afternoon."

"You too."

The man disappeared from the edge of the bridge. David went back to staring at the creek.

"You sure?" the voice floated.

David looked back up, mildly annoyed at the man leaning on the bridge. "Pretty sure."

"Okay. As long as you're sure. Because I can wait, if you'd like."

"No. That's okay. Thank you for the offer though."

"Sure thing." The man disappeared.

A minute later David heard footsteps. He didn't look up; he knew who it was. The man sat down next to him and offered his hand. "Nick Stavic."

David took it, a firm handshake. "David Rottingham."

"Welcome, David. I know a lot of people in River Bend but don't think I've seen you before. You new here?"

"Visiting. Lived here a long time ago. Thought I'd pay it a visit before I couldn't anymore."

"Explains the out of state plates. How long ago, if you don't mind me asking?"

David shrugged. "Twenty or so years. I decided it was time to see the world."

"Retirement gift to yourself?"

"Something like that."

"See some good sites?"

"Many."

"I've never been much of a world traveler myself. I was raised in Chicago."

"Chicago? You're a long ways from there. Why the move?"

"Too big. I was a cop and saw a lot of crazy shit, pardon my language. Decided one day I'd had enough. Took a road trip and stumbled upon this corner of the north woods. That's the short version."

"Why River Bend?"

"I'm still trying to figure that out," Stavic said with a grin.

David took his meaning. "Sort of the same reason I'm back. My wife passed, part of the reason I decided to leave, but the last several months I've been thinking of this place. Not sure if it's my time yet, but my wife is buried here. Figured that when I go I'd like to be near her."

"Where you staying?"

"Green Forest. Can you tell me... does Shelly Lynch still run it?"

"Shelly? No. She retired a while back. Her daughter runs it now. Amber."

David remembered Amber. Cute little girl with ponytails back in the day.

"Well, David," Stavic said as he stood. "I have to be getting to work. You sure you're okay to get back up there? I don't mind helping."

The moment gone, the emotions fading, David stood. "Sure. I'd appreciate it."

* * *

Claire sat slouched in the passenger seat staring vacantly out the window as Emily drove. The stranger she saw in those eyes while at the hospital was absent. It must have been her imagination. The day was clear with only a few clouds hovering in the sky. It looked warm out, but the autumn winds made a light jacket a necessity.

Her doctor had forced her to stay overnight—just as a precaution, he'd said—and with some coaxing from Emily she'd begrudgingly agreed. She wouldn't admit it to them but it was the right call. She didn't dream, and she did feel better, the soreness she'd felt yesterday had subsided substantially.

Emily had tried talking to her about what had happened. She knew Emily was convinced it had been intentional, regardless of how much she denied it, and was tired of going in circles. Finally, she just decided to stay quiet.

"Take a left at the light," she instructed Emily.

"Why?"

"I just want to." There was more to it than that, but she'd never admit it to Emily. What she was really doing was avoiding a conversation she knew was awaiting her when they got home.

Claire had begun to have trouble sleeping the last few weeks. Dreams of her adulterating husband plagued her, some good but mostly bad. She relived his betrayal, the night she confronted him, the accident, his abandonment… Not wanting to continually see his face she'd started to drink.

When she and her ex-husband had learned she was pregnant they thought it best to move away from the congestion and crime of a big city. Claire had lived in River Bend for several years as a child and had fond memories of it and the nice couple who treated her like their own. It was home once, why not again? They spent the weekend visiting and exploring, and by the end that was all they needed and agreed this is where they should settle down.

Emily turned left down 6th Street. Small shops passed by, many of which had stayed within families for generations. "Where are we going?"

"I don't know."

Claire sensed Emily's glance and ignored it. She stared out the window as the town fell behind giving way to golden fields of wheat and browning corn stalks.

Claire had acquaintances but no one she was close to. Moving around a lot as a child had taught her becoming attached to anyone was just cause for heartache. Then Devon had come into her life, and she thought she'd finally be able to settle down, to have those attachments everyone else around her took for granted.

How silly she'd been, trusting him.

One thing her parents instilled in her was self-reliance, and she'd managed to secure a job within a few months of Devon leaving. At least he'd left her the house.

She reclined her seat and closed her eyes, feeling the warmth of the sun caress her face. *Just a few minutes,* she told herself. *Just a few minutes to rest my eyes.* Claire was asleep seconds later.

* * *

Willem rode shotgun while his partner yammered on about…
what? Willem couldn't say. He'd tuned out five blocks back when
Justin started talking about his last night's hookup. They were headed
back to the firehouse after transporting an elderly woman who'd
suffered a heart attack to the hospital.

Either Justin hadn't realized he'd stopped listening or didn't
care, but he was content telling his story to no one. It wasn't that
Willem wasn't interested in the stories of sex and drugs—he was—
but something felt *off*. There was something in the air, and he was on
edge.

Justin was nearly three decades younger than Willem's sixty-
four, part of the reason Willem found his stories interesting. Willem
had never married and never had children. He got to live a young
man's life vicariously through Justin. While he was sure Justin would
have preferred someone closer to his age for a partner, Willem felt
younger because of it.

While most men in their thirties were trying to settle down,
Justin was the opposite. He showed no signs or interest in slowing
down his nightlife style. He loved women—apparently all types from
the stories told—and the idea of settling down with just one scared
the hell out of him. And why not? He was a handsome man, fit, why
not milk it as long as possible? Willem, on the other hand, had always
wanted a woman to fall in love with, someone to have children with,
grow old with. It seemed that was not in the cards. They say there is
someone out there for everyone, but if true then where was his
someone? The world was a damn big place, and Willem was not a
world traveler, so if she was sitting in a Siberian tavern somewhere he
was screwed.

Justin slowed to a stop as the light went from yellow to red. He
was still talking about last night when a white pickup truck drove
past.

"—she was using her… *holy shit!*" Justin bellowed. Willem
watched the pickup swerve, narrowly missing a man crossing the
road. A sedan in the right of way slammed on the brakes, the woman
behind the wheel laying on the horn. The truck swerved again. It was
almost through the intersection when a city bus plowed into it, the
impact a thunderclap of twisting metal and breaking glass. The
pickup spun twice and flipped to its side before coming to a stop at
the edge of the sidewalk. A stuck car horn blared.

Willem grabbed the CB and called dispatch. Justin turned the
van emergency lights on and drove the short distance to the accident.

Willem hopped out before the ambulance came to a full stop. He glanced at the bus as he ran past. Through the spider web of glass he saw the bus driver talking to the passengers; no one on the bus appeared to be injured. He raced past the sedan, the horrified driver had a hand to her forehead as she stood.

"You alright?" asked Willem as he passed. She nodded.

The driver of the pickup came into view as Willem rounded the crumpled front of the truck. The airbag had done little to stop the unbuckled man from being tossed about the cab. He now lay in a tangled mess on the passenger side, unconscious or dead Willem could not say, arm pinned beneath the truck through the open window. Willem banged on the windshield.

"Hey! Sir!" he yelled over the blaring horn. "Wakeup! Sir?" The driver, a man in his mid-twenties, didn't stir.

A pedestrian in a gray suit ran up. "Is he alright? Do you need help?"

Willem gave the guy a cursory glance as Justin approached. "Please stand back, sir," was all he managed before Justin crouched next to him, dropping a medical bag. To his partner, he said, "Unconscious. Looks like he's pinned."

"We won't be able to do anything if we don't get this truck flipped," replied Justin.

Willem looked at the man in the suit who was now on his cell. "Hey! Come here!"

"Gotta go!" Suit jammed his phone in his pocket and ran over.

"What's your name?"

"Jim." His voice quivered with adrenaline.

"We have to flip the truck Jim. Can you help?"

"Flip? How?" He looked tense and on edge.

"We push it."

Willem stepped to the middle, Justin the hood, Suit took the trunk. Willem looked to each man. "Okay. On the count of three." He paused, readying himself against the car, "One." He glanced at Justin who was watching him intently. "Two." Justin gave him a nod. *"Three!"*

The three men pushed into the pickup, straining their shoulders, putting everything they had into it flipping it. Two men who had been on the sidelines gawking ran over, throwing their weight into the truck too.

The truck tilted. Jim's penny-loafered foot slipped on the pavement, but he regained his balance quickly. "Keep pushing!"

Justin grunted through gritted teeth. The car began to tilt as more pedestrians collected like insects to a light. "We're almost there!"

The unconscious man's unnaturally twisted arm dangled from the window opening. It was covered in blood from a large cut across the bicep. Drops of crimson hit the pavement as distant sirens echoed through the air.

Gravity took over and pulled the car down with a solid *thunk*, broken glass falling away. Willem reached through the window and felt for a pulse as Justin opened his bag. For a few short seconds Willem feared the man dead, but then he felt a weak but stable heartbeat. "Got a pulse," he told his partner who was putting a stethoscope in his ears.

Justin pressed the stethoscope bell to the man's chest. Seconds ticked by. "Respiration is good," he said as he draped the stethoscope over his neck. Justin dug in his bag and pulled out gauze and handed it to Willem then raced back to the ambulance.

Willem dressed the laceration in the man's bicep, the red spreading outward. He made it as tight as he could and taped it down.

"Anything else we can do?" asked Suit.

Willem glanced at him and gave him a short smile. "No. Thanks for your help, sir. Now please stand back." The man did as told and was back on his phone. Sirens were fast approaching; the other emergency responders would be there in a minute.

The next few minutes were a whirlwind of activity. A police car arrived as Willem and Justin were pulling the man from the car. The officer began asking questions and taking notes. Two fire trucks arrived, another police car, a second ambulance. The woman in the sedan was giving a statement to another officer while they loaded the unconscious man into the back of their ambulance. The bus riders were filing off of it, some bruised but no one seriously injured.

Willem and Justin loaded the man into the back of the ambulance. Willem stayed in the back while Justin took the driver's seat. Seconds later they raced off to Mercy Hospital, sirens blaring.

* * *

After leaving David Rottingham by his car, Stavic drove to the two-story brown brick station. He parked in the back and walked in through its entrance. He grabbed a coffee in the kitchen before going to his desk, on which sat a manila folder. He sat, took a sip of the too strong coffee, and flipped it open. Perfect, and just what he needed to counteract the sleepless night he'd had. Three pages from the coroner were inside, the preliminary results for a John Doe.

The stripped and eviscerated body had been found near the Fox River by two boys on ATV's. They'd run prints and taken a mold of his teeth for dental records, but so far nothing had come up. The man, who looked to be in his late thirties, was a mystery.

Stavic scanned the coroner's report. Stavic couldn't imagine the excruciating pain this poor soul felt as he'd been gutted alive. When working in Chicago as a cop he'd never experienced something like this.

Kinney rapped his knuckle on Stavic's desk. "Good. Wanted to make sure you got that."

Stavic held it up. "Nothing that helps us though."

"No," agreed the slightly heavyset, balding, and generally very serious man.

Stavic didn't think he'd ever seen him tell a joke, let alone crack a smile. His shirts were fastidiously pressed, he was always clean shaven, and he held himself straight and tall. He'd become sheriff of River Bend three decades earlier when his predecessor retired. Stavic was indifferent to the man. "I'm thinking I might take a ride back to the scene, see if there's anything we missed."

"Don't bother. The area was scoured there's nothing there."

"Never say never." Stavic lifted the folder up, shook it. "Has his car been found? Any idea how he got there?"

Kinney's lip curled.

Dear God. Is he smiling?

"That's why you're going on a little boating expedition."

That gave him pause. "Me?"

"I'm thinking that the body may have been dumped elsewhere and washed downriver. I've asked Harold to take you on a little river tour."

Stavic's heart skipped a beat. He hated large bodies of water and tried to stay as far from them as possible. Sitting in a small boat on a river terrified him.

"But sir—"

Kinney held up a hand. "I know but, you know, orders. I give them." As he walked past he patted Stavic on the shoulder. "Harold's expecting you. Go to his shop and coordinate a time to do this, sooner rather than later. You know why?"

"Orders," Stavic said glumly.

Kinney looked back, made a gun with his finger and fired it at Stavic with a click of his tongue. "Bingo."

* * *

"You disposed of the body?" DeMarcus asked.

"As instructed," said his associate with a broken nose.

DeMarcus nodded in appreciation. Good. This man—whom he'd known only a few short weeks—was becoming an exceptional asset. So easy to manipulate and control.

"How's your nose?"

"Tender, but I'll be fine."

They'd both been through a beating a few weeks ago. DeMarcus was especially lucky Paul had come to when he did or he might have been killed. He owed him for that.

He wasn't sure what had brought Melson Waters snooping around, but it was troubling. The last time he'd seen the man was months ago running for the Wispy Mountains. As far as he knew there was only one way in and it was through this place, so either Melson had sneaked past somehow—unlikely—or there was another door. Regardless, and even more troubling, was how he got past the security entrusted to protect the entrance to this place. His best men were supposed to be guarding it.

DeMarcus closed his eyes. He must be getting stronger. In the weeks after his confrontation with Lilly and that good for nothing husband of hers, he was no longer able to sense her. But now... now he could. Barely. It was still a good sign though, one that eased his mind. If he'd lost her then he was stuck, and the last place he wanted to be was here. He had a world to get back to, one to rule, and he needed her.

It was supposed to have been so simple, if only her parents had followed through with their agreement... But that was neither here nor there at this point. They'd been punished for hiding her away and broken to reveal her whereabouts.

It was a genius move on their part, sending her to the *belere*. He never would have guessed they would damn their only daughter to the shadow realm.

Unless they have a way to bring her back.

That logic was the only reason he came on his own instead of sending someone. No parent would sacrifice their child, so there had to be some way for her to return. When he'd confronted her parents they'd given it up easily enough. Of course they did, considering the amount of pain they were in.

"Paul," DeMarcus called. The large man stood and approached. He'd been sitting with his back to the opposite wooden wall. "I'm beginning to sense her again, and I need you to go find her."

"You can't pinpoint her like last time?" said the man in the red trucker hat.

"Not yet… still too weak. In time, perhaps, but the sooner we find her the sooner we can leave."

"And you're still convinced she's the way?"

"Oh yes. Of that I'm certain. It's been a few weeks so hopefully they're guard is down. Start at their home. Do whatever it takes, but bring her to me."

"And her husband?"

"I don't care what happens to him at this point."

Paul nodded and walked from the room.

Marc Buhmann

two

Willem sat at the kitchen table, a piece of uneaten toast on a plate in front of him, and a steaming mug of black coffee between his hands. He was staring out the window watching the birds at the feeder dig out the seeds they wanted while scattering those they didn't on the ground. Later today he'd have to go and sweep up the mess.

He had tossed and turned all night, memories of his childhood dancing just out of reach. He remembered little snippets here and there, but much was lost to him. He remembered the big events but the smaller more intimate details remained behind an opaque veil.

Sam.

It had been so long since he'd thought about his baby brother, and now that he tried he had trouble remembering what he looked like. Sam had died at the age of eight when he'd fallen from Willow Creek Bridge. While he couldn't remember his brother's face the memory of his broken body, blood washing away down the creek, was vivid.

I should have protected him. I should have done something.

18

Yet there was nothing to be done. He could have stayed with his brother or left him to run for help. At that time River Bend wasn't bordering the creek, and it would have required at least five minutes at a heavy sprint to get to the nearest shop, then who knows how long to get back.

You could have done more.

Ever since then he'd kept telling himself he could have, but what? He was ten. There were no cell phones back then, no way of instant access like there was today. Had it happened today he was sure his brother would have survived, but in 1960 things were different.

Thinking of Sam brought up the memory of Elliott, his older brother, who was five years his senior. They'd had a falling out and had stopped talking. Whatever the fight was—he couldn't remember over what—it had been bad. They'd tried to reconcile once but that hadn't gone well, and that was the last time they spoke. He wondered how Elliott and his family were. Maybe he should call, but would he want to talk to him? They said blood was thicker than water but in his opinion memories were thicker still.

Willem glanced at the phone, debate raging. What's the worst that could happen? At least he would have tried.

Willem glanced at the clock. 7:20. The best way to avoid things you didn't want to do was do something else. He trashed his toast and went off to get ready for work.

* * *

Stavic stepped into the bait shop. Harold glanced up before going back to a fish he was cleaning on the counter. "Morning, Deputy. To what do I owe the pleasure?"

Harold was an old timer. He'd lived in River Bend all his life, and even at seventy had no plans for retirement. *If I did that people would be forced to go to Coops in Andersonville, and I'll be damned if I let that happen,* he was often overheard saying. Harold and Cooper were longtime rivals as well as cousins. They used to be close, but at some point in the last five decades something happened and no one knew what. Most figured even they didn't remember.

"Sheriff told me you were expecting me."

"Ah yes! River tour. Didn't tell me why though."

"We're in need of an expert."

"Expert, eh? What is it our esteemed sheriff thinks I'm an expert of?"

"We need someone who knows the waters."

"I just like to fish. Ain't no expert."

"Stop being modest."

"Pfft!" Harold said with a wave of a hand.

"You know that death we're investigating?"

"Sure. Not often we have a murder in town."

"Is that the word on the street, that he was murdered?"

"That it is."

Stavic pulled out a map of the area, unfolded it and lay it on the counter. His finger touched the town then traveled along the blue curvy line that signified Willow Creek where it merged with another blue line and tapped it. "This is where his body was found. No easy access—only an ATV trail a quarter mile away—so we're trying to figure out how he got there."

"Could have walked."

"Possible. It's also possible his body was dumped there. The only way I see how that could be was by boat. Now, I know the creek just outside of town is pretty shallow. A boat would just run aground."

"Canoe or kayak might be able to do it, maybe, but nothing with a motor, that's for sure."

"Right, so I'm wondering where the creek deepens enough that something motorized wouldn't run aground."

Harold rotated the map and scanned it. "Easy." He jabbed a finger where a second blue line intersected. "Fox River is the main waterway. Willow feeds into it. I'm guessing the body floated downriver."

That would definitely expand their search area. "Any way of getting a boat in there?"

"Oh sure. Plenty of landings along the river. Andersonville has a public landing people use, but it's right downtown."

"Anyplace else?"

"There's a landing here," he said, pointing. "That's off the beaten path a bit. Someone could have put a boat in there. And one here." Another point. "Couple folks also live right on the water, too."

"Anyplace else?"

Harold thought about it then shook his head. "Nah. That's it I'm afraid."

Stavic turned the map and marked where Harold pointed with a pen. Andersonville was too open, and the other was pretty far downriver. That left the one just south of where Willow Creek met the Fox.

"When are you available to give me that tour?"

"Tomorrow. 10-ish?"

"Sounds like a plan."

"Where you want to meet?"

Stavic stared at the map, then tapped the landing where Willow Creek and the Fox River met. "Here."

"Think you can find it okay?"

Stavic picked up the map, folded it. "Not a problem at all. See you tomorrow."

* * *

David stood over his wife's grave, a bouquet of lilies in hand. Birds chirped as the wind sang through the trees. Next to her headstone was one for him, though his was missing one crucial bit of information: the date of his death. After Lilly had been buried he'd purchased a matching headstone for himself. It was pre-engraved and placed next to hers.

He'd missed her every day since her passing, though standing here now was harder than he'd expected. They said time heals all wounds but that wasn't the case for him. Maybe it had at one point, but not today… not now. He missed Lilly more than ever.

I'll be with you soon enough my love, he thought as he set the flowers at the foot of her headstone.

When Lilly passed his grief was palpable. He'd barely slept those first few months, exhaustion becoming the only cure for insomnia. Yet even in those fitful nights he'd half-wake crying, sure it was all a dream and that Lilly would be sleeping next to him. He'd reach out to only find cold lonely sheets and reality would tumble back.

It wasn't until Lilly started visiting him in his dreams that his grief began to subside. He'd try to talk to her but he had no voice, so they would enjoy each other's company in silence. This went on for weeks, the two of them sitting on a grassy hill watching the sun rise, or beneath the willow tree as the creek trickled by.

It was during one such memory, this one a walk through the woods on an autumn day, that Lilly finally spoke. *When it's time, return,* she'd said. *Until then go out and enjoy the world.* They'd crested a hill and

21

she'd stopped to look at a cabin below. *Turmoore*, she'd said, and held up her necklace. *You will need this,* and placed it in his hand. He'd woken feeling calm and relieved, knowing Lilly wanted him to move on. He'd sold his house, packed up a few belongings he wanted to keep, and went out into the world.

Over the years one word Lilly had spoken continued to intrigue David: *turmoore*. He knew there was something crucial about the word he was missing but couldn't remember what, the meaning hidden in shadows. He began to research it, pouring over books and newspapers and searched the web, but he only gleaned tiny bits of information, very little that made sense. What he could gather alluded to something mysterious and terrifying and wonderful. It was a concept, a place, a thing—a convolution of all these and more depending on his source of the day. It made his head spin.

He'd spent several more years traveling Europe hoping to discover the secret that was *turmoore*, hoping he could solve the mystery before his time came. Then dreams of Lilly returned and with her his insomnia. Memories of past events that hadn't happened, yet seemed so real, swirled around in a cacophony of chaos, forgotten faces materialized.

Claire.

He saw her as the little girl he once knew and as the woman she was now.

Why are you showing her to me, Lilly? But no answer came. First Lilly and then Claire. David didn't believe in coincidence and knew it was time to return home.

We're born, we live, we die, he thought as a sadness crept through him. Sometimes it felt so pointless—it was hard not to—but when he started to feel down all he had to do was think of Lilly and the time they'd spent together. He wasn't sure if there was an afterlife, but he'd be overjoyed to be reunited with her. He'd felt lost and alone without her, but now he was beginning to feel a warmth within him.

Love.

David smiled to himself. "Thank you," he said. He took his time standing and made his way to the street. He looked towards the sun feeling it on his skin. Fallen leaves blew across the ground, and he breathed in deeply enjoying the smell of decaying leaves.

* * *

Willem and Justin sat at a booth in Manny's Diner having their usual, a BLT for Willem and a bacon cheese burger for Justin. Manny's still made their sodas like in the old days, mixing flavored syrup with cola. Willem favored the cherry. They were halfway through their lunch.

"Something is on your mind, Willem," Justin was saying. "I can tell." He tapped the side of his nose with his index finger. "Spill."

"Just didn't sleep well is all. It's nothing."

"Bullshit. Something is troubling you. I'm always telling you stuff—"

"Voluntarily."

"Yes, but I share. Something you rarely do. In fact, come to think of it, I don't know much of anything about you. How long we been working together?"

"Three years.

"Three *glorious* years, and all I know is that you've never married and you like old TV shows."

"I've shared more than that."

"Like?"

"Like…" Willem delayed answering by taking a bite of his BLT. Talking around a mouthful of food he said, "I'm 64."

"Hurray!" he cheered, holding up his hands in mocking jubilation. "Something I didn't know!" He put his hands down. "But seriously, what gives? People normally like talking about themselves. Why not you?"

Willem shrugged.

"How very noncommittal."

"What do you want me to say?"

Justin wiped the corner of his mouth, pushed his plate to the side, and leaned in. "Tell me something. Anything. Has to be about you though. Something I *don't* know."

"Anything?"

"Anything."

Willem sipped his cherry coke.

"We are not leaving here until you give something," Justin said, jabbing the table.

"Okay…" He picked up a fry and, right before taking a bite, said, "I'm a very private person."

"You're… you…" Justin's face turned red.

"You said share anything."

"Share anything I didn't know! I can put two-and-two together."

"You may have assumed, but it's nothing I've ever told you."

Justin leaned back, crossed his arms, almost a pout. "You're a piece of work. When was the last time you went out?"

"We're out right now."

"You know what I mean."

He leaned back, sighed. When was the last time he'd gone out? He couldn't remember.

"As long as I've known you you've never gone on vacation. When was the last one? Where?"

Willem didn't like vacations, preferred to stay right where he was. He was happy and content with that. "Never been on vacation."

"Why?"

"Don't see the point."

"You don't get burned out at work?"

"No."

"You don't want to see something new?"

"No."

"When did you last see a movie?"

"When it's on the TV."

"A play?"

"No."

Justin let off a throaty growl. "I give up! You want to live as a mystery? Fine. But know that when you die that's what you'll be. A mystery."

"And I'm content with that. I help people every day, and when I die I'll know I have made a difference. I did what I was put on this earth to do, and even if people don't know me by name or remember my face, I'm fine knowing I've made a difference."

Willem finished his BLT and drink, Justin staring at him.

"Ready?" he asked.

Justin grabbed the bill with a sigh. "Whatever. One of these days I'll get to know the real you."

"It'll be a letdown because what you see is what you get."

"You're an enigma, Willem."

"What do I owe you?"

Justin's color had returned to normal and he smiled as he stood, though he was obviously still annoyed. "My treat."

Willem watched Justin walk to the register to pay, dug into his wallet and fished out a couple of fives. Least he could do was leave the tip. He dropped the bills on the table.

An enigma? He really didn't think so—there was no mystery about him. He just didn't like to talk about himself or his past. What was the big deal?

The past is the past, and it wasn't worth revisiting.

* * *

"You did good," DeMarcus said to Paul. "Wise to bring him to me."

The man in the red hat nodded in appreciation.

DeMarcus turned his attention to the old bruised man who was tied to a straight-back wooden chair. First Melson Waters and now Patrick Deshanal, both part of the Shaw's security detail.

"Good to see you again," he said cheerfully enough. "Though I must admit I'm a bit perplexed as to you being here. The last I heard you'd been killed at Joshua Bay. Care to explain?"

No response, just an icy stare.

DeMarcus sighed. "You can make it easy on yourself by cooperating but, really, the choice is yours." He took a few steps and crouched so he was eye-to-eye with Patrick. "How did you get here? What were you doing at Lilly's home?"

Patrick eyes blazed.

"I'm giving you the opportunity to survive. I'm really not the monster the Shaw's made me out to be, but I will do what is necessary to ensure a fair and just existence for us. So, one last time, what were you doing at her home?"

"Do what you must," Patrick said, staring him down defiantly.

DeMarcus shook his head and sighed. "Let's start with something simpler. Where did you enter? Was it here? Somewhere else?"

Patrick didn't answer.

"What are you doing here? What did you hope to gain?"

Nothing.

"How did you know to look here? Did you sense her too? Did you find her?"

Silence.

"How many more have come through?"

When Patrick said nothing DeMarcus sighed, looked at Paul, and nodded. "Okay," he said, looking back. "Let's start from the beginning."

The man in the red trucker cap walked up behind Patrick.

* * *

Claire lay in bed, eyes closed. She'd almost fallen asleep when she heard the knock on the front door. She thought about going downstairs to see who it was, but the medication she'd taken made her drowsy, so she decided to stay put. Distant voices floated to her, though what they said she didn't know. Probably talking about her.

Sometime later the front door opened and closed again, followed by the creaking of stairs. Her bedroom door opened. Emily peeked in and, seeing Claire awake, her expression flashed disappointment before she smiled sadly. "I thought you'd be asleep."

"I almost was. Who was at the door?"

Emily hesitated. "Jessica."

Jessica was a friend of Emily's. The voice had sounded male, but because of a combination of being drowsy and the voices being muffled she couldn't be sure.

"Can I get you anything?" Emily asked.

Claire shook her head. "I'm fine."

"You should get some rest," she said as she sat on the edge of the bed. She took her hand in hers and gave it a gentle squeeze. "What happened, mom? What really happened?"

Claire looked down at her hand enveloped in Emily's. She'd known it was only a matter of time before Emily would want to have this conversation. "Can this wait? I *am* tired. The pills you know—"

"No, I think we should have it now."

"Fine. What do you want to know?"

"Why would you try and—"

"I told you I didn't try to kill myself."

"What then? Because that sure as hell is what it looked like. The mix of pills and alcohol... Do you know that you almost died?"

"I haven't been sleeping well lately, so my doctor prescribed me something. I must have forgotten I'd taken them, had a drink, took the pills again... it's nothing. Just a mistake."

"Is that what you call it? A mistake? Mom—"

"What else do you want me to say?"

Emily bit her lower lip, a telltale sign she had something to say.

"What?" Claire asked.

"Your job, mom. I know you lost it."

Claire's mouth dropped open, shocked Emily knew. "How?"

"I called to let them know you wouldn't be in and they told me. Why were you fired?"

Claire clenched her teeth. "Didn't they tell you?"

"They said I should ask you."

It had been a spiral effect. She'd shown up to work late a couple times smelling of booze, had been warned, and she hadn't followed through when she said it wouldn't happen again. When her boss had told her she was being let go she'd broken down and cried. *Please!* she'd begged. *Just one more chance!* He hadn't been phased. On the way home she'd picked up a fresh bottle of whiskey.

Claire looked down, ashamed. "You wouldn't understand."

"I'd like to. Really, I would." She hesitated a moment. "Was— was it something I did? Was it because of me?"

Claire looked up and saw the hurt in Emily's eyes, and her anger and annoyance melted to grief. "No sweetie. No. Of course not." She reached out and hugged her daughter. They sat like that for a while, a slow rhythmic rock, enjoying the comfort of each other. Claire hoped that was enough for Emily, at least for now.

"You're through, right? No more drinking?" When Claire didn't respond Emily pulled back. "Say you're done. For me."

She nodded, though she knew it was easier said than done. If it meant ending this weighty conversation—one she was too tired to have in any case—she'd agree.

Emily looked satisfied and wiped at her cheek. "Good."

"What about you?" Claire wanted to know.

"I'll be okay. Now that you're home…"

"I'm fine. Really. I don't need you taking care of me like this. You have school to think about. And college. It's really not a big deal."

"You keep saying that, but it *was* a big deal. At least to me."

"You don't trust me."

"In all honesty?" Emily shook her head. "No. I don't."

"Emily—"

"Just… stop." With that Emily stood and walked to the door. "Now get some rest." She gave a small smile and shut the door.

* * *

It had taken some time, but Patrick ultimately caved. They always did. DeMarcus knew what would break a person, a combination of physical and mental abuse. Sometimes only a few hours were needed, other times it was days or weeks or months, but in the end the person would spill what they knew.

Turns out another doorway was found that opened here in the shadow realm near a building in the woods. He didn't know its name but it looked like a communal place where people socialized. When he was a little stronger he was going to go and investigate this place.

What are you doing here? he'd asked.

To find Lilly. To bring her back.

And did you find her?

No. Just an old man.

How did you know where to look?

Sensed her.

On and on he asked his questions, and Patrick answered them until he began to sob, begging for the torture to stop. DeMarcus just shook his head. *No… you had your chance.* And the torture continued until Patrick was no more.

He didn't gain a whole lot of insight, yet knowing there was at least another doorway bothered him. Who knew how many more of Shaw's supporters would come through? And why was the essence of Lilly coming off some old man? That didn't make any sense. DeMarcus was going to have to pay him a visit.

He wasn't thrilled about traversing in the shadow realm but it was a necessity. While he trusted Paul with most of the tasks given him, there were some he needed to handle himself.

"Dispose of him," DeMarcus instructed Paul. "I need time to think."

Paul nodded and started to untie the limp body of Patrick Deshanal.

* * *

Stavic cut a line of coke and snorted it with a straw. He leaned back, closed his eyes, and let the bitterness drip in the back of his throat. His tongue numbed as he waited, letting the drug envelop him.

There was only one drug dealer in town. Stavic kept him out of trouble and in return he was offered a hell of a discount. He also knew the underbelly of River Bend. If a John Doe was murdered here then there was a good chance Charles Went knew something about it.

He really should get to bed. He'd been up for thirty-five hours and was beat. The insomnia had him on edge, and he'd taken the coke to try and curb the nerves. Bad idea.

Stavic ran his hands through his hair then brushed the coke residue off the manila folder onto the coffee table. He picked the folder up and flipped through the pages.

Nothing. Not a god damned thing.

He tossed the folder back and looked around his small cliché apartment. Dark, dingy, papers scattered about, liquor bottles piled on the tables… the epitome of every fucking pulp book ever written. The only thing he didn't do was smoke. That may have been because his mother was a chain-smoker, and he had always hated how their house smelled. Not to mention the walls had taken on a shade of piss over the years. Say what you wanted about his place now, at least it was only cluttered.

Stavic had never known his father; the man died before he was born. All he knew was that his name was Frank and was the result of an accident at the mill. His mother Abigail had done what she could to raise him right—gave him space to make mistakes and learn from them—and never hovered. He'd gotten into his fair share of trouble, but what teenage boy didn't?

In its heyday RIver Bend was a logging town, and to this day still produced a large amount of paper products that shipped nationally. Farmlands bordered it with not much north of them besides small tourist towns for outdoor enthusiasts. It was all fine by Stavic though: he'd take this any day over a big city. Too much noise, too much crime, too many assholes. He'd done his time in Chicago and it had nearly cost him his life.

Stavic went to the kitchen and filled a glass with ice then splashed in some whiskey. He had the glass to his lips when an image of Jennifer popped into his head. Her accusatory eyes glazing over as he tried to stem the bleeding from the hole in her abdomen.

Hold on baby! Hold on!

Stavic willed the image away. Poor sweet Jennifer. If not for her he'd be rotting in a coffin. He regarded his glass, poured in a bit more whiskey. He had a feeling it was going to be one of those nights.

three

Willem's eyes fluttered open.

Another restless night, another bad dream.

Two nights in a row. He was lying in his recliner and it was still dark out, the sound of crickets coming through the open window. He closed his eyes and waited for sleep.

It never came. The cricket chirps dissolved to cooing mourning doves. When the sky began to brighten Willem figured he might as well get up.

He showered and had breakfast then went out and filled the bird feeder. He swept up the mess of seed the birds had left on his patio. While he may not take care of his yard like he should he'd be damned if he'd let these poor little fellows starve.

The morning was sunny with small wisps of clouds drifting through the sky. It was days like this that Willem enjoyed, days that conjured memories of running through fields with his brothers, fishing in Willow Creek, and biking in the woods. Where had it all gone wrong?

Whenever he thought of Elliott he got angry, but now that had given way to regret. Maybe he should reach out to him, but what would he say? Those sorts of calls were always the worst, the uncertainty of where the conversation would go.

Maybe some fresh air would clear his head. What with the day being as beautiful as it was, and the nostalgia of childhood pulling at him, he decided a walk was just what he needed. He could follow the path he and his brothers used to take, detouring where needed to compensate for current development.

Three boys on the opposite shoulder were walking towards him. Each looked to be about twelve, and they were having a heated conversation about something called *Battlefield*. Willem had no idea what *Battlefield* was, but he guessed it was some sort of game. That conjured memories of him and his brothers playing cops and robbers.

As he walked he wondered how Elliott was doing. His wife and children were always pleasant to him, and he found himself missing their smiles and energy. *Maybe I'll give him a call when I get home.*

Sometime later he saw Willow Creek Bridge and more memories of his youth came back. This had been a magical place for him and his brothers to escape. One day it was medieval lands, a local hideout for robbers the next. It was their go-to spot for their ever expanding imaginations.

He stopped in the center of the bridge and gazed south. The creek meandered past a willow tree some distance down before disappearing into a wood. A memory came to him, one of the willow tree and his brothers.

It's our buried treasure, he remembered Elliott telling him. *You can't tell anyone about it.*

God! He had forgotten all about the tin box with their buried treasure. Couldn't be there anymore, not now, not after all these years. Some other kids must have discovered it by now surely. But maybe… And what had they buried? He couldn't recollect.

He heard the casting of a fishing line and looked down. A kid around ten-years-old stood at the edge of the creek, fishing pole in hand. "Any luck?" he called down.

The boy looked up, eyed him nonchalantly. "A few bites."

Willem watched as the boy reeled in the line and cast again. He wasn't very good at it. "How long you been fishing?"

"I dunno. Hour maybe?"

"No," Willem said with a laugh. "Not just today."

The boy looked up. "An hour."

The amusement dissipated, and Willem felt bad for laughing.

He watched the kid try again, the lure not getting very far.

"You ever fish?" the kid asked without looking up.

"Not in a long time, but yeah. I used to go with my brothers. Used to fish right about where you're standing as a matter of fact."

The boy looked up. "Think you, uh, could give me some pointers?"

He was in no hurry; what was the harm in helping this kid out? "Give me a second."

Willem worked his way down the embankment. It was steep, and the worn rut they used to use was hidden beneath long uncut grass. Several times he slipped on his way down. This had been easy when he was a kid, but at sixty-four not so much. The ground leveled off and Willem approached the boy who was reeling in again. "What's your name?"

"William."

Willem couldn't help but smile. "When I was your age I had a good friend named William. I'm Willem. You can imagine the confusion the two of us caused in a group." The boy smiled politely. "So let me see you cast."

The boy readied himself, pressed the release with his thumb, and flicked the pole hard over his shoulder. The lure only went half a dozen feet before smashing into the water. He looked at him expectantly.

"You're being too forceful." He extended his hand. "Let me show you."

The boy handed over the pole and watched and Willem reeled it in. "The trick is to be gentle. Start by casting sideways. Once you're comfortable with that you can go overhead. Like this."

Willem extended the pole, pressed the release, and flicked it. The lure glided through the air gracefully landing with a gentle *plop*.

The boy beamed. "Let me try!"

Willem reeled it up and handed the pole back over. The glint of the lure caught his eye and an image appeared from the depths of his memory. A green lure, much like this one. Maybe he had one like it when he was a boy? He shook it off. Didn't matter.

The boy readied the cast. "Like this?"

"Yep. Just like that."

The boy cast smoothly, the lure landing nicely in the creek. The smile on the boy's face radiated pure joy. "I did it! Thanks!"

"You're welcome. That's a nice rod you got there by the way. Who gave it to you?"

The smile dropped a bit. "My dad. Got it for me for my birthday."

"It's your birthday today?"

A nod.

Willem felt bad for the boy. He should be learning to fish with his father, not some stranger who just happened to pass by.

"Well happy birthday, William."

"Thanks."

Willem watched in silence as William practiced, each cast improving. "You're a natural."

"It's not really that hard once you get used to it."

"Very true."

Memories flooded back of his father taking him and Elliott fishing, then Sammy when he was older. Laughing, eating a picnic lunch their mother had made them. They mostly caught pan fish, but once he'd caught a bass. He remembered how excited and proud his father had been. That was before his father…

He shook it off. Why did he keep thinking about his family after spending so many years pushing those memories aside? Maybe he should just swallow his pride and call Elliott. It had been ten years since they'd last spoke. Perhaps it was time to let bygones be bygones?

"Keep practicing," Willem said, "and soon you'll be a master fisherman. Pleasure to meet you, William."

Willem turned and made his way back up the overgrown path. By the time he'd reached the top he'd decided he would go home and make the call. It was time.

* * *

As Stavic pulled into the parking lot of the boat launch, he noted that Harold already had the boat in the water and tied to the dock. He was at the end staring out at the river, a cigarette dangling from his lips. The launch was empty except for them. Harold's truck and trailer were parked at the edge of the lot next to a row of trees. Stavic looked at his watch: 9:57. Apparently Harold wasn't the fashionably late type.

Stavic snorted a dash of coke. If he was getting in an aluminum boat that had the stability and grace of a cicada he needed something to calm his nerves. Grabbing the two cups of coffee he'd brought with him he stepped out, gravel crunching beneath his feet. The day was sunny, but a bit on the cool side.

Harold turned as Stavic approached. "Morning deputy," and proffered a cup.

"Thanks. And just call me Nicolas. Or Nick. Deputy is too formal for my taste."

"Fair enough." Harold pulled the cigarette from his lips and graciously took the cup, sipping it. He flinched, almost dropping the cup. "Hot!" he said.

"Good to know," Stavic replied. He looked at the cigarette between Harold's fingers.

"Nasty habit, I know, but old habits die hard. Everyone is allowed one vice anyway, don't you agree?"

"Implicitly." The twelve foot boat was three feet lower than the dock and bumped against it with a metallic thump. Stavic noted the small Evinrude outboard motor on the back of the boat. It looked ancient. "How old is this thing?"

"I got it back in the seventies. Maintain it properly and these things will last a lifetime. I still have my father's old one horse, one of those you have to wrap the rope around top manually. Thing still putts like a champ." He took a final drag on the cigarette and flicked it into the water. "You ready?"

Stavic slowly shook his head. "No, but let's do it." He sat on the dock and stepped into the aluminum tin can. It leaned to one side and he nearly fell in. Stavic caught himself, moved to center, and stabilized it. "Is this thing safe?"

"Haven't tipped it yet." Harold got in effortlessly and sat, pulled the starter, and the engine roared to life. Once Stavic sat, Harold backed away from the dock, and then they were on their way. "So what are we looking for Nick?" he asked over the engine.

"Anything out of the ordinary. Waters' body was dumped most likely by way of the river, so we're looking for boats, launches, docks, anything that would make that easier."

Woods encroached upon the river on either side, and besides birds and ducks they didn't see any living thing. The engine was probably scaring away most of the animals. Stavic kept sipping at his coffee, looking from one side of the river to the other. Nothing stood out as being out of the ordinary. It was too early to think of this as a waste of time, but that's certainly what it was feeling like. It didn't help he was stuck on a boat the size of a large coffin. That said he felt comfortable with Harold's piloting. Or maybe it was the cocaine. Either way, he wasn't clawing to get off the boat like he'd expected.

"Anything juicy you can share? I know you don't tell the public everything."

They hadn't released many details of their investigation, and he wasn't sure how much he could trust with Harold.

"Come on," Harold prodded. "Give me something. You know what they say about bait shop owners? We're like shrinks."

"That's bartenders."

"Same difference."

Stavic couldn't help but laugh. He had to give Harold credit: intentional or not, he was doing a good job putting him at ease.

"Is it true he was skinned alive?" Harold asked.

Stavic stared at Harold shocked. "Is that the rumor?"

"One of them."

He shook his head in disbelief. "Unbelievable. No, he wasn't skinned alive."

"What then?"

"He'd been gutted."

Now it was Harold's turn to look shocked. "Oh that's much better." Harold paused, his eyes moving about as if searching. "It sounds similar to what happened back in the late 50's. Know anything about that?"

"First I'm hearing of it."

"Husband and wife murdered, much like you described."

"Did they ever catch who did it?"

"Not that I heard. I'm guessing if they had there would have been a parade for those who'd managed it. Lot of people were scared for a while, waiting for something to happen to them."

It definitely couldn't hurt to look into it. It wouldn't be the first time an old case came back out of the blue.

Stavic suspected Harold could be trusted to stay quiet, but he felt he had to say it just to be safe. "What I've told you you have to keep to yourself. Can you do that?"

"I didn't get to be this age by gossiping, Nick."

"Good."

They came to a point where a narrow waterway joined them.

"What's that?" Stavic asked.

"Lake Crescent. Only lake in the area that connects to the river."

"Anything in there worthwhile?"

"Nah. People's cabins—all good people I might add—and that bar, The Thirsty Whale. Other than that not much. Good fishing if you're into that sort of thing. There's a good rock bed—"

Stavic cut him off. "Let's keep going."

They continued on another fifteen minutes in silence. The drone of the motor soothed Stavic, and he'd almost dozed off when Harold said, "Look over there." Harold pointed to the right side of the river.

Stavic did as instructed, the engine quieting as Harold slowed. "What am I looking at?"

"A blind."

He didn't see it. "You sure?"

"Positive." He idled in towards shore and, sure enough, there it was, made of pine branches and leaves sidled right up to the edge.

"Pull in next to it," Stavic instructed. Harold ran the boat aground, the aluminum boat echoing the scratching of sand and twigs beneath. He jumped out, grabbed the bow, and pulled the boat in. "Stay here."

Stavic inspected the blind. It was made of thick branches tied together with twine. The roof and walls were pine branches with leaves thrown over to fill in the gaps. It blended in perfectly with the forest around it. "I'm going to go take a look. Be back soon."

"Should I come with?"

"No. I got this."

His walk was near silent over the earthen ground. The incline was gradual but long, and he started to get winded as he made his way up. Nature sang to him. As he climbed he tried to calculate where he was between town and where Waters was found. His rough estimate put him about two miles from Waters' body—eight from town, three from where they started. They were also on the other side of the river, an area he knew next to nothing about.

While he hadn't grown up in River Bend, he'd grown up in a rural community that had plenty of woods where a boy could be mischievous. His mother had never remarried, and she was protective but not smothering which allowed for him to get into trouble from time-to-time. There'd been a couple times a police officer had escorted him home much to the dismay of his mother. He wouldn't have considered himself a wild child, but he loved the adrenaline rush he'd get when jumping from the cliffs at the Eau Claire Dells into the cool water below, or drag racing out on a country road.

Ironic that he became a cop.

Stavic was ready to turn around when he crested the hill. Below sat a small log cabin no more than eight-hundred square feet. All was silent and still, no smoke wafting from the chimney. And while he did see a path running through the woods to the cabin he saw no vehicle. He was pretty sure he was alone and made his way down the hill quietly.

Curtains were drawn across the windows. He walked along the perimeter listening intently for any sound coming from within. He was pretty sure he was alone so climbed the front porch.

Should he knock or just enter? Best to play it by the book.

Was that…? Stavic thought he heard movement. He rapped gently on the door.

"Hello?"

He listened. This time he didn't hear movement but thought he heard something close. Maybe a cabinet or a door?

"Police. Open up please."

When no one answered he took the knob and turned it. The door swung open.

The dinginess made the hair on the back of his neck stand and he pulled his gun.

"Show yourself," he called out. From the stillness he knew he was alone in the dark cabin.

But then what was that you heard? he asked himself.

There was a kerosene lantern hanging on a rusty nail where he'd expected a light switch to be. This far off the beaten path there was probably no power. He found a book of matches on a utility shelf. He struck the match, the scraping sounded loud in the stillness. The flame flickered. He touched the match to the wick and the orange light illuminated the darkness.

With each step on the wooden floor his boots sounded like a cannon echoing through the room. Not much here save for a bed, a nightstand next to it, and a recliner.

And an eviscerated body.

It was slumped against one wall, pale and naked. With the head drooping he couldn't make out the face.

"Nick?"

He whipped around, saw Harold in the doorway.

"Jesus!" he huffed.

"Sorry, but I got curious. What…"

And then he saw the room and turned white.

"Out!" Stavic shouted, following after him.

"Who—?"

Stavic had his phone in hand. "I don't know, but I'm calling in the cavalry."

* * *

It was warmer out than it had been, and Claire had the cleaning bug. She'd let this place go over the last several months and it was time to tidy up. A fresh breeze came through the open window pushing the stale air out. She wanted this place back in tiptop shape by the time Emily returned home.

She began immediately after Emily left for school, starting on the first floor and working her way up. She dusted and vacuumed and mopped, and by ten o'clock she was onto the second floor. Claire went to her room, tackling the obvious things first. She stripped her bed and tossed old magazines; a chickadee sang outside the window.

She went to the closet—it had a slight musty smell to it—and stared at the mess. Claire needed to take an inventory and decide what to keep; there were way too many outfits she no longer wore. But first the laundry. She pulled out the hamper and sorted them into piles. After she was done in here she'd clean Emily's room, grab her laundry and add them to the mix.

All these old and outdated clothes. Maybe this weekend she could get Emily to go to the store with her and help her update her wardrobe. She could use a little of her savings, and it would be nice to have a mother-daughter day, something they hadn't done in… how long? Claire flipped through the shirts and dresses *tsking* herself. God! When did she become old?

Claire was about to close the door when a box caught her eye. It was shoved in the back corner, barely visible in the shadows. On the side was written in bold letters **DEVON**. She slid the box out and stared at it. She'd completely forgotten about this, a collection of her ex-husbands relics from before the divorce. She'd stashed a few things she hadn't been ready to part with, more for Emily than herself. While he had crushed her, Devon had been Emily's father and she deserved to have *something* from him.

She pulled the flaps and opened the box. On top were an assortment of photos, some group shots while others of just Devon. There were a few cassettes of her husbands favorite music, a couple of books, and other trinkets. And there was the manila envelope with the divorce papers, still unlooked at after all these years. At some point the metal fastener had broken free and the flap easily lifted, the white papers within visible.

Claire began to wonder if the divorce was legal if she'd never even looked at these papers. Maybe there had been something else she'd needed to sign and never did? But that was stupid, she realized. If that were the case her attorney would have contacted her. Claire was tempted to pull the papers out, finally cement the divorce by seeing it in writing, but couldn't bring herself to do it. She tossed the envelope back into the box and put it on a chair next to the dresser. Maybe she'd finally give it to Emily once she'd had a chance to sort through it all.

Emily's room was next. There was a slight dirty odor, so she opened the window. The room itself was decent enough, definitely not the best she'd seen of her daughter, but certainly not the worst. There weren't dishes caked in food or half-filled cups around the room. There were, however, clothes scattered about and a desk covered in papers and books. This wasn't typical of Emily—she was usually so meticulous with everything in its place—but she was a teenager and teenagers sometimes got lazy. And who was she to judge anyway?

Claire sorted Emily's clothes and tided up her desk and changed the sheets on her bed. The vacuum bumped something under the bed. She killed the power and reached under and pulled out an ashtray. Two stamped out cigarette butts were in it.

Smoking? When did Emily pick up that nasty habit? She was going to have to speak to her about this.

The nightstand drawer taunted her. If her daughter was smoking what else was she keeping hidden from her?

No! You're invading her privacy.

True, but she was still her mother, and this was her house, and she had a right to know what her daughter was doing. It was her responsibility to protect her.

Claire opened it. She breathed a sigh of relief, almost laughed, as nothing jumped out at her. She'd half expected to find drugs or drug paraphernalia stashed in here. Cigarettes weren't good, but there were far worse things Emily could be doing to rebel. Tobacco she could handle.

She stood and went to the trashcan next to Emily's desk, picked it up, and dumped the butts into it.

And her heart stopped.

She reached in, hand trembling, and lifted out a thin plastic bag. Through it she could see the contents. Hoping, *praying,* she was wrong she reached in and pulled out the box. A pregnancy test.

Her mind was a whirlwind, didn't know what to think. Was Emily pregnant?

She opened the box but it was empty.

Breathe, she told herself. *Don't jump to conclusions. Maybe it was her friend's. Jessica.*

But how could she not? The last thing she wanted was to see Emily making the same mistakes she'd made. If that happened then she had failed as a mother.

Claire sat there a while, unsure how to react. She was going to have to talk to her about this.

I need a drink.

Yes. She could really use one right now.

* * *

Willem shut the front door and locked it. A sunbeam streamed through the partially closed curtains, dust particles visible in the air. A cold beer would be good right about now, but since his estrangement from Elliott he'd sworn off alcohol. Instead he grabbed a cola from the fridge, popped the top and took a long drink, one that produced a hiccup.

No more delaying it; he opened and dug through a drawer finding a black address book buried under miscellaneous junk. With book and cola in hand he sat at the table. He stared out the window wondering if he was ready for this.

His hand hesitated over the address book. Assuming Elliott still had the same number would he even talk to him? Maybe not knowing was better.

To hell with it. He grabbed the book and flipped through it until he found Elliott's number, picked up the phone and dialed. Might as well get this over with.

The phone rang three times before a woman answered. "Hello?" Her voice was tinny and soft through the handset.

"Beth?"

There was a slight pause. "Yes?"

"It's Willem. Is Elliott there?"

The pause went on longer. Could it be she didn't remember him, or just surprised at his call? His tension washed away as her jubilation resonated through the phone. "Willem! It's so good to hear your voice. How have you been? God, it's been so long!" Hearing the happiness in her voice brought on a smile.

"Good, good. Is he around?"

"Yes. Hold on."

He listened as she walked, her footfalls barely audible through the phone. There was a *whoosh* sound as she covered the mouthpiece, though not enough.

". . . Willem. He'd . . . talk to you."

The silence continued, and Willem could only guess what was happening. Elliott was probably shaking his head no to Beth, not wanting to engage in a conversation with him. And then he heard Elliott's voice.

"Hello?" Elliott's voice sounded tired.

"It's Willem, Elliott. How are you?"

"Good," he said with a slow inhale. "It's been a long time. Ten years?"

"Something like that." Willem grew increasingly concerned. Ten years was a long time, but not so long that his brother would sound so... *aged*. "Is everything alright? You don't sound like yourself."

"It's been a long time," Elliott said again, as if that answered the question. He coughed.

"You still working in tech?"

"Nah. Got out of that years ago." He heard Elliott cover the mouthpiece and another cough. "It was a dead end job, no real career path. I started working as a consultant and never looked back. What about you? Still saving lives?"

"Trying. Elliott—"

"I've been thinking about you a lot lately," Elliott interrupted. "You and Sam, actually."

"Sam?" He found it interesting that they both were thinking of their brother in recent days.

"Yeah." Willem sensed some hesitation on his brother's part. "Whatever the reason for our fight, I think we should let bygones be bygones."

Willem was taken aback. He expected some resistance to making amends—Elliott was always a stubborn one. Maybe ten years had mellowed him out a little. "I agree. In fact, I don't even remember what the fight was about."

A phlegmy laugh came through the phone. "Really? Funny how that works."

"You said you've been thinking about Sam lately. So have I."

"Well isn't that interesting. You dying, too?"

That caught Willem off guard. "Dying?"

"Cancer. Docs say I don't have much time left. So that's my excuse, what's yours?"

"In all honesty, I'm not sure. Just... memories coming back." If Willem felt uncomfortable before now he was distressed. "How are Beth and the kids handling it?"

"Kids are adults now and are fine. They've all accepted the inevitable. In all honesty, I'd like this to be over with so that they could move on." Another cough through the phone. "Did you ever marry?"

"No."

"Well then you probably won't understand, but the pain I see in their eyes every time I look into them, it breaks my heart. They say the eyes are the gateway to the soul, and you know what? It's true. I never realized it, not until I saw how they look at me now."

It pained him to admit it, but Willem was jealous of his brother and what he had, for what he was losing. He'd never known love, the longing one feels for their wife or children, the smile received when returning home from work or a trip. The unequivocal joy on a loved one's face. That had eluded Willem into his adult life.

As if reading his mind, Elliott said, "It's never too late, Willem. Never." Elliott cleared his throat. "So why the call after all these years? Not that I'm complaining, mind you. I would have picked up the phone myself if I wasn't so damn scared you'd hang up or wouldn't answer."

"I've never known you to be scared."

"Eh." Willem could sense the shrug through the phone. "I put on a good show."

"How long do you have?" Silence on the other end. "Elliott?"

"A week. Two at most." The defeat in Elliott's voice was heartbreaking.

Willem needed to see his brother before the end, needed to talk to him, to make amends. He wanted to be there right now. It was a five hour drive, so if he could get on the road in the next hour or two he could be there before nightfall. "I'll be there tonight."

He'd expected an argument, but Elliott surprised him. "Okay. I'll let Beth know. But now I've got to go, Willem. I'm tired."

Willem understood. Elliott was his only remaining family and to set things right it was something he needed to do. "I'll make the arrangements and be there tonight."

Relief seeped through the phone. "Thank you."

"Goodbye, Elliott," and Willem hung up the phone.

* * *

It had been more difficult to find the cabin than he expected. It had been a long time since he'd been out this way—some fifty years—and his recollection wasn't what it once was. The road off the highway was overgrown and blended in with the surrounding forest so well he'd missed it the first pass. Back in the day it was easy to miss unless you knew what to look for, but now it was nearly impossible. When he finally did find the road he expected he'd be able to drive the entire way in. That wasn't meant to be. Just past the two boulders that blocked Oak—the abandoned road that went nowhere—was an age-old tree that had come down in the not too distant past. There was no way for him to maneuver the car around it, so he'd thrown it in park and got out.

Twelve feet up from the base of the tree it looked like lightning had struck snapping the thing in half. The wood was charred black. David could only assume that rain had been coming down at the time and had managed to keep the fire from spreading. Good thing, too. If it hadn't he'd probably be standing in a cemetery of trees right now.

When the cabin came into view he scarcely believed it. It was real! The cabin Lilly had taken him to in his dream existed. It solidified the fact that his hazy memory was in fact true.

David stopped dead in his tracks when he saw movement on the side of the cabin. He pressed himself against a tree hoping to blend in. He watched as a man approached the door with trepidation and knocked. It looked like… Was that the deputy he met the other day? What was he doing here?

With no response he watched Stavic open the door and step in. Another man, this one older, stepped around the cabin and crept up to the door and peeked in.

"Out!" he heard Stavic shout as he propelled the second man from the entrance. What was going on? Stavic put a phone to his ear.

He couldn't stay here. If he was calling for backup the last thing he wanted was to be found skulking around the cabin.

* * *

They had set up powerful lights that washed away all the shadows. Stavic and Kinney stood outside the cabin's front door. Everything was red save for Jim Patterson, the county coroner, who was dressed in a yellow hazmat suit. The floor and walls were splattered with blood. Once Deputy Reed arrived he asked him to escort Harold back to his boat. No sense in traumatizing him further.

"This is the worst thing I've ever seen," Kinney said, "and I've seen a lot. "How did you find this place?"

"Tour of the river like you asked."

Stavic felt himself being drawn back to that night in Chicago when he was almost killed. At the time he was a beat cop on the north side of the city. Not nearly as bad as the south or west sides, it still had its own gang problems. In honoring the Mayor's plan to crack down on crime, Stavic had volunteered to work undercover. It had taken sixteen months, but he'd managed to infiltrate one of the major gangs in the neighborhood, had them convinced he was a junkie living in squalor. Not that that wasn't far from the truth; he'd started hanging out with the right people that by the end he was living in a skeleton of a burned out three-flat gray-stone. Several homeless people lived there, all of them he'd considered friends by the end. One in particular, Jennifer, he'd become exceptionally close to. While that hadn't been the first time he'd done drugs it certainly was what got him addicted.

A major drop off was planned of which he alerted his superiors. He and his homeless friends—people who just wanted to make a few bucks to eat—went to the location, met with the runners. The cops were ready and a shootout ensued. One of the drug runners came to Stavic convinced he'd sold them out. Before he could react a muzzle was pressed against his temple. He felt the warmth of the fired weapon tremble against his flesh. Stavic closed his eyes, expecting death, when Jennifer lunged.

The bullet grazed his head and blew out his eardrum. Jennifer ended up taking a bullet to the gut, but it afforded Stavic enough time to wrestle the gun from the drug runner's hands and blow him away. When it was all said and done most of the criminals had been killed, the others caught. Stavic stayed with Jennifer as she bled out, the sparkle in her eyes fading.

She was gone before the ambulance arrived.

After the experience of being undercover, partial loss of hearing, nearly a bullet to the head, and the death of Jennifer it became too much for him and he put in his two weeks. He was told that when he was ready to come back just pick up the phone—he was a good cop.

To try and clear his mind he'd decided to travel. It was the seventh week being away from home and he was headed back to Chicago when he saw a sign for River Bend. Something about the name pulled at him so he decided to check it out. As soon as he crossed Willow Creek Bridge he felt like he was home. Everything about it was comforting and safe.

Once he got back to Chicago he called up the River Bend police station and inquired about a position. Turned out there was. One of the deputies was moving and the position needed to be filled. But, he was asked, why would a Chicago cop want to be a deputy of a small town when all the action was in the big city? Stavic answered, Sheriff Kinney nodding in understanding. Stavic filled out the paperwork, got glowing recommendations from his bosses, and met with Sheriff Kinney. He was offered the job on the spot. Less than a week later Stavic was packed and moved, leaving behind the disgusting nature of the human species.

Or so he thought.

The soft glow of an impending sunset illuminated the horizon. He breathed deeply, taking in the crisp autumn air. Wasn't sure how much longer until snow fell. Couple of weeks at most. He closed his eyes and stretched his back. It cracked. He let out a long throaty sigh, leaned forward, and opened his eyes.

"What do you think this guy was doing out here?" Stavic mused.

"That's a very interesting question," Kinney said, and patted him on the shoulder. "I think you should start figuring that out."

* * *

She didn't know how to broach the subject of pregnancy with Emily. This was new territory for her, and it scared the crap out of her.

The sun was down and Claire sat in the living room watching television. She stared at the flickering image, the sound low. Hard to believe only a few days ago she nearly died here. She looked at the spot where she'd been found, trying to imagine how she'd looked, what Emily had seen. Emily had told her how terrified she'd been, but she couldn't imagine it. Sure she'd been scared before, of things Emily did as a child—running into the street, falling out of a tree—but those resulted in moments of adrenalized panic, nothing like finding someone who was for all intents and purposes dead.

Claire wrapped her robe around her a little tighter, tugging the ropes around her waist. She took her cup of hot tea and sipped it wishing for a cocktail instead. But a promise was a promise, one she intended to keep.

Trotting footsteps down the stairs echoed from the hallway. "Mom?" Emily asked peeking around the corner. Her eyes focused on the steaming cup in Claire's hands.

Claire paid it no mind. "Yes sweetie?"

"Is it alright if I go to Jessica's? We have a test tomorrow and she wants help studying."

"That's fine. Just be back by ten."

Emily hesitated. "Will you be okay if…?"

Claire waited for her to finish, saw she was going to let the words linger. "I'll be fine. Just me and Earl here." She held up the cup with a smile. Though she wanted something stronger than tea she'd be hard pressed to find something in the house. Emily had cleared out all the booze while she'd been in the hospital; the place was alcohol free at the moment.

"Okay then."

Ask her. Ask her about the test.

Claire watched Emily put on her coat and realized she and Emily hadn't actually talked recently. They didn't even eat together anymore. When had things gone astray?

Why do you have a pregnancy test?

"Emily?"

"Yes?" her daughter said as she perked up.

"Could you come here a moment please?"

Emily stepped into the room, and Claire gestured to the seat next to her. "Sit," she said and turned off the TV. Emily did apprehensively.

"Am I in trouble?"

"No." Claire reached out and stroked Emily's cheek tenderly. "I just realized we haven't really… talked… in a while. I miss that."

"Okay…"

"How is school going? I haven't heard anything from your teachers, so I assume everything is good?"

"Peachy."

Silence fell between them. Had she distanced herself so much she couldn't have a normal conversation with her daughter? She was happy to see she still wore the necklace she'd given her, a necklace she'd received from her neighbor Mrs. Rottingham when she was eight. What with her parents always gone for work the gesture had meant a great deal to her. She and her husband watched her a lot and always treated her as if she were their own. It was when her family packed up and moved that Mrs. Rottingham had given it to her, telling her to wear it always for good luck. And she had. Every day she wore it until she'd given it to Emily after her father had left.

"I realize I haven't been a great parent, especially as of late, and I don't really know what's going on in your life right now. How's Dylan doing?"

"Dylan? We broke up like two months ago."

Claire's mouth dropped and she covered it with her hand. "Oh baby! I'm so sorry! I didn't know—"

Emily forced a smile. "I know you didn't."

"Why didn't you tell me?"

A sad nervous laugh escaped Emily. "Where is this coming from? You haven't been interested in anything I do in a while. Why suddenly now?"

Claire hadn't thought about it. "I think it's because of what happened."

"You said it wasn't a big deal. Now it is?"

"That's not... no. I mean—"

"If you suddenly want to get chummy after you died—"

"Nearly died."

"I'd say it was a pretty big fucking deal."

"Emily!" She'd never heard her use that language before.

Emily pushed herself up. "I'll be back by ten."

"Emily," Claire said following her to the front door. "Please wait." She felt an emptiness in her heart, the pressure of remorse. She felt she'd lost Emily and hadn't even realized it. That was something she was going to have to fix. After Devon, she couldn't lose her daughter too.

Emily opened the door and turned to her mother. "I love you mom, I really do, but don't pretend to care." She leaned in and gave Claire a quick peck on the cheek then left. Thirty-seconds later Emily drove off past a red Nissan parked on the opposite side of the street. Claire stood there a while—unsure what to do—feeling ashamed, alone, and abandoned.

* * *

Beth had greeted Willem warmly with a hug. She asked where his bags were, that he was more than welcome to stay with them, Willem feigned appreciation and told her he'd already checked into a hotel. Yes this was his family, but it was a family he hadn't seen in a decade, and with Elliott as sick as he was Willem didn't want to be a burden on Beth. He'd always liked her, and while she put on a brave front he could see the sorrow in her eyes.

When Willem first saw Elliott he was surprised his brother wasn't already dead. He was too thin, too frail, and his pale skin hung loose on its frame. His brown hair was gone, and if someone thought he looked like a walking skeleton that'd be kind. But what Elliott lacked in looks he made up for in spirit. Even at the end of life, be it days or hours, Elliott still managed to smile and put those visiting at ease.

Elliott turned his head when Willem entered the room and, upon seeing him, smiled weakly. He waved him over and Willem obliged, bending down to embrace the worn man before him. "It's good to see you," Elliott said quietly. "It's really good to see you."

And then Willem felt tears running down his cheeks. Whatever had happened between them was irrelevant. What mattered was the here and now, this moment. All was forgiven in that instant.

When Willem pulled away Elliott was grinning. "Knock it off you big baby."

He laughed and wiped away the tears.

"Would you like something to drink, Willem?" Beth asked from the door. Judging by Elliott's reaction he'd forgotten she was there too. Willem looked sheepishly at her. "Coffee, if you have any made."

"Sure." Beth pulled the door so that it was almost closed giving the two men privacy.

"Sit." Elliott gestured to a desk chair. "Bring that closer."

Willem obliged. "How are you feeling?" he asked as he sat.

"Like I've had my ass kicked half way to Timbuktu."

"You're not on morphine or anything?"

"I was, but it made me sluggish and stupid. I'd rather be alert and in pain over not knowing who is who and what is what. You look good, by the way. A little round around the pants though." His tone was in jest.

Shrugging, Willem said, "I'm doing alright. Is there anything I can do for you?"

"Aside from curing cancer?"

"Aside from that," Willem said with a half-hearted smile.

"Then no. There's not much more to do now but wait for the inevitable."

"Still one for dramatics I see."

"Indubitably." He laughed. "It makes me sound smarter than I actually am. Surprisingly, I think I've fooled most everyone."

"Except me."

"Except you."

"And probably Beth."

"And Beth."

"And your kids?"

"Oh shut up."

They chuckled together like they had so often as boys.

"I'm sorry I've been out of touch for so long," Willem said. "It shouldn't have been that way."

"It's not your fault alone. I was just as stubborn and stupid and could have picked up the phone anytime. I'd rather not go over all that. Let bygones be bygones, as they say."

Elliott grabbed a tissue and coughed into it, wincing in pain. He didn't complain. There was a knock at the door then it opened. Beth handed Willem his coffee.

"Thank you," he said. Beth nodded, walked away.

When he was sure she was out of earshot, Elliott said, "I don't know how she's doing it. If our roles were reversed I'd be a basket case. I keep trying to picture what my life would be like without her and I can't. We've had so many good times together, so many good experiences—how would I be able to go on without her?"

Willem said nothing. This was an emotion he could only pretend to understand. How would one feel if someone you've loved unconditionally for thirty-plus years was suddenly gone? Complete and total loss, he supposed. That was a feeling he'd rather not experience. Ever.

Elliott recited, "'Tis better to have loved and lost than never to have loved at all.'"

"And you believe it?"

"Without a doubt. Out of curiosity, why didn't you ever marry?"

"I never met the right person," responded Willem without hesitating.

"What a bullshit answer. Any single person who's never married always says that."

"It's true," Willem said quietly.

Elliott patted Willem's knee. "Well, there is still time. Plenty of people marry late in the game. Nothing wrong with that."

"You make it sound like I've never loved anybody."

"Have you?"

"Of course."

"Who?"

When Willem said nothing, Elliott continued. "You have to break out of your comfort zone sometime, Willem. You can't stay locked up in your house forever."

"I'm not locked up…"

"I'm just saying." He coughed again.

Elliott fixated on the window, and they sat in silence enjoying each others presence. Willem was about to excuse himself to use the bathroom when Elliott said, "You see death on a regular basis, right? Do you have any advice for me?"

It was then Willem realized his big brother had lied: he hadn't accepted what was coming, the inevitable end. He was afraid, terrified even. He was just putting on a brave face to make it easier for those he loved. He didn't want them to be afraid, so he chose that path to walk alone. He suffered in hopes of expediting the process, to stop the fear and pain. Understanding his brother's situation strengthened his belief in euthanasia further. Fuck morals: if it ended ones pain and suffering just a little sooner then why not?

"I don't know what you want me to say."

"I don't either," responded Elliott. "What would you tell a patient?"

"I'm not a doctor, Elliott. I don't see patients."

"Whatever it is you call them then. What would you say?"

Willem sighed. "I'd tell them to keep fighting, that they have something to live for. That's what I would tell them."

Elliott gently nodded. "Something to live for, huh?"

There was another lull in the conversation, but Willem didn't mind. It gave his brother time to rest and time for him to reflect. When he thought Elliott had fallen asleep he stood.

"I thought you wanted to talk about Sam. Isn't that why you really came here?"

Willem turned to Elliott who still had his eyes closed. "It's nothing. It can wait."

He opened them. "No it can't."

He doesn't have much time, Willem realized and sat.

"Earlier today—the reason I called you as a matter of fact—is that I met a boy at the bridge. He was trying to teach himself to fish with a gift his dad had gotten him. I don't know the circumstances, I don't know why, but his dad wasn't there teaching him, and I could see it bothered him."

"And that made you think of how dad treated you."

"Well, yeah. I still have no idea where it came from. I remember a time he was a good and loving father, but then at some point he changed. Maybe it's just me, but I remember I seemed to be the focus of his anger. He never seemed to have that with you or Sam."

"I wish I had an answer for you, Willem. I really do. But…" He grabbed a tissue and coughed several times into it. "Even mom didn't know what was up."

"You want to know what's really sad? As much as I've been thinking of Sam, I can only remember the events. I'm having a hard time remembering what he looked like."

Elliott pushed himself up and pointed to a box sitting on a dresser. "Grab that." Willem picked up the box and handed it to Elliott. Inside were photos of all sizes, some color, others black and white. "Beth found these a while back in the attic." He shuffled through the pictures, pausing on a few but not offering them to Willem, before settling on one. "Here," he said.

Willem took it. The black and white photo was of a young boy sitting in tall grass playing with several army figures. His eyes were squinted as he looked at the photographer, probably because of the sun.

"Ghosts only haunt our pasts, Willem," Elliott sighed. He leaned back and closed his eyes. "Sometimes I wish we could go back to our former lives. You know? Back when all you needed was a box for your secrets." The words came out slurred and tired.

"I'll come and visit tomorrow. Okay?"

Elliott nodded, never opening his eyes. "Tomorrow."

Willem stood and went to the door. "Willem?" He looked at his brother wishing they'd made amends years ago.

"Yes?"

Elliott met Willem's eyes. "It was good seeing you again."

Willem smiled. "You too."

And then he closed the door, not knowing if he'd see his brother again.

* * *

Beth was waiting at the bottom of the stairs. She stared vacantly out a window. The carpeted stairs muffled Willem's descent and it wasn't until he touched her shoulder did she acknowledge him with a flinch. She smiled sadly and patted his hand.

"He's resting," Willem said.

She sighed and stood, stretching her back. "Good."

"How are you doing?" Willem wanted to know.

"To be honest I'm tired and worn out."

"Where are the kids?"

"They've been flying back and forth on a rotation. Gregory left this morning, and Margaret is flying in tonight." He must have given her a condescending look. "Don't," she said, cocking her head. "I want no sympathy. It's been hard, I won't lie, and this is not how I thought our lives would end up, but life is full of uncertainties. Best to deal with these sorts of things on a day-by-day basis."

"It's getting late. I should be going."

"Where are you staying?" Beth asked.

"Motel near 51."

"I wish you'd stay. We have plenty of room. The company is always nice."

"I know, but I'd feel like I was imposing—"

"You're family, Willem. Regardless of what happened, you're always welcome here."

"I know, but I've lived alone for so long…" How did he tell her he wasn't comfortable staying under his dying brother's roof? "I hope you understand."

"Yes," she sighed. "I do. Will you be back tomorrow?"

They walked to the door. "I promised Elliott I'd come by. When is good?"

"Anytime is fine." She opened the door. "Well, until tomorrow then." She leaned up and gave him a kiss on the cheek.

He felt her watching him as he walked to his car, but it wasn't until he was getting in that he looked back and waved. As he drove away, the sun beginning to set, he wondered how much longer his brother had.

four

"Why did you run?"

Willem was seated in a chair next to Elliott's bed. He looked more alert than yesterday.

"I wouldn't say I ran—" Willem began.

"The moment you could you hightailed it out of River Bend."

"Honestly? I don't know. There was nothing there for me. At least that's how it felt at the time. Sammy was dead, dad had disappeared, you'd gone off to college, and mom had her own life. What was I going to do? I didn't want to be stuck there with her."

"Fair enough, but then why sever all ties the way you did?"

"Why is any of this important now?"

"Indulge a dying man."

Willem scowled at Elliott, sipped his coffee. "I've always felt responsible for Sam's death. If I'd been more careful in protecting him he may not have died."

"It wasn't your fault."

"So you and mom said, but hearing it and accepting it are two vastly different things. I was supposed to be looking out for him. If I'd done a better job of that he wouldn't have fallen."

"You don't know that."

"No, but I believe it."

"Ironic, isn't it, that you moved back after we left?"

"I had my fill of Milwaukee. It always felt like there was a sickness that seeped from the cracks. A simple life seemed more my speed, and it was more comfortable to move back to something familiar."

"I'm sure knowing we'd moved away made it easier."

"I'd be lying if I said that wasn't a factor. By the way, it was nice of you to take her with you."

Elliott shrugged then coughed. "Beth and mom got along great, so it made the decision easy. She got to stay close to her family and grandkids, and we didn't have to worry about her being on her own."

Willem sipped his cooling coffee, grimaced. Beth certainly knew how to make a strong cup of joe.

"We never really had a chance to finish our conversation from yesterday," Elliott said.

"It's fine."

"No. It's not." Elliott cleared the phlegm from his throat, winced. "I don't want you to go back home and never see your family again. My family is all you have, and I don't want you withering away and dying alone."

"I'm not alone."

"I'll haunt your sorry ass," Elliott quipped.

Willem smiled. He knew it was sad, but he didn't care. "What do you think happened to him?"

"Who? Dad?"

"Yeah."

"There's a lot of strange and beautiful things in the world, Willem," he sighed. "I like to think he found something that made his life less hateful."

His heart was heavy, and Willem didn't know he was crying until he felt the tears on his cheeks. He thought he'd flicked them away before Elliott had seen, but because of the look his brother was giving him he knew otherwise. Willem shrugged, trying to be nonchalant. "I was just thinking to myself what it was about me he hated so much. Why I was the one he singled out. I suppose that's pretty stupid, wondering about that now I mean."

Elliott shook his head. "No, not at all." There was a moment of hesitation, then he let out a long sigh. "The last few months before he disappeared even mom really had no idea what was going on with him." He opened his mouth to say more, closed it.

"What?" Willem wanted to know.

Elliott looked at him with intense eyes. "Dad lost it. There is no other explanation. According to mom he was becoming increasingly paranoid and agitated, part of the reason—she thinks—he began to drink so heavily. You want to know why dad singled you out? It's because he thought you weren't you, that someone different had taken over."

"Someone different? But that's crazy."

"That's what mom tried to tell him, but he wouldn't listen. She tried to calm him, to get him help, but he refused. That's why dad took out his anger on you. He was sick, Willem. Nothing more."

"She told you?"

"We talked about it, yes. She couldn't understand why you left the way you did or why you estranged yourself."

"Because she didn't do anything," Willem said coldly. "All that I went through and she looked the other way."

"But that's the thing—she didn't. You know the old adage 'love blinds you'? There's truth to that. She didn't know how bad it had gotten for you because she still loved her husband and was trying to understand what was going on. So she wasn't ignoring what was happening, she didn't see it."

"She had to have known—"

"Why? Because you told her?"

Had he talked to her about it at the time? He thought so, but now as he sat here he was second guessing himself. Regardless, the anger and disappointment he'd latched onto toward his mother and brother had grabbed onto him and wouldn't let go. "Never you or mom or Sammy. Me. It was only me." The tears began to flow again, this time freely, and without humility. And suddenly, in the blink of an eye, he understood why he'd become the man he had. "You want to know why I never married, Elliott?" He stood, wanting to be out of here, away from Elliott and the memories. He needed fresh air, the coolness of the breeze. "I was afraid."

Willem went to the door, opened it.

"Please don't go."

"I need to step outside for a few minutes. Clear my head."

"Have you ever considered that the accident gave him the excuse he needed to leave? Maybe he didn't like what he was becoming and left to protect us?"

Willem didn't buy it—*couldn't* buy it. What father would run off like that?

Elliott coughed and seemed to deflate into the bed. "Sometimes you just have to let it go, Willem. Sometimes there just isn't always an answer to be had."

Willem looked back. "You want to know what I think happened to dad? I think he ran away like you said, and I think it was because of me. He abandoned us all because of me." He hesitated a moment, then said, "I'll be back."

Elliott gave a slight nod. *I understand*, it said. *Go.*

And he did.

Elliott passed a few minutes later.

* * *

A few months ago David started to experience a longing for home. It was an intense feeling, one he couldn't shake. The days leading up to David driving into town revealed little more than hints. Dreams or visions, truth or fiction, he felt a yearning as if some great wrong would soon be set right.

David stood outside 462 Baker Street, the home he'd owned with Lilly. Before coming here he'd gone back to the cabin where things had changed. For one the roadway had been cleared of the fallen tree. When he'd crested the hill he saw the house taped off with yellow police tape, a squad car parked in front. A crime scene? He saw no one outside and backed away. Last thing he wanted to do was be questioned by the cops. With the cabin temporarily off limits he'd decided to go to his old home and search for the necklace Lilly had shown him.

It used to be a pristine white one-story box with a picket fence, but now both were rundown, paint peeling. It hurt seeing the home he'd shared with his wife for forty years decaying like this. This place was a trove of memories, but now it looked like death had crept in.

He wondered who owned it now, if it was the same family whom he sold it to twenty years back, or if it was someone new? He knew looks could be deceiving, but it seemed the place had been all but abandoned. That'd be a shame. They'd always taken such good care of the property, making sure it had a fresh painting every few years.

The picket fence door sat askew, the latch uneven and unable to stay shut. It groaned when David pushed it open, the bottom wood scraping on the concrete. He noted the window shades were drawn as he walked along the concrete path between overgrown sections of grass. Stepping onto the porch he knocked.

And waited.

No one answered. He tried again, and after a full minute decided that no one was home. The door handle felt familiar, but the door wouldn't open. It was too much to hope for, he supposed, to have it unlocked.

"Mr. Rottingham?"

He turned to the aged yet sweet voice. His old neighbor, Cynthia McCormick, stood on her porch, mail in hand.

"Is that you?" she asked.

"Indeed it is," he said stepping off the porch with a smile. "I didn't expect to see you."

The shock on her face was obvious. "I can say the same. What are you doing here?" She met him at the fence.

"Good will tour."

She laughed politely and slapped his arm with the mail. "Would you like to come in and have a cup of coffee?"

"Thank you, no. I have somewhere to be in a little while. Had time to kill so I figured I'd check out the old homestead."

Her warmth darkened a bit. "Shame what's happened to the place. You and Lilly always kept it up so nice. You were the envy of the neighborhood."

He chuckled. "I doubt that. What happened though?"

"The Reeds—they're the ones you sold it to. Frank ended up losing his job, and when that happened they fell into foreclosure. They ended up moving, and the place has been vacant ever since. Twelve, thirteen years. Something like that."

"Thirteen, huh?"

"Baker's dozen."

"So the bank owns it now?"

"Yeah. We've been trying to get them to have someone come out and do some work on it, spruce it up a bit, but so far they've balked. I don't know how they expect to sell it if it looks the way it does."

He couldn't hide the acid in his voice. "If they're going to let it go they should just tear the place down and be done with it."

Cynthia pursed her lips. "When did you get back?"

"Couple days ago. Staying at the inn." He looked back to the house. "Out of curiosity, let's say you saw a frail old man breaking into that abandoned house. You wouldn't call the cops, would you?"

"If such a man did break in then I didn't see it," she said. "I'm sure I was busy doing laundry."

He gave her smile. "It was nice talking to you again."

"You too. I don't know how long you'll be in town, but if you want a nice home cooked meal our door is open."

"Thank you. I might just take you up on that."

She touched his arm, turned, and went back to her house. When the door closed David walked around back.

The first thing he tried was the back door, but like the front it was locked. A worn mat lay at the foot of the door. Could it really be that simple? He kicked it to the side but, no, no key. Next he checked under the three pots that now only contained soil, the plants long since rotted away. Nothing. He looked up, thinking.

And then he saw it. Right in plain sight, hanging behind the back porch light, was a key. He reached up, took it, slid it into the lock. He heard the chambers turn followed by a click. When he tried the handle it turned easily, so he pushed the door open.

The abandonment had not been kind to his home. Some of the ceiling plaster had collapsed, littering the counter top in debris. The tiled floor was brown, mostly from water damage. Mouse droppings littered the corners and along the edges of the trim. He tried the light switch knowing nothing would happen. No way was there still power.

David walked into the dining room. Much the same—the carpet was covered in mold. The chandelier hung two feet lower than it should, the base having broken from the ceiling, dangling by the bare wires. Gone was the warmth he remembered, the Thanksgiving and Christmas dinners, just he and Lilly.

He explored the remaining rooms, his mind drifting to the past, sadness growing with each step, days long gone. Here the TV sat, his chair, the couch, watching *Jeopardy!* together, trying to solve the puzzle first. Lying in bed, he with a newspaper, Lilly a book.

This was to be their child's room before the accident. The crib was to go there, the dresser there. It was one of the brightest rooms in the house, a shining beacon of joy in their lives. But it wasn't meant to be, and in the end it had become a sewing room for Lilly.

Back in the kitchen he tugged on the stuck basement door. It finally gave, the smell of decay wafting from the darkness. Reaching into his coat pocket, he pulled out a small flashlight. He hadn't expected the place to be vacant but it never hurt to come prepared. With a press of the button the stairs came into dim view. A dry groan emanated from the old wooden stair as he took a step. He hoped the stairs would hold.

The stench was worse at the bottom of the stairs. He did a slow turn, the light cutting through the darkness. The basement was as empty as upstairs, nothing left behind. David crossed the room to a closed door. The knob turned easily, and the door opened. The stench hit him hard, and he took an involuntary step back covering his face. What in God's name? He shined the light in.

A decaying dog lay against the far wall. Judging by the maggots squirming in its eyes, nose, and mouth it hadn't been dead long, maybe a week. How had it gotten in here? No matter, a dead dog was the least of his concerns. Best get what he came for and get out of here.

This room had once been used to store coal for the furnace, though that was long before David and Lilly bought the place. For years it was used for storage, until David and Lilly needed a project one winter day. They decided to convert it into a pantry, so they'd worked together constructing shelves. Lilly had been the one to find the loose brick, and when she pulled it out she discovered a hollow area behind the wall.

The light danced over the bricks. He wondered…

David worked his finger into the small missing chunk on the underside of the brick and worked it out. With a little effort he managed to slide it out, then grasped the second and pulled it out, too. He shined the light into the compartment and, to his delight, saw a red cloth. He felt giddy as he pulled it out and unwrapped it: the dull and worn necklace. Or part of it. The pendant he remembered seemed to have been broken in half. Still, it was lovely.

After their confrontation with DeMarcus she'd said she'd lost it, yet now here it was. Why had she lied about it?

There was a scraping sound behind him; he turned just as the door slammed, the echo bouncing off the walls. The noise had startled him, and he dropped the flashlight and the necklace, the light going out.

"Blast it." He reached down and felt around, his fingers only scraped stone. No way was he going to find anything without the door open.

He went to it and grabbed the knob, but it wouldn't budge. Jammed! He slammed his fist on the door. In the gloom he could hear the slithering and sucking sound of the maggots eating the dog. It grew in intensity as he continued to hammer at the door.

The chewing, the gnawing.

BANG!

The squirming, the squealing.

BANG!

Fear was taking hold. A distant familiar screech, a horror from his past.

BANG! BANG!

Getting louder, closer. Sweat dripped into his eyes, burning. Full on panic taking hold.

BANG! BANG! BANG!

And then the door opened and David was staring into the concerned and beautiful face of Cynthia. "Mr. Rottingham! Are you okay?"

David put a hand to his chest, closed his eyes, calmed his breathing. He nodded vigorously. "Yes. I am now, thank you."

"What happened?"

"I don't know. Th—the door. Wind must have caught it or something and it jammed."

Cynthia directed her flashlight to the dog, her face contorting in disgust. "Come on. Let's get you out of here."

"Wait. I dropped something. May I borrow your flashlight?"

She handed it over and he swung around. His flashlight had rolled next to the dog; no way was he going near that thing. But where did the necklace go? He scanned the ground but it was nowhere to be seen.

"Where are you?" he muttered to himself, walking in circles around the room.

"What are you looking for?"

"A necklace. It was my wife's. Do you see it?"

There was a moment of silence, then, "No."

"I had it in my hand. Then the door closed, and I dropped it. It has to be here."

Yet he couldn't find it; it was as if it had disappeared. With a resignation he looked back at Cynthia. "I'm sorry," she said. "I just don't see it."

The pitter patter of feet echoed from a pitch black section of the basement they hadn't been in. Cynthia looked from the sound to David nervously. "We better go."

With a frustrated sigh, he stood and moved past her. She kept the light on the stairs so he could see the steps as he ascended. A minute later they were standing in the backyard.

"It's a good thing I saw a suspicious old man hanging around the back and decided to investigate," she said with a smile.

"So am I." He glanced around.

She grasped his upper arm and gave it a gentle squeeze. "You going to be alright?"

"I think so, yes." He turned and looked back at the house. *Strike two.* First the cabin, now the house. He was going to have to come back a second time to try and recover that necklace.

With Cynthia in tow he made his way slowly to the front of the house. He gave it one final look. "A shame."

"Yes," Cynthia said. "A shame."

"I must be going, Cynthia. Thank you again."

"Of course. About dinner—"

"I'll let you know."

"Okay," she said, then turned and walked to her house. David went in the other direction. He was being polite, and he knew she knew that. There would be no dinner.

* * *

"What do you mean you have no record of who owns the property?" Stavic asked into the phone. "There's a goddamn shack on some goddamn land next to a goddamn river. There's a little goddamn road that goes to it, too."

"I'm sorry, Deputy, but as far as our records indicate that is public land owned by the county and not any individual person. I wish I could be more help."

He slammed the phone down as Kinney walked up, coffee in one hand, a folder in the other. "Trouble?"

"County clerk is fucking useless."

"There's a lot of woods out there, Nick. Hard for anyone to keep tabs on everything that goes on in them." He sat down, the chair squeaking as he leaned back, and set his coffee on the edge of the desk.

Stavic took the folder and looked over the paperwork. Two dead bodies, both unknowns. He'd been meaning to pay his dealer a visit after the first John Doe but hadn't had the opportunity. While Charles Went wasn't secretive about his dealings, he did keep a low profile. Stavic didn't think Kinney knew about Went's side business, so decided it play it safe. Why ruin a good thing?

"During my little excursion with Harold he mentioned some murders back in the fifties. His description of it was awfully similar to what we're seeing now. Know anything about it?"

Kinney closed the folder, handed it back. "Nope. A bit before my time."

"Think we have files?"

Kinney exhaled an airy whistle. "Somewhere I'm sure, but don't go asking me where. All the old case files are in boxes in the basement. Never had a reason to go digging through that stuff."

Stavic didn't much relish digging through old moldy and rotting boxes looking for the paperwork on two murders fifty-plus years ago. "Who was the sheriff back then? Think he could help?"

"Maybe, if he were still alive. Man died of a heart attack years ago."

Damn. "You do realize we can have all that digitized, right?"

"Yes, but why? Haven't had to dig through those boxes in a long time. No justification for the cost."

Looked like he was going to have to do this the old fashioned way. He was going to need more coffee and a line before going down there.

"If you don't mind me saying so," Kinney said as he stood, "you really should do something with your desk. Personalize it."

"With what?"

"I don't know. A picture. A calendar. Anything."

"Why's that?"

"Helps you focus. Gives you a chance to look away from work for a minute and collect your thoughts. What you're doing right now forces you to focus on one thing: work. It can drag you down."

"I'll go for a walk if I need a break." *Or do a line in the shitter.* "Can we get back on track, please?"

"I'm telling you it helps."

Stavic grabbed another folder, opened it, and pulled out some photos and papers. "To make things more interesting it appears the cabin is on public land. No record of who owns it—"

"It's definitely old. Been there decades."

"At least. Bed was stripped down—no fluids. No garbage lying around."

"Any tire marks?"

"None, but with all the leaves coming down that's not too surprising. I think the more likely scenario is that whoever is going to that place comes by way of the river."

Kinney stood and took his coffee. "You might as well start digging through the old cases downstairs. A weak lead is better than no lead."

"Want to help?"

"Not on your life," Kinney chuckled and walked away.

* * *

Claire decided that she needed to try and repair the connection between her and her daughter. When she'd made the realization yesterday that they hadn't even had a nice meal together in a really long time, she'd gone to the grocery store to pick up supplies for one of Emily's favorite dishes. She hoped Emily would be as excited as she was to make it. She knew she'd disappointed her daughter, and she wanted to make it up to her. It was time for her to be a mother again.

She turned the corner onto her street. The car rattled; she'd have to get that looked at when her last paycheck was deposited. Her house was just a few blocks away, a black car parked out front. She watched Emily jog out the front door and get in.

As the car drove past she noticed the driver was a boy around Emily's age. Who was he? It wasn't her ex-boyfriend, and she didn't have any friends that were boys that she knew. Dinner forgotten she decided to follow.

Claire had never tailed another vehicle before, but she'd seen it done in the movies. She knew to keep her distance so as not to spook the other driver, but stay close enough so that they weren't lost. What looked easy in the movies turned out to be more challenging in real life. At one intersection she almost lost them when they turned right on a yellow light. She was two cars back and was positive she wouldn't be able to find them—they had a good lead on her after all—but there they were, several blocks ahead, pulling into a metered spot. When she was a little closer she did the same.

What am I doing? All these years she'd trusted Emily to make smart decisions, so why was she suddenly concerned? Maybe it had to do with the fact she didn't know who Emily was hanging out with. Emily had shown good judgment over the years because she liked all her friends—all smart girls—but something just felt… *off.*

Emily and the boy got out of the car and walked down the sidewalk. A boyfriend? Just a friend?

They rounded the corner, disappearing from view. Shit! Claire jumped out of the car and hurried along the sidewalk, slowing as she approached the corner. She peeked around and didn't see them. Had they gone in one of the stores? She hurried on, looking in stores as she passed.

Nope. No. Nothing. Where had they gone?

A red Nissan drove past and pulled into a slot a few spots down.

"Oomph!" she said as she bumped into the back of someone who let out a small cry.

"What the hell?"

Claire stared at Emily. The boy had a supportive arm around her, bracing her from a fall. She feigned surprise. "Emily? I am so sorry. I didn't see you there."

Emily glanced at the boy nervously then to her mother.

The boy was handsome, with just a hint of acne. His face had light peach-fuzz whispers that matched his blond hair. "You must be Emily's mother. I can see the resemblance." He pulled his arm from around Emily and extended his hand to Claire with a warm smile. "I'm Billy, Mrs. Whitmore. I go to school with Emily."

She took his hand and shook it. "Nice to meet you. Emily never mentioned you to me."

"Mom," Emily said with a hint of embarrassment.

"I—I'm sorry," Claire stammered. "That was rude."

Billy just shook it off. "It's alright."

Claire looked back to Emily. "I was about to head home to make dinner. Will you be joining me? Lemon chicken," she said in a sing-song fashion.

"Oh. Um, we were going to meet up with Jessica and a few others at Manny's. Is that alright?"

Claire eyed her suspiciously, forcing Emily to look away, uncomfortable. "But... lemon chicken..."

"Mom... I didn't know. Can we do it tomorrow?"

Claire was disappointed, but she had sprung this on Emily. "Be home by eight, okay? You have school tomorrow."

"I'm seventeen, mom. And it's Friday."

"Of course. Right. Midnight then, okay? Not a minute past."

"Fine," she said begrudgingly.

Claire looked at Billy. "Make sure she's home on time."

"I will, Mrs. Whitmore."

As the two walked away Claire realized that she didn't trust Billy. He was charming, yes, but he put her off somehow.

You're being silly. He was nothing but courteous.

Yet she didn't trust him.

* * *

"Hello, David."

His heart skipped a beat, couldn't believe his eyes. DeMarcus! "But… how?" he asked.

DeMarcus stood in the doorway of David's hotel room grinning. *That damn grin.*

"Come now. Let's be civil. May I come in?"

He knew he didn't have a choice. DeMarcus didn't look like he'd aged a day while he had one foot in the grave. There was no way he could fend off DeMarcus even if he tried. He stood aside and let him in.

DeMarcus looked around. "Nice. Quaint." He focused on David. "How long has it been?"

"Long…?"

"Since our last confrontation."

"Fifty years." It seemed DeMarcus was as equally baffled. "How is it you haven't aged?"

"How is it that you have?" David didn't know how to respond and was saved when DeMarcus held up a hand. "A silly question for an obvious answer. Our times are not in sync. What was years for you was weeks for me." He sat on the edge of the bed, brushed out a wrinkle. "How have you been?"

Confusion boiled away to anger and he shut the door more forcefully than intended. "Cut the crap, DeMarcus. Why are you here? How did you find me?"

"I sensed Lilly. Where is she?"

A pang of grief swept over him. "How dare you talk about my wife."

"Lest you forget she was mine before she was yours."

"She was never yours."

DeMarcus sighed. "I'm in no mood, so I ask again: where is Lilly?"

"Dead." He couldn't be sure, but David thought he saw a flicker of dismay flash across DeMarcus' face.

"Impossible. I know she's here."

"Whatever you think you know is wrong. She's been dead going on twenty years."

David watched DeMarcus' expression shift as he had an internal debate about whether or not he was telling the truth. "Do you mind if I look around to… indulge my curiosity?"

"If it gets you out of my room then be my guest."

DeMarcus looked in the bathroom and closet. It was slow and meticulous.

"It's not that big a place, DeMarcus. It shouldn't be taking you this long."

He turned toward David, the smile having dropped a little. "Where is she?"

"Whispering Pines Cemetery. Go look if you don't believe me."

"How long?" DeMarcus asked as if unsure he believed David.

"Twenty-one years."

The man was on edge, and he was sure DeMarcus was going to lunge at him. If he did would he be able to fend him off? Doubtful. And if that happened he wouldn't be able to figure out why he was back, why Lilly was guiding him here.

DeMarcus glided toward David and it took all his courage not to flinch away. When DeMarcus spoke he smelled of honey and licorice. "What you perceive as death is nothing but an illusion. She's someplace close, I can sense it. Two days… that's what I offer you." And with that DeMarcus let himself out.

Two days? Two days for what? What was he talking about? David knew he wasn't going to like finding out.

five

Willem stood at the back of the church watching his brother's friends pay their last respects. He knew none of them, and the few family present were all but strangers. Those first to arrive expressed their sympathies to him too for which he politely thanked them, but after the first dozen or so he moved to the back of the church to avoid any more awkward exchanges. He didn't feel right detracting from Elliott's wife and children, so he decided it best to blend in with the crowd—just another person in a sea of friends.

At the front of the room was his brother's open casket. He was in a black suit, and didn't look nearly as sickly as he did when Willem last spoke with him. Beth had come up beside him and gently placed a worn pocket watch in Elliott's hand. It was familiar though he couldn't quite place it. She'd looked at him with tired eyes and had asked how he was doing. Alright, he'd said. He felt the same as he did at his mother's funeral. Nothing.

Beth had asked if he'd like to perform the eulogy, but he'd declined. How could he accept? He knew his brother as a child, not as a father and husband. He knew next to nothing of him. Anything after his twenties was a fog of estrangement and occasional brief visits. Best eulogy duties go to someone who hadn't been absent the better part of his life, Elliott's son or daughter perhaps.

So strange, Willem thought, that he was the last survivor of his family. His father, if he were alive would be in his nineties now, but with his lifestyle Willem was all but certain he'd passed. Sam's death, his mother's passing, and now Elliott—it was an unusual sensation knowing you were the last in your family. How had he survived so long? He didn't eat particularly well nor did he exercise. He should have died of a heart attack years ago, yet here he was watching strangers grieve over his brother.

Reflecting on his past the last couple of days he saw where he'd made poor decisions. Willem never should have let things come between him and his family because, really, what was the point? He was more alone now than ever. While he hadn't been on speaking terms with his mother or brother they were there, and he could have called them if he needed to. Deep down he knew he'd been the one to distance himself, that he'd pushed them away. For all these decades he'd wanted to blame them, to not bear sole responsibility, but sitting in his small hotel room thinking about Elliott and his mother, Sam and his father, past and present relationships, everything that had come between him and other people was his own doing.

Memories of his mother's funeral flooded back. At the time he'd felt hollow and empty, unsure what emotions he should feel. He'd hated the woman for so long that he'd almost not gone, but after prodding by Elliott and Beth he'd succumbed to a need for closure. He'd hoped that by going he'd have a better understanding of the choices she'd made and be able to forgive her. Better late than never, he'd supposed. As Willem had stood outside the church the cold wind blew at his back and the gray skies above only further soured his mood. It was only when the organ started playing he begrudgingly entered the church.

Like Elliott his mother had been in an open casket, the polished dark wood reflecting the fluorescent lights. The turnout had been good, great in fact, for a woman in her eighties. He figured all of her friends would be long dead, but he had been wrong. There were scores of people there of all ages, people that his mother had somehow affected in a positive way. It seemed she'd been more a mother to these strangers than him. Seeing these people, these *strangers*, swooning about his mother gave him pause. Had he been wrong all these years? Was his animosity toward her misguided?

He'd sat through the service feeling nothing, then he'd gone to the cemetery and witnessed her being laid to rest. While the rain had stopped the afternoon remained gray. The priest said a few more words, and then she was lowered into the ground. That evening, after more than a few drinks had been downed, the years of bubbling anger hit a tipping point for Willem. He and Elliott had their final blowout ending with Willem storming off. They hadn't spoken since.

First Sam and then his mother. Now here he was, years later, doing the same thing all over again. Funny all that time he'd been disconnected, never wanting to talk or see them, only to lose them and... miss them. He felt alone. *I am alone.* All this time he'd thought that that's what he'd wanted, and now he found himself wishing they were all back. Even though he hadn't been in contact with them he'd felt secure in knowing that they were there.

What had he done? Why had he allowed himself to go on like this?

Anger is a funny thing—such a strong emotion that it could make you hate someone for so long and not remember why. Well, that was going to change. He was going to be a better uncle and brother-in-law moving forward. A better friend, too. When he got back he was going to make an effort to be more social with Justin. Hell, maybe he'd even go out with him one night.

Willem was brought back to the now when he realized that the chatter had stopped. Gregory, Elliott's son, stood at a podium. He shuffled some papers, took a moment to collect himself, then looked out across the room.

"My father..." Gregory paused, wiped at his eyes. "I'm sorry." He turned away to collect himself, turned back after a sigh. "I'm sorry," he said again, the room remaining quiet. "My father was a good man, a compassionate man. He was an amazing grandfather, father-in-law, brother. He always put himself before others at work and at home. I suppose that's why so many of you are here today, because this man touched your heart in some way. But there was a side many of you didn't see—that of a father, a husband, a family man. That's what I'll be talking about today.

"My father didn't have an easy life. He was born in 1946 and was the oldest of three brothers. Their father abandoned them leaving their mother to pick up the pieces and do what she could. The house wasn't paid for, and she only had a high school diploma. Samuel, the youngest brother, died when he was just eight.

"I never knew my grandfather. My grandmother was a bitter woman, a hard woman, yet compassionate. She had had a hard life so it was no wonder she was the way she was. My father started working at a young age, as a stock boy if memory serves." Gregory paused a moment and bit his lower lip, eyes distant. "The name of the store escapes me at the moment, but I know the owners name was in it." A smile came to his lips. "The reason I mention this is because many of you know how tight my father was with money." A wave of chuckles moved through the room, people nodding in agreement. "He made a dollar an hour, and he worked every day after school and on weekends to help the family. He told me once that he would have liked to have gone out for some sports, spent more time with his friends, but he felt a responsibility."

Gregory's steely gaze focused on Willem. "He had to become an adult far earlier than any teenager should have to, but he did it so the burden was not his mother's alone. He gave up his childhood so that they could stay in their home." His nephew's eyes bore into his, and he felt ashamed. "It killed him not to be the big brother he wanted to be, but it was a sacrifice that he felt needed to be made." And then his eyes drifted away across the crowd.

Willem couldn't help but feel terrible. He'd distanced himself from his mother and his brother when all they were doing was trying to allow him to have a normal childhood, and he blew it by being a selfish idiot.

"What he learned those years—about working hard and saving, to not live lavishly—was how he lived his life. He managed to put himself through school, he worked exceptionally hard, and became successful. By his example my sister and I both got jobs while in high school. While he didn't force us he definitely encouraged it because he felt it was an experience one had to learn to appreciate what you had, not what you wanted. If we wanted something that wasn't a necessity we had to work for it, earn the money to buy it, to appreciate it. It was a hard lesson, a shitty lesson…" Those chuckles again. "But we are better people because of it.

"Not many people know this but he also served in Vietnam. He was drafted when he was nineteen and deployed at twenty. He served his country for four years until he was honorably discharged. He didn't agree with the war, he felt it a lost cause, but he also felt it his duty as an American. I never talked to him much about what his experiences were. I tried, but when I did he always managed to change the subject. Another skill I'm sure some of you have experienced." People laughed this time—a good sound.

"Now, how he met my mother is a story I've always liked." Willem glanced at Beth and only saw the back of her head, yet he sensed she was smiling at the memory. "As I understand it, my mother was out for a walk downtown when she came across a bird. She sees this little goldfinch on the sidewalk—people walking by ignoring it—and she knew something was wrong. Although the bird tried to get away she managed to pick it up. It then occurred to her she had no idea what to do with it. So she has this tiny little bird cupped in her hands, and my father stopped to see what was wrong. She showed him, and when most people would have thought this lady nuts for picking up a dirty bird, he offered her his handkerchief to wrap the bird in. He walked with her to a nearby park and together they took care of this tiny yellow bird until it flew off. Anyone who's seen their backyard knows their passion for birds. It's more than appreciation and affection, but served as a reminder of a chance encounter that brought them together.

"I'm sure they had difficult times as all marriages do, but their compassion and love—not just for each other—is a reminder of how wonderful my parents, my *father*, was. He never yelled at us, never struck us, was never too busy for us…" He looked across the room, again focusing on Willem. "And he never gave up on any of us. He was what every man should strive to be, and the world is a lonelier place now that he is gone."

Gregory looked away from Willem, folded up the paper and walked back to his seat.

* * *

Stavic had every intention of visiting Charles Went last night, but after being stuck in the station's dingy basement digging through case files for hours, all he'd wanted to do was go home and get blasted. He'd thought about going after, but he had a reputation to maintain. Crashing his truck in a stupor would have ended his career real quick. And yes, he had his vices, but he enjoyed his job. In many ways he felt he was doing the community a service—by maintaining relations with the local dealers he could keep an eye on them. It was all for them.

After waking he'd showered, had his breakfast with an extra strong coffee, and dressed, then headed for the truck. Unsolved cases from the fifties could wait another day; a visit to The Thirsty Whale could not.

The Whale is what the locals called the secluded little dive bar off Lake Crescent. It was a little ways out of town down a two-lane winding road through the woods. They had a dock set up for those who preferred to boat in.

He turned off onto a gravel road that was just barely wide enough for two cars. Trees hugged the road, their branches slapping the truck along. And then he was in the lot with only three other cars. It was early enough in the day that people had yet to come and drink, smoke, and snort their money away. The Thirsty Whale had been designed to look like a log cabin—a style many used in this area—the exterior painted a nice dark tan. He kicked up gravel as he walked to the door and opened it.

The lights were on inside, but it was still dim. Adorning the walls were long dead taxidermy fish. A buck's head was mounted above the bar.

At the far end of the bar was Fred, a grizzled old man who practically lived here. He did odd jobs for the owner in exchange for drinks on the house.

"Charles here?" Stavic asked.

Fred pulled the half empty glass from his lips, white foam stuck to his whiskers. He licked it away. "In the back." A cough, then he called out, "Charles! Someone's here to see ya!"

"Give me a sec!" a deep voice boomed.

Fred gave Stavic a sideways glance. "He'll be out momentarily." He pronounced every word perfectly as if to make sure Stavic understood, then took a drag on his smoldering cigarette, the ember glowing a bright orange.

Stavic sat on a bar stool. The place smelled of stale smoke, staler booze, and cleaning products. It made him want a drink. A few years back the state implemented an ordinance forbidding smoking in public places. Went decided not to comply, something Stavic had to occasionally issue a ticket for. I scratch your back, you scratch mine was the mentality. And, so far, it seemed to be working out.

Charles Went was lumberjack big. He looked more a bouncer than a bar owner, but if he could handle the crowd then why pay someone else to do it? "Afternoon, Stavic. What can I do you for?" He glanced around. "You come alone?"

"As always."

"Alright. Give me a sec and I'll grab your bait. Grubs?"

'Bait' was the code Charles liked to use for drugs. Grubs was cocaine, worms marijuana, leeches was acid, and minnows LSD. He didn't deal with injectable drugs or so he claimed. Stavic had no reason to doubt him—he was the honest sort.

"Actually," Stavic sighed, "I'm here on another matter." He lowered his voice. "You happen to know if there's someone new in town dealing?"

"New?" Charles shook his head slowly. "Not that I know of. Why?"

"Case I'm working on."

"You talking about those two fellas that got murdered?" asked Fred from down the bar. He was looking ahead, staring at the liquor bottles against the back wall.

"What about them?" Stavic asked, glancing from Charles to Fred.

A shrug. "Nothing I haven't seen on the news."

And news it was. It wasn't often citizens of River Bend died mysteriously. They'd tried to keep it as hush-hush as possible—releasing only the names and mentioned they'd died of unknown causes, but that was all. They'd tried to keep the details as obscure as possible so as not to cause a panic. But, as things were in a small community, people talked and word spread.

"You sure about that? Haven't heard anything?"

"Nothing but farts in the wind."

Stavic wasn't sure if that was true, but he'd let it go for the moment. He turned his attention back to Charles. "What about you?"

"Nah. Same shit as always."

"Nothing about two bodies?"

"Is there something you're after, deputy?" Went was more curt than usual.

Stavic had the feeling something was amiss here, something Charles wasn't telling him. Another look around the room and his eyes fell on the unobtrusive door that led to the basement. Or that's what people assumed. For those in the know it led to a private section of the bar—a real underground place for those who wanted something more than just a night of drinks. He didn't know all the details—never went down there. Easier to play ignorant that way.

Stavic looked back to Charles. "Nothing on the other side of the world?"

"I wish I could help. I'll keep my ears open though."

"I'd appreciate that." He wrapped his knuckles on the bar and stood. "You know… maybe I will take you up on that bait after all."

"Sure thing. Usual?"

"Yeah. I didn't come prepared today—"

"Let me stop you right there. I know you're good for it."

"Thanks." Stavic stared at the shimmering lake through the back door. "You know, I think I'm going to take in the view."

"Knock yourself out. I'll have your bait right here for you when you're ready."

Charles excused himself to the back, and Stavic stepped out the back door onto a wooden deck that led to the dock. Ripples glided along the surface, the sound of a motor boat echoed in the distance. Across the way he saw a boat come around an outcropping of trees. That must be what Harold talked about the other day, where the lake joined the Fox River.

"How much do you really know about what happens in this town, deputy?"

Stavic started. Fred had followed him out and stood only a couple feet behind him looking out across the lake. "Enough."

"More than you know, I'd wager."

"What do you mean?"

"You know Charles pretty well I suspect which means you probably know he don't scare easy." He took a drag on his cigarette. "Everyone gets scared of something. I've seen the face of the man that scares him."

"Who?"

"I've only seen him once, the first time he came in here." His voice dropped to a whisper. "I never want to see him again."

"When was that?"

"The other night."

"And you're sure you've never seen him before?"

"No."

"Who is he?"

"I don't know, but he's a jovial fellow, or at least pretends to be. You see… he's always smiling. But there's something in that smile that's unsettling. It's not real," Fred said.

"Not real? You mean like false teeth?"

"No. The smile… it's a mask."

The door screeched behind Stavic. "You boys need more private time?" Charles voice boomed. Stavic and Fred looked at Charles who had the door propped open.

"We're just shooting the shit," Stavic replied. "It ready?"

"Has been." Charles pulled his head back and the door closed.

Stavic turned to Fred. "This... smiling man... he have a name?"

Fred took a final drag of his smoke. "DeMarcus. That's what I overheard at least." Fred dropped the butt and ground his heel into it. "Nice talking with you, deputy."

* * *

After the funeral Beth had come up to Willem and told him that she was hosting an intimate gathering for Elliott's closest friends. Would you please come? Willem had politely refused, citing his estrangement from the family, but she'd hear none of it. After a few insistences he'd agreed. He'd sat behind the wheel of his car, stopped at a red light wondering what in God's name he'd talk to these people about. He knew nothing of Elliott in his later years. Willem had settled on an appearance before excusing himself a half hour later. Yeah... that would be best. Let those closest mourn.

Now here he was two hours later with a cocktail in hand—the first in many years—watching the last of Elliott's friends leave. When the door closed Beth's shoulders slumped and she turned to Willem. With a weak smile she said, "Thank you."

"For what?"

"For coming. It means a lot."

Willem nodded as glass shattered in the kitchen. "Shit!" a woman's voice came. When they entered the kitchen Elliott's daughter Margaret was crouched picking up shards.

"Are you okay?" Beth asked.

Margaret sniffed, running the back of her hand under her nose. "Yes. It just slipped."

"Here... Let me." Beth got to her knees and helped her daughter pick up the broken glass. Willem set his drink down and went to the pantry where he'd seen a broom and dust pan earlier in the day. The two women stood and threw the larger pieces away as Willem swept up the remainder.

"Everything okay?" Gregory asked as he entered the kitchen.

"Fine, fine."

Gregory went to the fridge, pulled out a beer and offered it to Willem. He looked at the bottle, shrugged. "What the hell," he said and took it. What's one more?

"Anyone else?" Gregory asked as he opened another.

Margaret and Beth shook their heads no.

Gregory shut the door and stood at the counter next to Willem. He took a pull from the bottle. "I didn't get a chance to tell you this before, but that was a nice eulogy," Willem said, Gregory glancing at him. "Your father seemed to be very popular."

"He was well respected," Gregory agreed, "and will be greatly missed."

Beth looked at him sympathetically. Was it because of lost time? How his life had turned out? He noticed Margaret looking at him with a hint of curiosity. "What is it?" he asked her.

"It's just... I always wondered what happened between you and dad. I know it's none of my business but..." She shrugged and let the words hang in the air.

Willem felt all eyes on him and sipped his beer. What to say? There was too much to tell about his past, too much emotional baggage to give, and he didn't want to relive it now. The other problem was that he couldn't remember the specifics of the argument, what had sent him storming off the night of their mother's funeral. It was as much a mystery to him as it was to her.

He shook his head. "I don't know."

Margaret's brow furrowed. "What?"

"I don't know."

"Seriously? You and dad have barely spoken over something you can't remember?"

"That pretty much sums it up."

"Unbelievable," Gregory mumbled.

Willem glanced at him. "Your father and I have been through a lot together. A lot. Our father running off, our brother's death... We started to grow apart when we were still teenagers, but if you want to know what single thing happened that caused us to stop talking?" He shrugged. "I don't remember." Willem looked down to the bottle in his hands. "Have you ever heard the saying that anger is a poison?"

"Of course."

"It's true." He looked to Gregory again and felt tears on his cheeks. "It's true," he repeated, a lump forming in his throat. "Anger is a cancer. Once it takes hold it's very hard to get rid of. That's a lesson I'm only learning now. A very painful lesson."

* * *

Stavic was at his desk, feet up, looking at the old case files. A married couple, Harold and Joan Shaw, were killed in a horrific brutal slaying much like his two John Does. Harold worked as a traveling salesman and Joan was a housewife. A criminal background check yielded nothing out of the ordinary. They did have an adult daughter named Lilly that had recently married. He made a note to try and track her down.

He looked at their backgrounds again. They'd moved here from Albuquerque over a decade earlier; nothing strange there. Stavic compared the reports for the umpteenth time and noted both had moved here as well. While they were transplants as well not a goddamned thing connected them. If it was the same killer—he felt it unlikely—he or she would be in their seventies now, minimum. Copycat maybe? But who would be copying a series of murders from fifty-plus years ago, and why?

He tossed the folders back on his desk, rubbed his eyes. None of this made sense. Except...

Stavic pulled the old files out, skimmed them. There it was. The Shaw's bodies had been found in the woods near what had been the remains of a cabin. The cabin itself was no more—only the foundation had survived—and had been nestled in a wide indentation. He flipped to a faded black and white location photo.

The cabin was indeed gone, but he could clearly make out the layout of the structure. Off to the side he noted the crumbling remains of a well. While it could be the same cabin they'd found a few days back, how was it that there was a cabin there now? Had the owner rebuilt what once was there? But to do that you'd need building permits, and there was no record of this place at all.

He rubbed his sore eyes. Enough of this. He'd been burning the wick at both ends these past few days and he was burned out. He needed sleep, especially if tomorrow would be as busy as he suspected. It was time to go home.

* * *

Willem shut the door behind him and stepped off the front stoop. It was cool, the sun setting, a classic contradictory Midwest autumn much like his mood. He was almost to his car when he heard, "Willem?"

He turned. Beth walked toward him, her hands rubbing her arms in the chill. A pair of birds swooped and passed overhead.

"Will we see you again?" she asked.

"I don't know. I'd be lying if I said I did."

Beth nodded in understanding and looked away at the changing leaves. "This was always Elliott's favorite time of year. The Peak, he called it." She smiled. "Every year around this time we'd take a drive in the country, make a day of it. All the back roads winding through the woods, along the river. It reminded him of his youth he said." Her smile fell and she bit her lip. "Is it true what you said? About not remembering?" Beth looked at him expectantly.

"Yes."

She nodded in understanding and gave a weak smile. "Elliott took it pretty hard that you never said anything. He figured after his letter you'd understand, let bygones be bygones."

Perplexed, Willem couldn't help but ask. "What letter?"

"Elliott," Beth said slowly, "he sent you a letter after your fight. He spent several nights writing it, sure that it might help with, well, whatever it was you were going through."

"Did he tell you what was in it?"

She shook her head. "No. Just that he hoped it would help."

Had he received a letter? He didn't remember getting one. "Just after the fight?" he asked.

"Yes. Didn't you get it?"

Willem searched his memory. For months after that fight he'd used booze as a Band-Aid for the memories, for the pain. Much of that time was a foggy mess. Just because he couldn't remember a letter didn't mean there hadn't been one. But if he had received it what had he done with it?

Then the past began to creep back. It had been a few weeks after the fight, and he'd come home from the bar well past what a responsible person should drink, and found an envelope from Elliott in his mailbox with an assortment of other mail. The envelope from Elliott had a small object sealed within. He remembered it slid back and forth the length of the envelope. What had it been? A key! That's right. There had been a small key in the envelope. He had ripped open the side of the envelope and dumped the key and its double-vision partner into the palm of his hand.

After that he drew a blank.

"What's wrong?" Beth asked.

Willem offered a friendly, if not entirely comforting, smile. "Sorry. Just lost in thought. I did get the letter, but never read it. It came at a time…" He shrugged. "There was something with the letter though. A key. Do you have any idea what it went to?"

"No. I don't know anything about that."

"Well," Willem said dragging it out, "I better get going. Thank you again for the hospitality, and I'm sorry. About everything."

Beth reached around Willem and gave him a gentle hug. He tensed, but then wrapped his arms around her. "It's okay. The important thing is that you came and the two of you got to say goodbye. That's what's important." Beth pulled away and looked up into Willem's eyes. "Should you ever want to talk you have my number. And *please*… don't be a stranger."

"I won't," Willem said. He wasn't sure he would stay in contact, but he knew it was the polite thing to say. And who knew? Maybe he would. It had felt nice to rekindle a relationship with his family.

"Goodbye, Willem." Beth turned and walked back to the house, never looking back. Willem stood a while thinking about his brother, the letter he had sent, the key. That god damned key. What had he done with it?

He'd make a quick stop at the hotel to collect his things, and then he'd head back to River Bend tonight. He didn't know why, but he needed to find that key.

* * *

"Smells good," Emily said as she walked into the kitchen. "So what's the occasion?"

"None, really. I just know we haven't spent much time together. I want to try to start making it up to you, so I figured I'd make one of your favorite dishes." Claire stopped, concerned. "It is still one of your favorites, right?"

Emily flashed a reassuring smile easing Claire's tension. "Can I help with anything?"

Claire shook her head. "No. I've got it. Just take a seat. Finishing up now."

Emily did as asked, and Claire put the chicken next to bright green broccoli already on plates. She carried them to the table and sat, placing the meals in front of them. "Looks delicious," Emily said, readying her fork and knife.

"I hope so. It's been a while since I've made it."

They each bit into the chicken, the juice teasing their palates. "Yes. This is exactly as I remember it."

Claire smiled, proud of herself for bringing a smile to her daughter's face. It'd been so long since she saw genuine happiness there. "I'm happy we could do this."

"Me too, mom. It's nice."

This felt like a date. Had she become so disconnected with Emily she couldn't even have a conversation with her? "Thank you for being home when I asked."

"Midnight. Just like you asked."

"What did you do?"

A shrug. "Hung out."

"Just you and Billy?"

Emily inspected the chicken on her fork. "Yep."

"So... Billy... He seems—"

Like a good-for-nothing charlatan.

"—nice. Where did you meet him?"

"School."

Claire could sense Emily closing up, not wanting to talk about it. Still, she needed to connect, had to push through. "How long have you been dating?"

"We're not dating. We're just friends."

"Okay. How long have you two been *friends?*" Claire tried to say it in a teasing way, dragging out the word. Emily gave her an "are you serious?" glance.

"A while. Look, mom, I know what you're trying to do. I appreciate it, but it's really not necessary."

"What?"

"This!" Her hand flip-flopped between them. "I know your trying, but I'm just not ready. Not yet."

"You should trust me. I want you to trust me."

"I know I should, and I *will*. But not yet."

This wasn't how it was supposed to be. Daughters were supposed to be able to trust their mothers, not be evasive. "I'm just... concerned. You're hanging out with a strange boy I don't know. I'm just—"

"Parenting. I get it. You've raised me to be smart and make the right decisions. I'm a big girl, mom. I can take care of myself."

They ate in silence, their silverware clinking on the ceramic plates. It was then Claire made a decision. If Emily didn't want to share her life with her fine, but she was going to abide by her rules.

"What can you tell me about him? What class did you meet him in? What do you do together? Who—"

"Mom! Knock it off."

"You won't see that boy again. Understood? Not until I meet him."

"You're being unreasonable!"

"You're seventeen, Emily, and I'm your mother. I've let you be your own person for too long, not interfering in your life, but no more. No… I'm *not* being unreasonable."

Emily slammed her fist on the table, the dishes vibrating. She stood and stormed for the door.

"Where are you going?" Claire demanded.

"Out."

Claire stood and followed. "No you're not. Until further notice you're grounded."

Emily whirled, jabbed a finger at her mother. "Where is this coming from? How dare you make demands of me!"

"This is my house, so it's my rules."

Emily's face turned red. She retreated for the door, opened it.

"Get back here!"

"No!"

Claire slammed the door closed before Emily could leave.

"Get out of my way!" Emily cried. Claire just glared. She could see the muscles in Emily's jaw clench. "Fuck you, mom!"

"What is going on with you? It's like you're not even my little girl anymore."

"Little girl? Dad would never have treated me this way!"

"How would you know? Your dad left us when you were two!"

"I wish it had been you!"

Claire slapped Emily across the cheek. Hard.

What just happened? She'd never hit Emily before, not even a spank.

Emily turned toward her cupping her reddening cheek, tears glistening at the corner of her eyes. "Emily, I…"

Emily pushed past Claire and yanked the door open. "I hate you," she whispered as she breezed past.

"Emily, please wait."

Claire stopped herself from following knowing the damage was done. No matter what she said or did now would only exacerbate the problem.

She stood there in the night chill long after Emily had disappeared down the street. What had happened to Emily? It was as if her little girl was becoming someone else.

* * *

DeMarcus sat in the dark backseat of his idling car. After his meeting with David yesterday he couldn't get the words he'd uttered out of his mind. How could she be dead when he could sense her? No… she was hiding here somewhere. He just needed to find her.

Yet he couldn't shake the feeling David had been telling the truth. He could see the hurt and pain on the old man's face, so he'd taken a trip to Whispering Pines Cemetery today. It had taken some time, but with the help of Paul he finally found the headstone.

He couldn't wrap his head around it. If Lilly was dead then he shouldn't be able to sense her. How was it possible? He seethed with confusion and anger. Was it possible there was more to the the excommunication than was known?

DeMarcus instructed Paul where to drive. He focused his senses following the dim beacon that was Lilly and found David coming out of Wood Court Homes, which looked to be a community home of some type. Maybe he was visiting someone from his past, or maybe…

He told Paul to stop. When David had driven away DeMarcus went into the building, the lobby clean and inviting. Several elderly people sat on what looked to be comfortable chairs talking quietly amongst themselves. A middle aged woman was working on a computer. She looked like she worked here.

"Excuse me," he said. The woman looked up, her forming smile faltering.

"Can I help you?"

"I'm looking for Lilly Rottingham. I was told she was here."

"Lilly…" she looked confused, turned to the computer and typed on the keyboard. "I'm sorry sir, but there's no one here by that name."

"Are you sure? Could you check again? Maybe you spelled it wrong."

She turned back, tried different variations, shook her head. "I'm not finding a Lilly here. Are you sure you have the right place?"

He focused again and sensed Lilly's presence dimming. Annoyed, he said, "Perhaps you're right," and left. Once back in the car they resumed their driving. He spotted David again, this time in Manny's Diner. But then he sensed something else—very faint—as if Lilly's presence was in two locations. Curiouser and curiouser. It took some time, most of the afternoon driving in circles and up and down streets, until he was confident he'd found the source of the second beacon. He had Paul park a few houses down and there they sat, waiting.

The sun had set and he was becoming anxious, was ready to go up to the house and investigate, when the door was flung open and a young girl stormed out. He didn't understand, why would Lilly's essence be coming from here? And then an older woman came out and somehow he knew instantly it was that damn neighbor child Lilly and her husband had latched onto. What was her name? It didn't matter. That was who he was being drawn to; that was where he was sensing Lilly.

This woman and David.

He needed to mull this over, figure out why he was sensing Lilly coming from two people. If she was in fact dead she should have transcended back to Turmoore. Having her here...

"Let's go," he said to Paul. "I need to think this through."

"Anywhere in particular?"

DeMarcus considered the question. They had found the place Patrick had talked about, the communal place for socializing. He'd enjoyed the seediness of it; the underbelly was exquisite. "That place we went to. What did you call it? A bar? We don't have places like that where I come from, and I quite enjoyed it."

"The Thirsty Whale it is," Paul said, put the car in drive, and drove off.

six

Willem stood in the mess that was his bedroom. He'd pulled everything out of his closet, dumped packed away boxes out on the bed, emptied drawers, looking for the key his brother had sent him. Every other room in his house looked exactly the same, as if a tornado had blown through.

He sat on the edge of the bed and rubbed his tired eyes. He'd been at this all night, and it would probably take twice as long to put everything back, a prospect he was dreading. He again found himself wondering why he was so hell-bent on finding something his brother had sent him years ago. Was it worth getting this worked up over something he hadn't remembered existed twenty-four hours ago?

He stood, stretched his back, and sauntered to the kitchen. A breakfast break might do him some good. He pulled open the fridge and was greeted with barren shelves. Shit. The cupboards weren't any better, and there was no coffee. Looked like he was going to Manny's. It was just past eleven according to his watch. Thankfully the diner served breakfast all day.

After a quick shower he filled the bird feeder with fresh seed—couldn't let the little guys starve to death after all—hopped in his car and headed to town. As he drove his mind wandered to Elliott and why he had sent him a key. That made little sense to him. Perhaps the letter that had come with it would shed some light on it.

The willow tree stood majestically in the distance as he crossed Willow Creek Bridge giving him pause. His foot relaxed off the accelerator, and he pulled onto the shoulder as he slowed. He stared out the window at the tree, its thin branches swaying gently in the breeze.

Something from his childhood…

Willem put the car in park, got out, looked at the bridge. In the last week he'd been drawn to this place twice—first by a boy who was fishing, and now this moment. He felt something pull at him, something he couldn't explain. His gaze fell upon the tree again.

The tree. That's what he was being pulled to, but why? The tree had been there since he was a boy, and he had some vague recollection of it, but other than that the tree held no special meaning. He wanted to turn away, to just go get his breakfast, but he knew that it was useless until he investigated. Best to quench the insatiable urge and be done with it. Two minutes later he stood in the spongy moss field that surrounded the tree. The shadow beneath looked safe and welcoming; nothing appeared out of the ordinary, and nothing from his past came back. He parted the branches and entered.

The sensation he'd felt dissipated—not fully, but now it was just a dull throb in the back of his mind. He circled the tree taking it in. Nothing out of the ordinary. A squirrel had made a nest in one of the branches, though at the moment it was vacant. The base of the trunk was surrounded by rocks as if to weigh the tree down and prevent it from falling in a storm. Willem looked at the creek ten feet away trickling by.

Waste of time, coming here like this.

Yet while the drawing had subsided he felt a connection to Elliott and Sam. This place held a special meaning for him, or had in the past. Why couldn't he remember spending time here?

Because you've chosen to forget, a voice whispered.

No. If it was important he would have remembered.

The voice stayed silent as if challenging him.

He was tired and hungry, and all he wanted was some warm food and then a warm bed. He'd figure it out later.

He left the security of the willow and headed back to the car, a tiny voice following on the breeze. *You have to remember! Please remember, Willem. Please!*

* * *

It was time to go retrieve the necklace he'd been unable to collect two days prior. David dreaded having to enter his old home again knowing the poison beneath, but Lilly had insinuated it was necessary. If she said he needed it then by God he was going to get it. After that he needed to pay Claire a visit.

Claire. His heart warmed thinking of the little girl he once considered the daughter they'd never had. The smile, the dimples, the happy go lucky attitude of that adorable little girl. Yet something had happened over the years, something he couldn't quite figure out. Lilly had shown him what had become of her and she looked... troubled. Like something was eating away at her inside.

He wasn't sure how he'd approach her, wondering if she'd even remember him after all this time. He wasn't even sure what he was supposed to do with her but, like most of what was happening these last few weeks, it was a leap of faith.

David grabbed the hotel key off dresser and put on a light jacket. It looked nice out, but this time of year could be unpredictable. He opened the door and was taken aback by DeMarcus, poised ready to knock. Behind him was a man in a red trucker cap.

"Hello, David," he said and pushed his way past. The man in the cap guided David away from the door and closed it. "So have you thought about our conversation from the other day?"

David looked between the two men nervously, finally settling on DeMarcus. "Not particularly."

"I'm sure Lilly wouldn't want me hurting you but I will if that's what it comes down to." He looked around the room, said, "Do you hear me Lilly? Come out or your sweet sweet husband will suffer the repercussions of your defiance."

"I've told you she's dead."

DeMarcus wagged his finger at David. "I went to the cemetery as you suggested and did see the headstone. A well-played ruse if I do say so, but if she's truly gone then why can I still sense her? She's here, close by. I can sense it."

"You're mistaken."

"And you're naive, unless..." A quirky expression crossed DeMarcus' face, one that showed confused amusement. "She made you forget."

"You're talking nonsense. Please leave," David's voice quivered.

DeMarcus approached David and reached out to him. He stepped back and bumped into DeMarcus' friend who grabbed both his frail arms.

"What are you doing? Don't…"

DeMarcus laid his hand on the side of David's perspiring face. "Shh… Let me see." DeMarcus' eyes bore into his, the grin drooping as his eyes danced. Then the corner of his lip curled, and David felt as if a levee in his brain buckled. Memories long hidden washed over him in a torrential onslaught. His brain felt beaten.

"Nooo," he moaned and grabbed at his temples as DeMarcus stepped away. "Stop it, please! Take it back!"

But DeMarcus just stood and stared as David fell back onto the bed, images drowning him, suffocating him. It was too much for him and he began to to feel his mind shutting down.

"Lilly," he moaned. "Why?"

"Why indeed?" DeMarcus asked.

David felt his body seize. The last thing he saw was DeMarcus leaning in with his shit eating grin.

* * *

"Where are you going?" Claire asked as Emily breezed past without saying a word.

Emily was at the front door, jacket in hand. "Out."

"Not until I say so," Claire said.

Emily rolled her eyes.

"I'm serious." Emily stared at her as if challenging. "Come here. Sit down for a minute."

She badly wanted a splash of booze to take the edge off.

"What?" Emily asked as she leaned against the door frame.

Claire pursed her lips. "I'd like to talk about last night."

Just a sip to make this easier.

"Are you going to hit me again?"

The words were like a slap. "I deserve that." She sighed. "Do you want to know what really happened to your father?"

"He left you. What more is there?"

Whiskey. Vodka. Anything.

"Yes, but its *how* he left me. Us." Claire gestured to the other chair. "Please. Sit."

Emily did. "Can we make this quick?"

"Billy can wait."

Emily looked at her phone then leaned back in her chair, pouting.

"When I was young my parents moved a lot. My dad was in the military and every few years he'd be transferred someplace new. Except when we moved here. Here we stayed twice as long as usual. That is part of the reason when we had you we moved to River Bend—it felt like home.

"My parents weren't around much... even though I was young I still knew enough that they were having trouble. Because of that I spent a lot of time at the neighbor's house, a nice couple who couldn't have their own children. I had a fantastic bond with them, a connection, until one day my parents packed up and moved again. That was the one and only time I ever had a strong connection. Until I met your father, of course.

"When I was a senior in high school I went with a friend to a college party. It was my first time drinking alcohol and I was stupid. My friend ditched me after hooking up with a guy and I was left to fend for myself.

"I woke the next morning in the bed of a stranger. I was mortified and disgusted with myself, but when I realized nothing had happened, and the guy whose bed I was in was sleeping in a chair on the other side of the room..." She shrugged. "When I tried to sneak out..." The memory brought a smile to her lips, then a chuckle. "I tripped and landed face first in his lap."

She could tell Emily was loosening up a little, that she wasn't as mad.

Claire continued. "Our friendship blossomed into a romance. Your father was about to graduate from college, me from high school, and it was about that time that my parents told me they were moving again. It was the perfect excuse to stay put and move in with him.

"We rented a small apartment after graduation and got married a few months later. It wasn't anything fancy—just us and witnesses in the courthouse. I became pregnant with you early on and played the good little housewife and stay-at-home mom. When you were born I thought things couldn't get any better. I had a loving husband, a beautiful daughter, and a roof over our heads.

"But then your father started working later and later, and flew out of town for business more and more which allowed us to save enough to buy a house. Since he was always gone he let me find a place. River Bend always felt like home—probably because of those nice neighbors—so I decided that's where I wanted to raise you. Your father seemed fine with the idea so we bought this place."

The next part was harder to talk about. While the wounds had calloused they still brought a deep throb of resentment.

"I'm not sure when you father's infidelities began," Claire said. "But I'm sure they'd gone on for a year or more.

"Earlier in the day we were at a friend's birthday party in Deerbrook. I can't remember exactly how I found out that he had cheated on me—it's a blur at this point—but the drinks I had were enough for me to confront him about it.

"We were driving home—you were in the backseat looking at a picture book if I recall— and I asked him outright who the woman was. He played dumb of course which infuriated me more so I lashed out. Stupid in hindsight, attacking someone who's behind the wheel." Not the hard part. "He lost control of the car and it flipped."

Emily was sitting up and watching her mother wide-eyed.

"When I came to, you and I were in the hospital and he was gone. He never checked in on us, never visited, never called. Divorce papers came a month later which I happily signed. I got the house, custody of you, but no child support. That was fine though; I wanted nothing from him. The final paperwork came a short time later and I filed it away without even opening it.

"I managed to get a job working as a receptionist. It didn't require a college degree, and I was able to work hours that still afforded me time to be there for you." She reached out and took Emily's hand.

"Why are you telling me all this?"

"Because, sweetie, I don't want you to make the same mistakes I made."

"Why do you think I will?"

Because I found your pregnancy test. "Let's just call it a hunch."

A car horn sounded outside. Emily glanced out the window, said, "He's here."

"It's just—it's Sunday night. You have school tomorrow."

"I'm just going over to his place to study. That's all."

"Why not study here? I can give you the living room, if you like. Or the kitchen—"

Her daughter stood with a sigh. "Not tonight. You've already passed judgment and I really don't want to deal with an awkward introduction tonight." She leaned down and kissed her mother. "I'll be fine, mom. Really. You've trusted me this long, you can trust me now."

And with that she walked out of the house.

Claire was shaking. She was angry, terrified, ashamed, contemplating what to do. She felt something else was going on besides teenage rebellion, something more troublesome. Maybe she'd gotten involved with a bad crowd, was doing drugs. Her paranoia exploded.

Claire made up her mind. She grabbed her coat and keys and ran from the house to her car. Time to find out what was really going on.

* * *

She followed Billy's car to Jessica's house. Emily's friend was standing on the sidewalk waiting and jumped into the backseat when the car rolled up. Claire hadn't noticed it until she'd gotten closer, but another boy was in in the car too. Keeping a safe distance she followed them through town and across Willow Creek Bridge, River Bend receding in her rear-view mirror. A pair of headlights winked.

Where were they going? The next town was Deerbrook, a smaller town than River Bend. God! She hadn't been out this way since…

She didn't want to think about it. That was in the past, and the only thing that mattered was Emily.

Did Billy or that other boy live out this way? A few miles later they turned left onto another two-lane highway. The farms gave way to silhouette forests, the road twisting and turning. She had no idea where they were now; she'd never been out this way before. She decreased her speed not wanting to startle them. But, then again, if they weren't doing anything wrong why would they suspect anyone of following?

A car passed them from the other direction. She glanced up and watched as its red taillights disappeared around a corner far in the distance passing a vehicle in her lane.

She snapped her eyes forward as a deer shot across the road. Her foot reflexively stomped on the brake, the anti-lock mechanism ratta-tat-tatting.

You son of a bitch! The memory of her hitting Devon flashed. *You goddamned son of a bitch!*

Claire yanked the wheel to the left swerving into the other lane, narrowly missing the deer.

Jesus, Claire! STOP! Emily started crying in the back.

She let off the brake, accelerated, and pulled the car back into her lane.

The vision clouding over, Emily's cries echoing into nothing.

That was close, She'd seen the damage done to a car when it hit a deer at sixty, and it was not pretty. Not for the car, and especially not for the deer.

Panic ripped through Claire as she realized there was no sign of the car ahead of her. She stepped on the gas, the speedometer needle pushing seventy-five—an unsafe speed on these narrow roads—praying they'd disappeared around a bend or down a hill. Her prayers went unanswered and she silently cursed herself for losing them. Where had they gone?

The inside of the car lit up drawing her attention to the rear-view mirror. A pair of bright headlights barreled down on her.

"What the—" she managed before the car behind slammed into hers. She let go of the wheel from the jolt, her car veering onto the gravel shoulder. "Hey!" she cried, grabbed the wheel, and turned from the shoulder, trying to get back onto the pavement. The car behind hit her again, this time the left side of the fender. Claire lost control of the wheel, the car spinning a hundred and eighty degrees. She felt the car tip, tried to regain control.

She failed.

The car flipped, whipping her around as it rolled down the embankment of the road. Her head hit the driver side window, spider-webbing the glass.

Emily cried. She felt warm stickiness running down her face. In her peripheral vision she saw the steering wheel smash into Devon's chest, the sicking sound of pounded meat.

The car righted itself, flipped again, came to a rest on its side. The world spun, darkness seeping in.

What just happened? What's going on? she wondered as she tried to fight off the inevitable, a fight she was losing. Her eyes felt heavy, the taste of rust ran across her tongue.

The last thing she saw before being consumed by the warm embrace of unconsciousness was a red car pulling up, a shadowed figure stepping from it.

There was no car. There was Devon, glazed eyes trained on her. Emily's cries faded.

Then the world disappeared.

* * *

DeMarcus slid from the car and walked to the edge of the highway. In the ditch was Claire's car, a metallic clanking coming from it. Paul stopped beside him.

Something was off. Lilly's presence was fading. Was Claire dying?

Panic ripped through him for only a moment until he realized that what he sensed was wrong. Lilly wasn't fading out of existence but moving away. But if Claire was here then…

The daughter! How could he have not seen it? That which he sought was in the daughter, not the mother.

"Back in the car. Quickly," he instructed.

Confused, Paul said, "But the woman…"

"Leave her. She's not who I need."

* * *

The sun was down and Willem was driving along a two-lane highway in the woods. He'd been told by Justin to meet him at The Thirsty Whale. He'd never been there but had heard of it.

It's a ways out there off the beaten path and sort of obscure, Justin had told him, *but keep your eyes open. There's a sign on the left side of the highway you can't miss.* And so here he was, high beams on, driving slower than normal, keeping an ever watchful eye for the sign.

Willem wondered how far "out there" was, and if he did miss the sign would he take it as a sign to just go home? That wasn't really fair to Justin who seemed excited to hang out with him outside of work. He didn't want to let him down. He was starting to think he'd missed it when it swam in from the shadows declaring "1/4 Mile Ahead on Left". When he saw it he turned.

The road was narrower than he'd like—he could only imagine how two cars would pass—when the drive opened into a clearing. A dozen or so cars were parked haphazardly creating a crescent, those at the back perpendicular to the bar. Willem killed the engine, stepped out, the gravel crunching beneath his feet as he made his way toward what looked like a log cabin. Two men stood outside the door, smoking, looking under the hood of a rusted pickup, engaged in a conversation on how to get another couple years out of the god damned engine. They didn't even acknowledge Willem as he breezed past.

The Thirsty Whale's decor was what he expected. Faux wood—knots and all—was a staple of the north woods, and was standard for many homes and businesses. It added to the natural look tourists expected. The design added a light brown color to the illumination of the room. Stuffed fish and deer heads adorned the walls, as did a large framed photo of an aerial view of the lake—presumably the one this cabin sat on. A group of men in their twenties, hung in the back by the pool tables and dartboards. Others sat around tables or at the bar drinking. Country music played from a jukebox, though Willem could hear faint bass and feel its rhythmic vibration coming from something other than the song—it didn't match.

At the bar sat Justin, a frosted mug of beer in front of him. He was chatting with the bartender. Willem sat on the circular stool next to Justin who looked over. Mild surprise flashed across his face before dissolving to joy. "Willem!"

"You look surprised to see me."

"I am. I wasn't sure you'd actually show up."

He spread his arms and laughed. "Well here I am."

"And what is that ridiculous thing on your head?"

Willem patted the hat on his head. "Never seen a fedora?"

"I've never seen *you* wear a fedora."

"Don't like it?" he asked as he took it off and set it on the bar.

"I don't know yet." Justin rapped his knuckles on the bar, looked at the bartender. "Charles my good man, would you please bring us two Malort and…" He glanced to Willem. "What would you like as a chaser?"

"MGD is fine."

Justin pointed to Willem with his thumb and clicked his tongue, said to Charles, "My tab."

The bartender set two shot glasses on the bar and poured an amber liquid in them. As he filled a mug with beer Willem asked, "You weren't kidding about this place. Definitely off the beaten path. How'd you find it?"

"Friend of a friend of a friend." His tone was mysterious and secretive. A grin formed. "It's more a neighborhood place—they don't really advertise. Keeps it more private that way."

"The way I like it," the bartender said, delivering the beer. "Can I get you anything else?" They shook their heads. "Flag me down if you need anything," and he went to check on others down the bar.

Willem brought the drink to his nose, sniffed. "What's this stuff again?"

"It's called Malort. German, I think. Doesn't matter. What matters is what's in it."

"And what would that be?"

Justin twitched his eyebrows, curled the corner of his lip into a quirky smile. "Drink first. To the confusion of our enemies!"

Willem laughed, clinked his glass to Justin's, downed it. The Malort burned on its way down, leaving a bitter sweet taste. Willem nearly coughed, pinched his face in disgust. The taste was revolting. He grabbed his beer and took two chugs. "What in God's name is that? It tastes like bug spray!"

Justin laughed. "That my friend will grow hair on your balls."

"More like burn it off. What's in it?"

"Wormwood. Same shit that's in absinthe. I believe it's the only drink in our great nation to allow it. That's what I've been told anyhow."

"If you're trying to convince me that getting out more is a good idea you're doing a poor job of it," he teased.

"Sorry. Just trying to start things off on a high note."

Willem took another drink, the taste finally subsiding. "How long you been coming here?"

Justin shrugged. "Couple of years. It's sort of like that bar on *Cheers*."

"How's Susan working out?"

"Competent and easy on the eyes."

Willem smiled. "Unlike this old geezer."

"You said it, not me." Justin's smile melted. "I have to admit you're back sooner than I expected."

"Me too. He went fast."

"When?"

"Yesterday."

"Yesterday? And you're already back?"

"What was I supposed to do? Me and his family aren't particularly close. I'm thankful my brother and I got to make our peace, but I can tell his kids have no interest in their uncle."

"No hope of rekindling some sort of family bond?"

"Maybe—I don't know. Even if there was it wouldn't have happened overnight."

"More reason you should have stayed there a little while. Try and reconnect."

"I had to come back, take care of something."

"What could possibly be more important than being with your family in a time of mourning?"

Willem didn't want to go into the details of his visit—old habits die hard—so instead said, "Just some personal stuff I needed to take care of."

"Cryptic."

"Others might say private. But it was a good visit. It was nice to talk, to put to rest some of the animosity we'd held onto."

Justin finished off his beer, held it up and teeter-tottered it to Charles who nodded. "You too?" he hollered at Willem. Willem downed what remained. Charles refilled their mugs.

"It's so weird seeing you like this," Justin said after Charles left. "I figured you were an alcoholic or something, maybe just didn't care for a drink, and preferred to stay in so you didn't have to be near it."

"No," Willem shook his head. "Not an alcoholic, just preferred to stay away from it." He could feel the shot and beer mixing in his belly, his vision clouding ever so slightly. Since he drank so infrequently it didn't take much to get him tipsy. "My dad may have been—he drank a lot—so I just preferred not to tempt fate and end up like him."

"And how did he end up?"

He shrugged. "Don't know. He disappeared when I was ten never to be seen again. Could be unknown bones in the woods, or maybe he lived a spectacular life in Mexico. We never found out what happened to him."

"Really? Man that sucks. I'm sorry."

"Nothing to be sorry for."

"Bullshit. I can't imagine what it would have been like if my old man hadn't been around—pretty lonely I can imagine."

"I managed. My mom had to start working as did my brother. I ended up pretty much on my own."

"It makes sense, you being sort of a loner." Justin must have realized what he'd said might have offended Willem. His mouth fluttered open, "I—I'm sorry. That came out wrong."

Willem waved it away. "No, you're right. I'm sure that has a lot to do with how I live. I watch TV, I feed my birds… nothing much to it."

"You're a bird watcher?"

"It's comforting," he said defensively. "Just watching them out the window… it's relaxing."

"Never much cared for birds. Doesn't help I'm allergic to them."

"I can see where that might be a problem."

"You think?"

"I do."

Justin held up his glass, Willem clinked his mug. They drank. A misty aura added a softness to Willem's vision. He told himself to stop after this one, but he had to admit it was nice getting out and spending time with someone other than the Bunkers. With nowhere to be tomorrow it wouldn't hurt him staying out. You only live once after all... might as well start enjoying it.

"What are you going to do when you retire?"

"What do you mean?"

"I mean you can't keep doing this forever. Hell, you're nearing retirement age anyway. Aren't you looking forward to doing something else?"

"Haven't really thought about it. I like what I do. I like helping people, and I can't imagine doing anything else."

"So you want to do this until the day you die?"

"I don't know. Maybe."

"You banking on a heart attack taking you?"

"I don't follow."

"I mean it seems you're expecting to live until you just keel over one day of a heart attack. But you realize most of us, as we grow old, start to deteriorate. We get slower, our memory fades, some get the shakes. You could suffer a stroke and not be able to walk anymore. At that point you'll live your life sitting in a nursing home watching those precious birds of yours."

Willem realized that in many ways he was living the life of an invalid. He left his house to work and grocery shop, but mostly he just sat at home and did nothing. Pity started to creep into the back of his mind. His life really had no meaning. Sure he helped others, but he did nothing for himself. And then he wondered: did he want to? What was it all for?

He drank the rest of the beer, waved Charles over, saw Justin was almost through with his. "Another?"

"Definitely."

"Two beers and—" What was the hard stuff Justin had ordered? "Two of that hairy balls shit."

Charles' eyebrow arched, looked at Justin who burst out laughing. "Malort," he told Charles. "You keep talking like that and some dude is going to get the wrong idea and hit on you."

"I will graciously decline the invitation." He was starting to feel tipsy, and the words felt heavy in his mouth. The shots and beer were pushed in front of them, Willem held up his shot. "Now it's my turn to do a toast."

In the distance a bell rang and Willem looked toward it. Through the front door breezed four people—they looked younger than the required twenty-one—two boys and two girls. They laughed but seemed nervous.

Whatever. Could look younger than their age, or maybe the bar looked the other way, in either case it was no concern of his.

"You drift off to la-la-land there Willem?"

"Not at all."

"Good. What's your toast going to be?"

"To the confusion of our friends!"

Justin laughed. "No, no! It's 'To the confusion of our enemies.'"

Willem smiled. "Not so, because if friends weren't confused by our lives then we wouldn't have friends at all."

"That makes zero fucking sense."

"Probably not," he said and brought the drink to his lips and downed it.

* * *

The place wasn't hopping, but it was far from dead—not like the other day he was here. Granted it had just opened, and most people didn't get their drink on until they'd suffered for a day at a job they hated. Still, the number of cars outside seemed excessive for the number of people here. Maybe everyone drove themselves instead of coming in twos and threes.

Stavic stood in the doorway taking in the room. Charles was laughing with two men until he saw Stavic. Fred was at the other end of the bar, sitting in the same seat he had been in his last visit, staring at the TV, twirling a bottle. Music echoed throughout, its gentle twang and warbling of a singer bringing a certain atmosphere to the room.

He hated it. He hated country music and everything it represented. How anyone could stand it was beyond him. Give him Pink Floyd or The Doors or some other classic rock any day.

He sat two stools down from the pair at the bar, a fedora next to one of them. The one closest to Stavic looked younger by a least a couple decades.

"What are you doing here?" Charles asked.

"Just want a drink. Nothing more."

"A drink, eh?" His eyes shifted to Fred who continued to gaze at the TV. "Fine." He looked back. "What'll it be?"

A grin formed on Stavic's lips. "Surprise me."

Charles stared him down as if challenging him. Charles turned, picked a bottle off the top shelf, poured it into a glass, and presented it to Stavic. The caramel liquid looked good. Stavic picked it up, smelled. The aroma stung his nose. "Whiskey?" A nod.

The drink was smooth—too smooth—which meant this was going to cost him. He didn't want to know. Stavic smiled, said, "Good choice."

He'd planned for a long night, so before coming to The Thirsty Whale he'd had a couple of shots and snorts at home. That mixture was already making him feel pleasant, energetic, and he suspected this would push him along further.

"I was at home and realized that that was the last place I wanted to be tonight. I'm not sure why, but there was this *need* pulling me here. Do you know that as long as we've known each other I've never paid you a visit in the evening hours?"

"I much prefer our daytime meetings. I'm more in my element now, and one thing I don't like when I'm in my element are cops." He smirked.

"The only people who don't like cops are guilty people. Are you guilty of something, Charles?"

"Me? Oh no. My nose is as clean as a whistle." He cocked his head, focused on Stavic's nose. "How's yours?"

Paranoia set in and Stavic wiped his nostrils across his sleeve, the cloth tickling him causing him to sneeze. Charles laughed, the sound threatening.

"Fuck you," Stavic said.

"The feeling's mutual." Charles jabbed his finger from the drink to Stavic. "Finish that and go. I don't want you here tonight."

"Such hostility. Actually, I'm here to meet a good buddy of mine. Goes by DeMarcus. Know him?"

Charles' eyes flashed, his lips tightened. "No."

"Really? Because he said he'd meet me here."

"No one here by that name."

"You sure? You know everyone who's here in this room?"

"Everyone here is a regular."

Stavic glanced at the two men to his right. "You guys regular?"

The one closest to him grunted "Yep" as his fedora buddy watched on.

"Don't bug my customers. Finish your drink and leave." Charles walked away, stopped in front of Fred, leaned in. They exchanged words, Charles slightly more animated. His presence had definitely touched a nerve. Fred stubbed out his cigarette in an ashtray, as he stood nearly knocking his stool over, and walked out in a huff.

Stavic sat a while soaking in the atmosphere, listening to the various conversations, waiting for a word or phrase to set off his alarm. Charles continued to serve the patrons, the music continued to play, and soon he was just another face in the crowd—except to Charles who kept an ever watchful eye. Stavic made sure to sip his drink. He planned to stay as long as possible.

The wait paid off. The men next to him started to have a conversation, one that piqued his curiosity. The one closest to him said, "You ready to call it a night?"

"What time is it?" asked Fedora.

"Uhh... looks to be around 10:30. Not too late, not too early."

"I think I'm good for a bit yet."

"So... how far you wanting to go tonight?"

These two homos? he wondered. There was an awkward pause, then Fedora answered his question by slowly stating, "It depends on what you mean."

The other man laughed. "Not what I meant..."

"Because if you swing that way I by no means will judge."

"Seriously? I've told you stories—"

"You could just be protecting your ass."

"Anyway," exhaled the man, "you were saying your brother talked to you about getting out and living a little. I wanted to know how far down that hole you're interested in going?"

"You said it yourself I'm near retirement. I think I have some catching up to do."

He couldn't see it, but he sensed the man smile. "Then grab your hat my friend," he said as he stood, slapping Fedora on the shoulder. "Because we're going underground."

The man did as asked, and the pair walked along the bar to the back to an unobtrusive door. The younger man opened it, music with a heavy bass spilling out. They entered, the door closed, and the room returned to normal.

Stavic had seen the door before, figured it was a closet for supplies, never considered it went anywhere. Now he did, and he wanted to know where. He polished off his drink, waved Charles over. "Done. What's the damage?"

Charles looked relieved. "Too rich for a cop's salary, I'm sure. Leave now and we'll call it even."

"A bribe?"

"A gift."

"If you insist." Stavic stood, turned, and walked out.

The cool autumn wind hit him, cutting through his outfit and into his bones. He glanced through the window and Charles was preoccupied. Good. He thought Charles might watch him, make sure he got in his car and drive away. Stavic was happy the big man trusted him enough to think he wasn't a threat.

Sorry, Charles, but I'm still a cop. Friendship can only go so far.

He moved along the side of the building to the back, saw no one was out on the deck in this cold weather, hopped over the railing. Two boats were tied to the dock.

Stavic looked in the back window and watched Charles. All he had to do was bide his time.

Five minutes went by. The cold seeped into Stavic's blood. He started to think he might have to abort when Charles finally went into the back room.

Stavic opened the door quickly yet quietly so as not to draw attention to himself. A couple people looked over. *Probably from the blast of cold,* he told himself.

He didn't know how much time he had, so Stavic walked directly to the door as if he belonged. With only a hint of trepidation he opened the door and was greeted by loud music and a wooden staircase that descended under the bar. The door closed behind him and he started down.

* * *

"What is this place?" Willem yelled over the loud music.

Justin spread his arms out proudly. "This is The Underground!" he laughed.

It was one giant wooden room with space heaters spread throughout. A heavy duty extension cord extended from the stairwell along the roof to various power strips throughout. It was haphazard in execution—done most likely after the building had been erected—and clearly broke half a dozen safety codes. Those here seemed not to mind, seemed to relish in it in fact.

Two naked women danced on a stage, their movements timed to music that caressed and lulled. They teased the audience—made up of mostly men—with titillating touches. The audience cried out for more when the women nearly kissed.

"Time to fade away!" Justin said, his voice barely audible over the music.

He led Willem to a large open cooler filled with ice and bottled beer. A man, who Willem guessed doubled as a bouncer, stood behind the cooler collecting bills and serving drinks. Willem had no idea if this man was related to Charles upstairs, but he was equally large. He did not want to get into a fight with anyone for fear this man would break him in two. Justin gave the man a ten, grabbed two bottles and gave one to Willem. They found a table and sat.

Justin said, "This is the real party!" and pulled out a bag. He opened it, various drugs within. "I got your uppers, your downers, your lefters, your righters. You want an orgasm of the mind or the dick, I got you covered."

Willem was surprised if not impressed. He'd assumed Justin was into drugs but not to this extent. How had he managed to become a paramedic what with their rigorous drug testing? He didn't care what people put into their systems—it was a free country after all—but Justin had seen what this sort of stuff could do to a person. Why would he do it knowing the inevitable outcome?

And yet he found himself not caring. Justin was doing something more than work and going home. Regardless of the danger he was putting himself in, he was going out and living a life. He lived up to the motto "you only live once" he spouted every so often.

"You want something to open your mind to unimaginable beauty? Something that will fire up your synapses and remember memories long forgotten? Or are you more interested in something that will dull your senses and let you forget?"

The room spun.

An idea occurred to Willem. "Remember. Something to help me remember," he slurred.

He looked around the room. The kids he'd seen earlier were there, sitting at a table, talking to some unknown man. Definitely seemed too young to be here. They seemed nervous as they took something from the man. He laughed, probably at them, and walked off.

Justin tapped his arm, handed him a pill.

"What is it?" Willem asked.

A shrug. "A little of this, a little of that. Don't worry about it, and enjoy the ride."

What the hell. You only live once, right? And he'd lived sixty-four years with nothing to show for it. Perhaps whatever this cocktail pill was would help—nothing to lose.

Willem took the pink pill from Justin's palm, placed it on his tongue and swallowed.

He felt it almost immediately. A hollowness crept out from his chest, moving along through his extremities. A vibration in his hands, a tingling in his toes. Oh yes… this was good. He closed his eyes and leaned back, letting the drug do its thing.

What would he remember? What would he see?

The music faded and slowed. He opened his eyes a crack. Justin was watching the two girls on stage, his hand moving below the table. He didn't want to know.

Movement by the doorway. A man stood there, an authoritative presence.

A light flickered.

A new song began, the pulsing beat infectious.

The girls danced, hips grinding. Touching flesh and breast, teasing, eyes half closed in the erotic and exotic.

The monotone singer sang about a tired man.

He could relate; he felt tired.

A couple started dancing near the stage.

Correction. It was the moon, not the man. The moon was tired.

He felt like the moon, a waxing crescent expanding toward half then gibbous then full. Illuminating and enlightening.

And as the room grew dark, the moon lit up, and Willem's mind awoke.

* * *

What in God's name is this place?

Stavic wouldn't have been surprised to see something like this in Chicago but in River Bend? And how was it he—or anyone in the police department for that matter—did not know about it? Unless he wasn't the only cop taking favors.

He felt a little ashamed now. If he'd been more diligent, more alert, and not so easily swayed by nose candy he may have been more observant. This could not stand. Unfortunately he was alone and off duty—not much he could do now, especially if he wanted to track down DeMarcus. Couldn't well do that if there was a raid going on. No… another night wouldn't hurt anything right now, though next time he'd bring the motherfucking army.

The music would have been comforting if not for the atmosphere. Sex, drugs, and who knew what else was happening in this dingy basement of a bar. Big city shit in small town America. It was an ever expanding infection.

The room had a good number of people, more than upstairs. It explained why the parking lot was so full yet the bar had seemed relatively empty.

He spotted the two men he'd sat next to upstairs at a table. Fedora was either sleeping or stoned out of his mind, his friend was jerking off while watching the dancers on stage. *Odd way to spend your night,* Stavic thought.

He glided through the crowd, trying to blend. He spotted a man selling beer—bought one.

He's a jovial fellow, or at least pretends to be, Fred had said. *You see… he's always smiling.*

No one on this side of the room by that description. Only pervs and freaks as far as he could see.

The people here focused mostly on themselves. Stavic suspected a couple could be fucking in the middle of the room and no one would bat an eye.

He turned, looked left to right. Nothing! Where was the son of a bitch?

Stavic swiveled, checking every face. No one looked like the man he was looking for.

He was ready to grab a seat when a figure in a white suit descended the rickety stairs. Beneath the white suit was a pristine black button down shirt and bright red tie.

There's something in that smile that's unsettling. It's not real. The smile… it's a mask. Stavic now understood what Fred meant.

DeMarcus scoped out the room and focused on four kids that had no business being in a place like this. Stavic watched as DeMarcus approached them, said a few words, then sat down.

He wasn't sure what was going on but it couldn't be good. Stavic made his way through the crowd. "You DeMarcus?" he asked with a firm tone.

DeMarcus looked up, his smile never wavering. "I am."

"I have some questions I'd like to ask you."

Out of the corner of his eye he saw the kids exchange a look. "You're interrupting a fabulous conversation I was just about to have with my new young friends here," DeMarcus said.

"No," interrupted one of the boys. "It's cool. We can leave you—"

DeMarcus flashed him a look. "No," he said with acid in his voice. He looked back.

"I'm Nicholas Stavic with the River Bend police." He noticed DeMarcus' eyes flick to the kids who were shifting away from him. "I'd like to ask you a few questions."

"How dull."

The two men stared at each other, sizing each other up, DeMarcus' smile never faltering. Stavic asked, "Are you aware of the two murders that have happened recently?"

"Murders? Why no! How sad for them."

"Eviscerated. Cut end-to-end and gutted. You wouldn't happen to know anything about it?"

"Tragic, and no."

"No?"

"No. I'm a kitten. Wouldn't hurt a mouse."

"Cats eat mice."

"Dog, then." DeMarcus shifted in his seat.

"There were two murders back in 1960—"

"Are you implying I had something to do with a series of murders that happened more than fifty years ago?" His grin widened. "How old do you think I am?" DeMarcus' eyed the kids again, only briefly. Stavic was pretty sure it was the girl with the dirty blond hair DeMarcus kept his eyes on. He decided to shift tactics and addressed them.

"You kids alright?"

They nodded but didn't speak.

"This man threatening you at all?"

Head shakes.

"What are your names?"

"Em—" the dirty blonde started but was cut off by one of the boys.

"Don't. You don't have to tell him anything."

A chair clattered to the floor, and the man in the fedora hurried up the stairs. His friend didn't seem to notice.

Stavic looked back. The girl looked from him to her friend. "You sure about that?" asked Stavic. "How old are you?"

"Twenty-one," said the boy.

"And you?" Stavic asked the girl.

"Same."

"Got ID?" The kids looked at each other as if having a telepathic conversation. Stavic gave an "it doesn't matter" head shake. "Why don't you four get out of here."

DeMarcus' nonchalant tone dropped. "Don't," he warned the kids.

Stavic was startled as a rough pair of hands grabbed him. He looked back at the man in a red trucker cap. DeMarcus stood and said, "No. I think we'll all go together."

interlude

So close! She'd been so close and DeMarcus had to interfere. What was she going to do now that her poor David was in a coma? *Think!* she screamed to herself. *There has to be a way.*

She wracked her brain, looking at the situation from all angles, trying to figure out her next step. This was unknown terrain, and she wasn't sure what would happen should she ascend. She'd never heard of a time that a person divided. No... best not to sit it out and wait. She had to find a solution.

With her mind she reached out and searched. Maybe she could get those involved to interact somehow, to work together. But how? She was trapped.

Or was she?

She reached out and found Claire, represented by a forest green shimmer. While she couldn't influence her directly, she could perceive her surroundings from a series of images and emotion. Claire was unconscious and being transported somewhere in an ambulance.

Next she focused on DeMarcus. He was angry about something and...

Emily! she hollered. Yet she could do nothing to warn or help her. If DeMarcus knew what he had, and she suspected he did, would it be too late?

No. He has only half.

A shimmer appeared near DeMarcus, that of an unconscious man. She didn't know him, nor did she know why she was seeing it. He must have been angry or scared because it was a muddied red. Could she help? She reached out and realized she could sooth him, his red turning to a soft blue. Interesting she could influence him like this. Was he in some way connected to the situation?

DeMarcus left with two others—another man and Emily—while three kids struggled to drag the strange man out of the woods. She watched this all with fascination. While she couldn't do anything directly, maybe there was a way indirectly?

A third shimmer appeared near Willow Creek Bridge. Another man—this one with a brown aura—was passed out at the foot of the bridge. She didn't know him either.

Who were these unknown players?

She watched as they all converged at the hospital, where David was.

Where she was.

Too many questions, too many unknowns. She was seeing them for a reason, and she was confident it wasn't a coincidence they were being drawn together. They had a unified purpose, though of what she didn't know.

And then she discovered she could go into their memories and began to explore, started to see the pattern. She followed the trail in each of their memories and found the catalyst, the one event that tied them all together, and it shocked her. Never in a million years would she have attributed it to her and David and that terrible night. She had to make them see and understand.

Lilly connected them all, chose the relevant memories, and began to share.

II
past

**seven
(1957)**

Willem sat at the kitchen table playing with his toy soldiers. Elliott was in his room studying, and Sammy was in the living room watching *Howdy Doody*. While their mother didn't seem to like the show all that much she put up with it to spend time with "her baby".

The sun was setting casting the world in a deep orange, and a nice evening breeze came through the screen door. The weatherman was predicting storms tonight, but if one was headed their way Willem couldn't tell. The sky had few clouds and the smell of impending rain had yet to materialize.

The engine of a car moved along the house, its brakes squeaking into the back. A minute later his father stepped through the door, the spring squeaking as it was pulled open. Although his back was to the door Willem could sense his father's hesitation, his eyes boring into him.

He entered without a word, the door slamming shut behind. He walked past Willem and tossed his red trucker cap onto the table. He never looked at his son—seemed to ignore him—and went to the refrigerator and pulled out a beer, popped the top and drank.

The distance between the two had started gradually several years ago and had escalated to where they barely spoke. Willem didn't know why and often wondered what'd he'd done wrong to anger him so.

Willem had been trying to work up the courage to ask his father about it, but the animosity he felt radiating from his old man filled him with terror. He'd talked to Elliott and his mother about it but both told him the same thing: it's your father, not you. Don't read too much into it; it's been hard at work for him.

He didn't buy it.

He'd been sitting here waiting and going over and over in his head what he would say when his father got home. How to broach the subject?

Kids cheered and laughed in the background, Sammy giggling madly.

It was now or never.

He opened his mouth yet no words came out.

Blank! His mind was blank! What was it he was going to say? All the words he'd planned, all the positive memories he'd intended to share gone.

"What?"

Willem looked up and saw his father staring at him, bottle hovering an inch from his mouth.

"Either shut that mouth or say something."

Willem closed it.

Pfft! The sound whistled between his father's lips. The sound of disappointment. The sound of knowing.

Another gulp of beer and Mr. Amberson headed out of the room.

Say something! his mind cried. *Stop him!*

"Why—"

His father stopped, whipped his head around. The movement was so sudden and unexpected it stopped the words momentarily.

Tears bubbled up. "Why don't you like me?" He hated the meekness of his voice. He felt like a baby.

For a long moment his father stared at him, judging him, challenging him. Willem refused to break eye contact even to wipe away tears. His father turned fully and faced him.

"What did I do wrong?" Willem asked.

The hardened expression on his father's face refused to soften—he just stared.

"Please dad please! Tell me what I did!"

Mr. Amberson stepped toward him, a mask of hatred and distrust.

"Whatever it is I didn't mean to! Whatever I did was an accident! I swear! Just please stop being mad at me!"

A few more steps and now he was standing next to him, the kitchen table a dividing line. Willem stared up at his father, tears flowing freely. He snorted back snot, his mouth contorting to try and stem the emotional outburst.

Laughter from the television in the other room felt like taunts.

His father crouched, came down to eye level.

He's sorry! his mind screamed. *He wants a hug! It wasn't me at all! I love you dad!*

Willem leapt from the chair and wrapped his arms around his father's neck, hugging him as tightly as he could. He felt his father move, the sound of the beer bottle being put on the table.

He's going to hug me! Thankyouthankyouthankyou!

He'd missed the closeness he'd once had with his father, had felt a part of him had been taken away. But now his father was finally going to embrace him, let bygones be bygones, wrap his arm around him and tell him it was all going to be alright.

Instead he felt his father's hands grab his arms and pull them away from his neck.

No! Nonono! Hold onto him! Don't let him go!

But he couldn't. The crushing hold his father had weakened him; he couldn't hold on. Mr. Amberson pulled Willem's arms away, pushed them to his sides, and held him at arm's length.

"You," he said in a quiet gruff voice, "are not my son."

Willem felt like he'd been punch in the gut and all strength flowed from him. The tears were torrential, his mouth hung open wide, no sound escaping.

His father stood, took his red cap, and walked back outside.

Not your son? Of course I'm your son!

Far off in the distance the sky flashed blue.

What does he mean? What?!

Seconds ticked by. It felt an eternity.

Howdy Doody sang, the kids joined in.

A roll of thunder joined the car engine turning over, and then Willem's father was gone.

* * *

David was behind the wheel of a 1954 blue Chevy 210 DeLuxe, a nice sized sedan he and his wife had purchased used last year. They were on their way back from dinner at The Lodge, a restaurant two towns over from River Bend. It was one of the fancier places in the area, a bit out of their price range, but they'd decided to splurge this one time in celebration.

The sun had set an hour ago, the full moon the only light. They traveled along Highway 49, a two-lane road that wound around rolling meadows, through thick woods, and around several lakes. Minnesota may be the state of ten-thousand lakes but that was nothing compared to what they had.

David glanced at Lilly, an attractive petite brunette. She wore a gentle smile on her lightly painted red lips oblivious to David eyeing her. He couldn't help but smile too. He reached across and took her hand in his.

Pregnant! They were going to be parents. Lilly had sprung the news on him last night after he'd returned home from work. The foul mood he'd been in had washed away, her joy infectious. He'd rushed to her and swept her into his arms, picking her up and spinning her, she laughing sweetly.

They'd been trying for a year to get pregnant and after two miscarriages they'd started to think it wasn't meant to be. It was sad—they both wanted to be parents—but there was nothing they could do to change it. Then yesterday, Lilly had told him she was three months along. That had been a shocker.

David's mind wandered to when they'd first met. It had been a few weeks after the Shaw's had moved in next door. His parents wanted to welcome them to the neighborhood properly and invited them over for dinner. Harold and Joan Shaw accepted and came over with their daughter Lilly the following Friday.

David was a senior in high school, handsome, and into sports. He played football and wrestled, was considered one of the better competitors by many. Lilly was a sophomore, beautiful, and quiet. She didn't have many friends and stayed mostly to herself.

Lilly wore a blue dress and gold necklace with an unusual pendant, the same one she wore now. She'd been quiet at first, but as the night wore on she opened up a little. He wasn't sure what it was about her, but he'd become enamored. There was an alluring mystery about her, one that pulled at him.

All too soon the evening was over, and David was sorry to see Lilly go. She was intoxicating, and he wanted to soak in her presence. But they were two years apart—such a big difference in high school.

A week later Lilly approached David. As they talked it turned out they had similar interests. Both liked hiking in the woods and loved the music of Perry Como. She was surprised he watched *I Love Lucy* and he equally shocked to learn she adored *Alfred Hitchcock Presents*. From that moment on they spent much of their free time together studying or just hanging out. It was relaxing knowing you didn't have to put on a façade to try and impress a person.

Their friendship blossomed, and when David went off to college they made it a ritual to write each other weekly. When she was looking at colleges he helped her by offering suggestions but, in the end, she chose the same school as he.

The school had a dance night the day after mid-term finals where they encouraged the students to unwind, and both David and Lilly thought it would be fun. They'd dressed in their best—their best being their Sunday clothes—and met outside the gym. Lilly had arrived first and was by the steps clutching her purse in both hands. Her back was to him and when he'd called her name she'd turned and his breath caught. It was as if he was seeing her for the first time, her aura enveloping him. He could smell her perfume on the breeze, saw her radiant smile and gently blowing hair. It was in that moment he knew he loved her and wanted to spend the rest of his life with her.

The two had a great time in the gym dancing, and when Perry Como started singing "If" the lights dimmed and they moved in close. At the songs refrain he leaned in and kissed her. When they pulled away they looked into each other's eyes, she smiled sweetly, and put her head to his chest.

They married immediately after Lilly graduated college. The first time she missed her period she was overjoyed. When the test came back positive she shared the news with David who was ecstatic. Then she'd lost it. Just one of those things, the doctor had said. The second miscarriage had crushed her.

When she had become pregnant the third time she hadn't told him. She didn't want the weight of a third miscarriage on his shoulders too, so she'd waited three months to make sure the pregnancy had stuck. She explained all this to him last night, blubbering in excitement and joy. And now here they were, finally going to be parents. Six more months and they'd be welcoming a new life into the world.

The moon dimmed as clouds passed in front of it. A flash far off in the sky brought David's attention back. Looked like a storm was moving in. His watch read 10:42. Another fifteen minutes and they'd be home—they should be able to beat the rain. *Looks like it'll be a doozy,* David thought as several more flashes illuminated the black clouds.

He glanced at Lilly. "Are you feeling okay?"

She laughed. "It's still early. I'm not even showing yet."

"I know," he said with a smile. "It's just… You know…"

Lilly nodded in understanding. "I'm fine. Really. If I feel anything… strange… I'll be sure to let you know. Okay?"

"Okay. Did you mention anything to Doug today?" Doug was her boss, a doctor who appeared abrasive to strangers, but was actually kind. He didn't like people to know, though.

"Not yet. I'll tell him tomorrow."

"You think he'll be okay?"

She rolled her eyes. "Why wouldn't he be?"

"Because I don't know if he'll want to lose you, if even for a few months."

"It's really not his decision, now is it? Besides, there are other girls who can do my job."

"Maybe, but not as well as you."

"You flatter me," she said slapping his arm. Her eyes darted to him and she bit her lower lip.

"What?" he asked. She looked surprised—probably didn't think he saw her do that, her telltale sign she had something to say.

"'What' what?"

"I know that look."

"You know no such thing. You can't see anything anyway. It's nearly pitch black!"

A flash of lightning coursed through the heavens. A raindrop hit the window.

"Damn," David said.

Lilly looked over. "What?"

"It's nothing. I was just hoping to make it home before the rain."

Droplets began to pelt the windshield leaving streaks of water running down. David turned on the wipers in a futile attempt at better visibility.

"Just drive carefully," Lilly instructed. "It's not a race."

"I know."

They drove in silence, farmlands giving way to silhouette forests that hugged the shoulder. David looked at his watch again: 10:45. Why did time always move at a snail's pace when you were in a hurry?

Another flash of lightning, the trees and their shadow mates visible briefly. A roll of thunder echoed across the land.

Ahead of them the refracting lights of an oncoming car crested a hill. Looked like the other driver had his brights on. David slowed a little in anticipation of being blinded. *Probably will wait until the last second to turn them off,* he thought. He hated people who did that.

The car was now a quarter mile away and the brights were still on. That was enough. David flashed his lights hoping to alert the driver, but it did no good. He gave it to the count of ten and tried again. The lights were now washing out the wet windshield.

Asshole. David looked to the shoulder on the right. Instead of the usual gravel was just tall grass. At least he could see and had some reference as to where he was on the road. Just a few more seconds and the car would pass them and he would be able to see again.

Then there was movement on the road.

In David's peripheral vision he thought he saw a deer. He swerved to the right, his foot pumping the brake. As soon as the tires were on the grass he had no traction. Lilly let out a squeal.

The other vehicle swerved into their lane, tires screeching on pavement. A flash of lightning and a crack of thunder.

David tried to regain control of his car, tugged the wheel left, but it was no use. The other driver smashed into the rear passenger side of the Chevy, blue paint peeling away, jackknifing them. David grunted as the car spun out, tilted, and flipped. The car rolled off the road into the ditch.

David hit his head and there was a flash of white across his vision. The world was discombobulated: up was down in a confusing vortex of strobe lights.

There was a final bump and the car caught itself and stopped, coming to rest on its side.

The white dissolved and he could see, but then blackness began to overtake him.

No!

He fought to hold onto his consciousness, looked to Lilly. Her eyes were closed, blood oozing from a dozen lacerations on her face.

No! No! No!

David tried to reach for her, to take her hand in his, but his arm was weak. He tried to lift his arm but exhaustion won out. He was tired. He needed to take a nap. Just a short one.

No!

His fingers inched closer to her, eyelids heavy.

Have to… to stay awake… Have to…

The outside world blurred then faded. His finger brushed Lilly's hand.

And then unconsciousness washed over him.

* * *

When David had first entered the hospital room Lilly's parents had been here. They updated him on her status—there was none—before they'd excused themselves to the waiting room.

"If you need anything just come find us," Mrs. Shaw had said.

David sat in a chair next to Lilly's bed. She lay unconscious under white sheets, strange medical devices connected to her. David didn't know what it all was, but he was assured they weren't hurting her.

It had been two weeks since the accident. He'd come to in the back of someone's car. A Good Samaritan stopped when he saw the cars and had pulled them from their car and got them to the hospital.

Lilly was still in a coma and, even more heartbreaking, she'd lost the baby. The accident had caused serious internal trauma resulting in a hysterectomy. Whatever hope they'd had for children was now gone forever.

The doctors prepared him for the worst, that Lilly may never again regain consciousness. They'd done all they could, and now it was up to her and God. He believed that if she fought hard enough that she would come back to him, and he would be at her side when she did. She was a strong woman and he knew that she would fight for as long as she could. All it required was patience.

The police had been by to see him the day after he'd woke. They were still looking for the other driver—who appeared to have run off into the woods and disappeared—but after checking on the plates they were in contact with the family.

Who was it?

We're not at liberty to say until we've located him.

Fifteen minutes later they were gone.

A fucking deer. If not for that then this entire thing—this entire *tragedy*—could have been avoided. And what of the other driver? Where had he gone? Why couldn't they find him? Surely he wouldn't abandon his family over this.

People do strange things when they're scared, he told himself. *People disappear all the time.*

David grabbed Lilly's warm soft hand and gave it a gentle squeeze.

* * *

Willem's father had been missing for nearly two months, and the police had stopped coming by. No one seemed to know where he'd gone after the accident. Secretly he didn't care though—after the horrible things his father had said he'd just assume he never come back.

He still thought of that final moment. At some point his mother had come into the kitchen, asking, *Did I hear your dad?* That's when she saw him sobbing on the floor. She'd swept him into her arms, cooing and comforting, not knowing what was wrong, until he'd finally told her.

Maybe you misheard him? she'd said. He wished that were the case, but no matter how much he'd tried to convince himself his mother was right and he was wrong his father's words kept coming back, stabbing him in the heart. When he'd calmed down enough he'd excused himself and gone upstairs, wrapping himself up in his blanket on his bed, and drifted off to a fitful sleep.

As the days turned into weeks the family had become increasingly worried. At one point Sam had asked both Willem and Elliott when daddy was coming home. While it was looking more and more likely that their father had run off they didn't want to tell their six-year-old brother that, so instead they tried to reassure him while steering away from the conversation.

One evening Willem was upstairs playing with his brothers when he suddenly felt the urge to piss. On his way back from the bathroom he'd heard his mother and Mrs. Shelby's voice downstairs. Mrs. Shelby was a peacock-like woman they knew from church and the closest friend his mother had. The woman was the type to be acquaintances with everyone yet friend to none just to keep tabs on the parishioners. Can't have riffraff in the church, after all. That said, she was a God fearing woman who was eager to show her worth when the time came. She was not one to gossip and was the next best thing to a confessional.

"I don't know what I'm going to do," his mother was saying. "The police can't find him, and our savings are drying up..." She sniffed.

"Have you looked for a job? If not it might be time to start."

"I don't have any experience," his mother conceded.

"It'll be alright, Kathy," Mrs. Shelby sympathized. "Everything is meant to happen for a reason."

Willem's mother hesitated, then asked, "Why is He punishing me?"

"I don't think He is. I think He's challenging you." There was a lull, and Willem could picture Mrs. Shelby taking his mother's hand sympathetically. "How have the boys been?"

"Confused. Especially Sammy. I don't know how to talk to him about this."

"But you *have* talked to them..."

"More or less."

"Kathy," Mrs. Shelby sighed, "I don't think you're giving your sons enough credit. Children are smart. You should sit down and really talk with them about it. It could be good for them and you. You need to be honest and alleviate their fears which I'm sure they have. Love is the foundation of family."

"You think so?"

"I know so. They're children."

"That still doesn't help with money. I have enough for one final mortgage payment and then, after that, we're out. How am I supposed to support them?"

"I've heard rumblings..."

I'll bet you have, thought Willem.

"Do you know Mr. Robinson?" asked Mrs. Shelby.

"I don't think so."

"He owns Manny's Diner. Nice man. Fair. I know one of the staff is going to be leaving soon, so let me talk to him. Would that help?"

"Oh yes! Yes! Thank you, Nancy! That would be wonderful!"

"Don't mention it." There was a moment of hesitation, then, "Kathy... have the police offered any ideas of what happened to your husband?"

"No. Nothing but speculation."

"I see. I don't mean to gossip—"

"Do you know something?" his mother asked.

"Nothing definitive, which is why I hesitate to say anything anyway."

"Is he alive?"

"I don't know, and that's the God honest truth. All I do know is what I heard, and what I heard was that, well, when this person last saw him he'd been roughed up."

"Roughed up?"

"He got into a fight. Managed to get kicked out of The Fat Trout is what I heard."

"By who?"

"I don't like to gossip, you know that, but this seemed like something you should know."

"Do the police know?"

Willem tuned out. His father had been in a fight? Served him right as far as he was concerned. Willem felt exposed on the stairs and headed back to the bedroom, the urge to pee gone.

"Get lost?" Elliott asked.

"No."

Elliott looked up, the smile falling when he saw Willem. "You okay?"

Sam looked back, big eyes wonting.

"I was just listening to mom and Mrs. Shelby."

"You shouldn't listen in on other peoples—"

"It was about dad," he cut Elliott off.

"What about him?" Elliott said slowly.

Willem looked at Sam again. Should he say anything in front of his baby brother? But then the words of Mrs. Shelby came back, about children being smarter than they were given credit for. "I guess dad got into a fight the night he disappeared. Even got kicked out of a bar."

Elliott shrugged. "So? Doesn't explain what happened to him."

"Do you think whoever beat up dad could have, you know…"

"Killed him?" Sam said.

"I'm sure the cops would know about it," Elliott cut in, "so I doubt it."

"But then where is he? Why can't they find him?" He hadn't realized his mother was having such a difficult time. He was still happy his father was gone—the tension he'd been feeling had eased since his disappearance—but he was starting to wonder if the family was better off without him. His father was the sole moneymaker of the family. He hadn't realized the adult world was so much more complicated. A mortgage? He had no idea what that was, but he knew it had something to do with the house.

"I don't know." Elliott's soft demur hardened. "Now come on. Let's keep playing."

Willem sat down and picked up some army toys but was no longer in the mood. His thoughts were on his mother and father. He remembered picnics, flying kites, swimming... all the things a picture perfect family did. And then the way his father treated him had changed. He couldn't remember exactly when, but he knew it had been gradual.

They played quietly until there was a knock on the door. Their mother opened it and peeked in. "How's it going?"

"Fine," Elliott said lightly. "Sammy here is about to infiltrate my army."

"Ooh," she emphasized with just the right amount of motherly love. Sammy looked over with a smile. "Aren't you my brave little captain?"

"I'm a soldier, mom!"

"My brave little soldier, then." She squatted next to him and ruffled his hair.

"Is Mrs. Shelby gone?" Elliott asked.

"She is. She just left."

Elliott stood and went to the door.

"Hey!" Sam cried. "You can't just leave in the middle of a battle."

Elliott turned with a smile. "Consider this my waving the white flag. You won fair and square."

"Were you staying up here while she was here?" she asked.

He shrugged. "Yeah."

"That wasn't necessary."

"I know," he said and disappeared. A few seconds later his footfalls descended the stairs.

She turned her attention to Willem. "So is Sammy beating you, too?"

"Kind of."

"Kind of?"

"If he's not careful I'm going to kick his ass," Sam proudly proclaimed.

"Sam!" Their mother feigned shock, trying hard not to laugh. "Where on earth did you hear that?"

"Elliott."

"I'm not surprised," she said light heartedly and stood. "Fifteen minutes to finish the war and then its bedtime, okay?"

When she was at the door Willem asked cautiously, "Is—is every alright?"

A look of surprise crossed her face. "Yes. Of course it is. Why do you ask?"

He shrugged and looked down. "Just curious."

"Uh-huh." She didn't believe him, he could tell, but what was he supposed to say?

"Fifteen minutes then it's bed."

As he listened to her walk down the stairs he wondered why she had lied to him. Was it because she didn't think he would understand, or was it because Sam was in the room? He didn't know, but he felt a pang of sadness knowing she'd lied to him. She'd always told him it was best to tell the truth, so why was she doing the opposite? He decided he'd talk to Elliott about it later when Sam wasn't around.

"Alright Sam," he said. "Time for me to beat you."

"Never!" Sam cried and knocked over one of Willem's army men with his own. Willem laughed.

* * *

Dead!

David still couldn't believe it. He'd been visited by the River Bend sheriff the other day while at work, inquiring about Harold and Joan Shaw. He'd had to return to work, hated to do it—the thought of leaving Lilly alone was unbearable—but what little savings remained had dried up. Keeping focus had been a challenge, but it was something he had to do.

"Is there someplace we can speak in private?"

Why were the police interested in his in-laws? "Sure," he'd said, and guided him to a small conference room.

Once he'd shut the door the sheriff had delivered the bad news. "I'm sorry to tell you this, Mr. Rottingham, but they were found dead in their home this morning."

He'd felt sucker punched. "Dead? How?"

"We're still investigating, but..." He paused, seemed unsure of how to proceed. "Someone was involved in their deaths."

"Murdered?"

The sheriff nodded. "We've never had a murder in River Bend."

David had sank into a seat. Harold and Joan? They were the nicest people in the world! Who would want to harm them?

After a fifteen minute conversation the sheriff thanked him for his help and let himself out.

First Lilly, now her parents. What else could happen?

He'd left work and gone immediately to the hospital. Whether or not Lilly could hear him he owed it to her to tell her the news. They were her parents for God's sake. Telling her had been more difficult than he'd anticipated, but he finally had been able to get the words out. Even though she showed no reaction he'd felt a weight lift.

The sheriff made it official three days later. **Murder in River Bend!** screamed the newspaper headline. The police were following every lead, but at this point still had no suspects.

His mind was still reeling from the news as he walked into the small waiting area of the hospital. It had been an exceptionally long day coordinating the Shaw's funeral, and he needed a caffeine boost before visiting Lilly. An overweight woman in her sixties was knitting in a chair, her brown nylon socks clumped around her ankles. Her concentration never wavered. Another woman, younger and prettier, was pouring herself a cup of coffee.

As David stepped up behind her she turned and bumped into him. She let out a short "Oh!" and dropped the paper cup in hand, the dark liquid splashing to the tiled floor. The knitter looked at them over her too thick glasses, then went back to work.

"I'm sorry," David said.

"No, it's…" The woman touched her face in embarrassment. "You just startled me is all." She turned and grabbed some napkins.

"Let me."

"No, really, I made the mess."

"But I startled you," he said pleasantly. She hesitated then handed the napkins over with a smile.

David cleaned up the spill as the woman poured another coffee. "How do you take it?"

David glanced up, saw she was looking at him expectantly. "Two sugars." He finished cleaning, stood, tossed the napkins, and accepted the coffee when it was offered. "Thank you." He extended his hand. "I'm David."

She politely accepted it. "And I'm Abigail."

The silence was uncomfortable, neither sure what to say, so David just held up the coffee and said, "Thanks."

She nodded—*you're welcome*—and he turned away, walking down a hallway. He heard footsteps behind him, looked back, saw she was following. He paused. "You visiting someone?"

She caught up to him and David met her stride. "Yes. My husband. You?"

"My wife."

"Is she alright?"

"I hope so. The doctors aren't sure. What about your husband?"

"He's... not doing well."

"I'm sorry to hear that."

He decided it best to steer clear of an uncomfortable conversation and instead asked, "Do you live in town? I don't think I've seen you before. Not that River Bend is all that small," he finished with a half-hearted chuckle.

Her smile was sad. "We do but only just recently. My husband got a job at the mill a few months ago," she said with a sniff. "I told him to be careful. I told him it was dangerous, but he wouldn't listen to me, said it was perfectly fine, that no company would intentionally put their employees in harm's way. And then this..."

As if on cue Abigail stopped and pointed through an open door. David looked in and saw a bandaged body lying in a bed, the face three quarters covered, the remaining skin raw.

"What happened?"

Abigail led him in. She moved to the other side of the bed and pushed a strand of hair from her husband's eye. "He was working with a splitter. They're still not exactly sure, but somehow the log was ejected from the machine and hit him in the face, knocked him out instantly. A fire broke out and, well, you see... They said they're still looking into it but I don't believe it. How long does it take to figure something like this out?"

Sometimes never, he wanted to say. The police still couldn't find the man who'd crashed into Lilly and him. He hadn't returned home, his family swore he hadn't contacted them. The police thought he might have fallen in the Fox River and drowned, but even after an exhaustive search they'd come up empty.

"David?"

"Hmm?" He looked up. She was staring at him expectantly.

"Your wife?"

"My wife..." he exhaled. "Car accident."

"Bad?"

"Pretty bad. She's been in a coma for over a month." He had nothing left to say and wanted to get back to Lilly, so he politely excused himself. "Well, it was nice meeting you, Abigail, but I really should get going."

"Oh. Okay. Well, it was nice to meet you."

"You too. And I hope your husband pulls through." He was about to turn, then said as an afterthought, "I'm sure he will." With that he left the small and lonely room.

He was deep in thought walking on autopilot back to Lilly's room when a soft voice coming from his wife's room brought him back to reality. He didn't recognize the voice, and when he entered a man in a white suit, pressed black button down shirt, and radiant red tie stood at the side of his wife's bed. He was leaning over and speaking quietly into her ear, arms at his sides. David was suddenly nervous, an instinct to protect his wife from an unknown predator.

"Excuse me?" he said approaching the bed. "Can I help you?"

The man cocked his head and gave a tight smile. He erected himself fluidly. "Hello."

"Hello," David responded cautiously.

The man's smile never wavered, just watched David from the opposite side of the bed, head swiveling as David came to the opposite side of the bed.

When the stranger said nothing David asked, "Is there something I can do for you?"

"I was just visiting your beautiful wife, Mr. Rottingham."

"I'm sorry, but I don't think we've met."

"We haven't, but your wife and I are old friends. We knew each other as children."

"And how did you know she was here?"

"The papers. I would have been here sooner, but work prevented it." He glanced at her, touched her hand. "We were having the loveliest conversation."

His expression softened with hope. "She... has she spoken?"

"Oh yes. In fact, she's speaking right now."

Hope dissolved to disappointment. This man, whoever he was, was obviously not well. "I think you should be going, Mr...?"

The man glided around the bed, offering his hand. "DeMarcus."

David didn't accept his hand, so the stranger dropped it back to his side, seemingly unfazed by the rejection.

"Why are you here?"

"To visit is all."

David didn't buy that he was just here to visit, didn't get that vibe. There was a malicious lust in his eye. He'd have to let the staff know that under no circumstance was Lilly to receive any visitors without his approval. "I think you should be going."

"Very well, Mr. Rottingham. But before I go, what's your wife's prognosis?"

"They haven't given one."

"I see. Good day." DeMarcus headed for the door then stopped and turned. Still smiling he said, "I look forward to seeing you again, Mr. Rottingham," and breezed out the door.

A shiver went down his spine as David glanced at Lilly—she seemed unmolested. He wanted to know who this stranger was that was in his wife's room. He walked out but DeMarcus was nowhere to be seen. David hurried to the nurse's station where a frumpy woman was reading a magazine.

"Excuse me, but who was that man visiting my wife?"

The nurse looked at him over the magazine. "Man? You're wife hasn't had any visitors."

"But… there was a man in her room. Surely you saw him."

"I'm sorry, sir, but no one came by."

"Are you sure you didn't miss him?"

She gave him an annoyed look. "I'm sure," she said, and went back to her magazine.

Knowing it was pointless to argue he went back to Lilly's room and sat down in the chair next to the bed. *What a strange man,* he thought, *and obtuse.* Who was he, and why was he visiting her?

He gave Lilly a sideways glance, took her hand in his. "Lilly? Can you hear me sweetie?"

Your wife told me.

"Give me a squeeze if you can hear me." Yet there was no movement, not even a twitch, no indication she had heard.

She's speaking right now.

How could he possibly know that? The man was delusional, had to be. The nurse said no one was there, but she'd probably been too engrossed in her magazine. Yes… he certainly needed to make it clear to the hospital that their security was lax and unacceptable.

I look forward to seeing you again.

We'll see about that, DeMarcus. The next time we meet you better be more forthcoming.

* * *

127

Willem and Elliott walked through their neighbor's field. It had been a dry season, so the normally tall stalks of corn where truncated and gold instead of their usual green. They were careful not to break any for fear of the wrath of Mr. Feltcher, an ill-tempered man who was always cussing and complaining about the difficulty of farming.

The brothers were headed to the old willow tree. It was a sanctuary of sorts; a place they liked to pretend was a secret hideout. It was a ways off from Willow Creek Bridge—along the edge of the creek itself—and offered good shade and good fishing. It wasn't hard to find, yet they never saw any other kids there so claimed it as their own.

Mrs. Shelby had come through and their mother had started working at Manny's the previous week. Sam had been invited over to his friend's house for the day, so on her way into town she had dropped him off. It was odd not having her home, but both boys understood why it had happened.

Willem looked for the umpteenth time at the flask Elliott carried. "Can I see it again?" he asked.

"Sure," Elliott said and handed it over.

In the last month their mother had started to clear out their fathers things, storing some of it, tossing the rest. The things she decided to get rid of they sifted through, looking for anything that caught their attention. The flask had probably been a sore reminder of the decay that had been her marriage. Willem didn't understand why Elliott wanted to hold onto something like this.

One side was an etching: *Amor Meus*. "What's it mean?" He looked up at Elliott.

"Beats me."

He shook it but whatever liquid it once contained no longer existed, either drunk by his father or poured out by his mother. "Why do you want to keep it?" Willem held it out to Elliott who took it back.

"It was dad's." He said it as if that made perfect sense, an obvious answer.

"I know, but *why?*"

"Because it was dad's," Elliott repeated, slower this time. "I can't really explain it any more than that." He must have had a confused look on his face because Elliott sighed. "This is something that was his. He touched it, he drank from it. Keeping it, I don't know, makes me feel closer to him."

The words made sense, but Willem had no such emotional connection to an object once possessed by his father. In fact, the idea of an emotional connection through a physical one was foreign to him. He had fond memories of his father, memories from before, but the pain the man had caused him over the last several years trumped those.

Time for a change in conversation.

"You know how mom always said it was better to tell the truth?"

"Sure."

"Do you believe that?"

"Of course I do."

"Remember the night Mrs. Shelby was over?"

Elliott stopped and turned. At first Willem thought his brother was mad, but the softness of his face was understanding. "It's okay to be worried, Willem. I am, mom is, and I'm sure Sam is too. The best thing we can do is help her around the house, okay? She's got her hands full."

"But she lied."

"She didn't lie, Willem. She was protecting you. She's protecting all of us."

"I don't follow."

His brother chose his words carefully. "What she told you was a lie, yes, but the reason is because she doesn't want you worrying about her. She's dealing with grownup stuff is all. Does that make sense?"

"Kind of."

"Don't worry about it, okay? Mom's got it under control."

Elliott put a reassuring hand on Willem's shoulder and gave a gentle squeeze. They continued their walk in silence, the sun beating down warming their skin. Cicada buzzed in the field, the stalk leaves rustling.

"Do you think we'll ever see dad again?" asked Willem.

"I don't think so."

"Do you think he's dead?"

"Dead or ran away, not sure which."

Willem had wanted to run away but never had worked up the courage. Where would he go? How would he survive? His father disappearing had alleviated that desire.

"Why would he do that?" Willem wondered aloud.

"Sometimes people just decide it's best, either for them or for their loved ones."

"Who do you think he did it for? Him or us?"

Elliott didn't respond. Willem was afraid his brother wouldn't answer the question, but it was important to him. His brother finally said, "I like to believe he did it for us. What do you think?"

Up until this point he'd figured his father had died. He didn't have an answer for his brother, not one he was satisfied with. He told Elliott as much.

"When you decide let me know," Elliott finished.

They walked in silence a good ten minutes before seeing Willow Creek Bridge where someone was at its edge. A few minutes more and Willem recognized him—William—a boy in his class. Because their names were so similar their classmates often called them brothers. It annoyed Willem, but there wasn't much he could do. Once something like that started it was almost impossible to stop. The two boys shared only one common interest and that was comic books, but Willem preferred DC while William liked Atlas Comics. They'd gotten into heated debates about it in the past. He didn't want to pass him because he knew it would most certainly lead to another heated debate, one he preferred not to have today.

"You know, we don't have to go to the hideout today. We can wait," Willem said as nonchalantly as possible.

"Wait? Why? We're almost there."

"I know, it's just... William."

"Since when did you start using your own name like that?"

"*Will-ee-um!*" he enunciated.

"Oh! *Will-ee-um.* Got it. Who's that?"

"Kid on the bridge."

"You afraid of him?"

"Not afraid, I just don't like him."

"Why?"

After Willem explained, Elliott said without hesitation, "Well that's silly."

"It bothers me."

"That they call you brothers or the comic thing?"

"Both."

"Is he a bad person or something?"

"Not that I know of."

"Then come on."

A few minutes later they were at the bridge. William was leaning against the side, fishing pole in hand, watching his bobber bounce along the surface of the flowing water. He glanced over. "Hey, Willem."

"Hi." He looked sheepishly at his brother who nudged him with his elbow. "What are you doing?"

He realized how stupid the question was the moment it escaped his lips. If William thought so he didn't say.

"Fishing. Haven't caught anything yet."

"Do you ever?" he asked with mild contempt. Elliott nudged him again, this time hard. Willem glared.

"What do you pull out of here?" Elliott asked politely.

"Crappie mostly. Sometimes perch."

"Willem here pulled out a bass once." Willem looked at his brother who smiled at him. "Didn't you?"

"Yeah. Once last year," he begrudgingly added.

"Really?" William seemed genuinely impressed. "Never caught a bass here. How big?"

"Fourteen incher."

"Cool! Hey... you check out this month's Uncanny Tales?"

Here we go, thought Willem.

William had a strange liking for the weird and often picked up comics that focused on horror like *Uncanny Tales, Journey into Mystery,* and *Strange Tales.* Willem preferred the rival publisher who put out the likes of *Superman* and *Batman.*

Willem said, "You know I don't read those."

"Have you ever tried?"

"Well, no."

"You really should. You might like them."

"I don't like horror just like you don't like superheroes."

"It's not that I don't like them. Scary is more interesting to me. I like the stuff that gets my blood pumping. Superheroes just don't make me feel anything."

Willem said unmaliciously, "You're weird." William just laughed.

"I know. I find the unknown creepy and wonderful. It's more real to me than a man who can fly."

"Why's that?"

William shrugged. "Just is. The idea of Caroline's Cottage, while unlikely, makes more sense."

"Ca—Caroline's Cottage?" He tripped over the word.

William looked over with mild shock. "You've never heard of it?"

The way he was being looked at made him feel like he'd grown a third eye.

"No. What is it?"

"I heard some older boys talking about it at school." William glanced to Elliott and said, "Have you heard of it?"

"Just stories," Elliott responded.

Curiosity was getting the better of Willem. "What is it?" he asked again.

"Well, the story goes that there once was a couple who had a farm house—not sure why they call it a cottage when it's a farm house. Had a well and everything. Anyway, one night the husband went off and disappeared. For three weeks they looked for him until they found his body in the woods. He was naked and gutted." He emphasized this last part by speaking slowly and succinctly. "The lady—Caroline was her name if you hadn't already figured that out—was devastated by what happened to her husband and locked herself in her house. Over time she convinced herself that the body that had been found wasn't her husband, and that he would return one day. She never left, never even came outside, just sat by the window... watching.

"I guess a local woman's group brought her food and stuff so that she wouldn't starve. Well, one day one of those ladies came to visit Caroline only to find her and the house gone."

"Gone? Like burned down?"

"No. *Gone.* As in not a trace of it anywhere."

"But how is that even possible?"

"Beats me, but it gets weirder. They say that if you walk in the woods at night you might stumble upon the house, a single candle burning in the window next to Caroline, who still waits for her husband to return. It is always moving, never appearing in the same place twice, and if you try to approach, it moves away."

"Come on," Willem said credulously. "A house that moves?"

"That's what they say—that if you approach it it always stays out of reach."

Willem turned to Elliott. "That can't be true," he said with a hint of nervousness. "Can it?"

"That's pretty much how I heard the story, though I have heard that on rare occasions the house doesn't move. Sometimes a person can approach, but if they do—and if they enter the house—they are never seen again."

Willem and William were staring at him, awe on their faces. "Seriously?" said William. "Cool!" A big smile came to his lips and he looked at Willem. "That would be so neat to see!"

Willem shook off the story. "Hold on. How is any of that even possible? A ghost house?"

"Why not?" William said. "Ghosts exist. It's been proven."

"No way would I go near a place like that."

"I think it would be exciting to see. Exciting and *scary*. When I'm older I'm going to go look for it."

"Let me know how that goes." Willem looked at Elliott and asked, "Ready?"

"If you are."

"Good luck with the fishing."

"Thanks!" Then: "You know… I think I'm going to try and catch a bass today, only mine will be fifteen inches."

"If you do, keep it. I want to see."

Willem and Elliott crossed the bridge then descended the embankment, following a small worn dirt path down to the creek edge. William asked, "Where you going?"

Willem looked up. "Just along the creek."

"To where?"

Willem pointed in the direction they were headed. "That way. See you at school."

He hated to admit that that stupid story made him nervous. When they were out of earshot of William, Willem asked, "Do you believe it?"

"Caroline's Cottage? No. It's just a ghost story. It's not real, just told to scare kids. Okay?"

"Okay," said Willem, not believing it. Already his mind was swirling with images of his father stumbling through the woods after his accident, getting lost, and coming across the farm house. Had he followed it looking for help? Maybe he was one of the few that actually managed to get to the house and enter it. That would explain why his body had never been found. He was now a guest of Caroline, never to be seen again.

Before long they were at the willow tree. Elliott led the way, spreading the hanging stalks and entering. They went from sun to shade, the temperature dropping noticeably.

The willow tree sang to them, its tiny leaves rustling in the breeze. It was relaxing, hypnotic, comforting. "What did you want to show me?" Willem asked.

Elliott looked at him and smiled. "This," he said. He crouched and moved rocks out of the way. "I found this a couple years ago and thought it would make a swell hiding place, but at the time I had nothing to hide. Now…" He held up the flask. "Mom doesn't want this stuff in the house—can't say I blame her—but some of it I wanted to keep, and then I remembered this place."

He moved a final rock revealing a hole at its base. Elliott reached in and pulled out a tin box with a keyhole. It had an intricate design on it, a pattern that resembled vine leaves that wove in circles.

"Here," Elliott said and passed it to Willem, dug into his pocket, handed him a small ornate key.

(The key! a distant voice cried.)

"Open it."

Willem did as asked, the key turning smoothly. The lid opened to reveal their father's worn pocket watch.

"What is this?"

"Our buried treasure," Elliott replied. "This is our secret stash. Anything you want to keep hidden put in here. It's better to keep this stuff than to toss it and regret it later." Elliott handed Willem the flask. "Go on."

He set the box down onto the mossy ground and took the flask. He fought the urge to throw it into the creek as hard as he could.

He ran his thumb over *Amor Meus*. One day he'd have to find out what it meant.

Willem placed the flask in the box, closed it, the clasp latched too loudly to his ear, echoing. He locked it and returned the key to Elliott then handed him the box.

Elliott took it and placed it back in the hole. Willem guessed that if they didn't have a body to bury then burying some of their fathers stuff was the next best thing. He watched as his older brother replaced the rocks and sticks.

"How do you know this stuff will stay safe here, that someone won't find it?"

He stopped a moment and looked up at the tree. "Can't you feel it?"

Willem looked around trying to grasp what his brother was talking about. Elliott looked over his shoulder and must have seen Willem's confusion.

"There's something special about this place," he continued, patting the trunk of the tree. "She doesn't give up her secrets, and this box… it is a secret, Willem."

"If you say so."

"I say so," Elliott said. "A very special one."

* * *

An upbeat instrumental rendition of *Deck the Halls* played on the portable radio David had set up on the nightstand next to Lilly. Through its tinny speaker the trumpets blared accompanied by a piano, trombone, and percussion. David stroked Lilly's arm knowing this was her favorite Christmas song, singing alone to his unconscious wife.

It was Christmas Eve and snow was falling in River Bend. Out the window flakes drifted lazily into oblivion. David was chilled just looking at it. The last few days hadn't gotten above twenty-degrees, and he wasn't looking forward to going back outside when visiting hours were over, even less enthused about going home to his cold bed alone. He missed Lilly, and he wanted her back. Her smile, her laugh, her warmth. Was that too much to ask?

In celebration of the holiday he'd brought in a small artificial Christmas tree to decorate the room in some holiday spirit. He'd put her favorite ornament on top of the tree, dressed it in colorful lights, and positioned it on the nightstand the radio played from. It was the best he could do short of bringing her home. Next year, he kept telling himself, they'd celebrate Christmas properly.

David stood, leaned over and kissed his wife's forehead. "Until tomorrow sweetie." He caressed her cheek and, for a moment, thought the corner of her lip curled as if trying to smile. When it didn't his heart sank.

The hallway was desolate, most people having abandoned their loved ones for the evening. One lone nurse sat at her station reading a newspaper. "Got the short stick?" he asked trying to sound upbeat and pleasant. She looked up with a hint of annoyance.

"No time off for good behavior it seems," she replied. She pushed a blond strand of hair behind her ear.

"How late are you stuck here?"

"Eleven. Two more hours."

"I left a radio on in my wife's room. I was hoping it could stay on, at least for a while longer."

"Sure," she said with a nod. "I'll leave it until I'm off."

"I appreciate it. Merry Christmas."

"You too," she replied, and went back to her paper.

David looked down and saw he was squeezing the brim of his hat in his fists, knuckles white.

You too, she'd said. How was he supposed to enjoy Christmas with his wife stuck in this place? Come back to me, Lilly. Please! He put on a brave face for no one in particular and walked along the tiled hallway, his footsteps echoing louder than usual.

"David?" Abigail was leaving her husband's room dressed for the weather. "You headed out?"

"Yes." They walked side-by-side toward the void awaiting them outside. "How's he doing? Anything?"

"Nothing."

He understood how she felt. The loneliness was palpable as the days stretched into weeks then months. Unless you'd gone through it, it was hard to imagine the loss one felt. That's how the two of them had become friends. They could relate and in that be supportive.

Abby, please, she'd told him after spending a few days together. *My mother was the only one to call me Abigail, and that was when I'd done something wrong.* Yet he couldn't bring himself to call her by such an informal name. It seemed wrong somehow.

"I know it's not how one should spend Christmas," he continued, "but I'm headed out for a drink. Not really in the Christmas spirit if you know what I mean."

"A drink sounds good," Abigail said, putting on her gloves. "Would you like some company? I really don't feel like going home to an empty house again, especially today of all days."

He'd planned to sit at the bar, get properly drunk, and hope— like he'd done so many times before—that this was all a bad dream. "Not at all. The company would be nice. But, just so you know, Loafers is not a classy place."

She feigned shock. "With a name like Loafers? You lie." He smiled, almost laughed. "I'll follow you." she said.

They walked from the hospital to the parking lot. Snow continued to descend joining the half inch already there. With each step the powdered snow crunched beneath, their footprints joining several half covered ones. David saw Abigail to her car, held the door for her, then went to his own. He led her out of the parking lot and down the road, taking it slow because of the slippery conditions. Last thing he wanted was for her to join their loved ones in the hospital.

There was almost no traffic out, most people now warm with their families in the shelter of their homes. Some would be opening gifts, others drinking eggnog or punch, parties, roaring fires, all the things that made this night so special, a night he thought he'd be spending alone. Now he had Abigail's company for the time being, and the loneliness he knew that awaited him had been postponed temporarily.

Loafer's was a corner bar that sat on the outskirts of town. Only two snow covered cars were parked in the lot. Men who worked at the lumber mill were the main patrons of the bar as it was the closest place to get a drink after a long work day, but on a night like tonight it was limited to the bartender and bachelors.

The room wasn't particularly spacious, but it was long. The bar hugged the right side with tables spaced in the middle of the main room. A pool table was at the back along with two dartboards. It was dimly lit, the wood finish darkening it further. David escorted Abigail to a table and pulled the chair out for her.

"I think I'd prefer the bar," she said. Abigail leaned in to him, as if to reveal a secret. "It's closer to the booze."

"Alright," laughed David. "Bar it is."

They sat on the tall stools, the bartender wiping the wood in front of them clean. Why David didn't know; it's not like anyone had been sitting here.

"What can I get you?" the bald heavyset bartender asked politely over wire-rimmed glasses.

"Tom Collins, please." Abigail looked at David.

"Gin. Neat."

The bartender stepped away to make the drinks. Abigail asked, "So how did you find this place?"

"I've driven past it a couple of times, and it always intrigued me. It's not a place Lilly would ever go to, so I never really had an opportunity."

Abigail looked around the room. "I like it. It's definitely not a place I'd visit on my own, but it has its charm."

"Charm?" David said with a smile. "I doubt the regulars will agree with you there."

"I wonder if Frank ever came here?"

She pulled out a handkerchief from her purse and dabbed at her eye. The light mood they'd been sharing dissipated.

"I didn't mean to upset you."

"It's not that," she said glumly. "The doctors… they don't think he's going to make it."

"I… I'm sorry. I didn't know. When did they tell you?"

"Today. Merry fucking Christmas, right?" She pulled a pack of cigarettes from her purse, lit one.

The bartender brought them their drinks then left them to talk privately.

"Of all days," he said more to himself. Then: "Why do they think that?"

"Readings, I suppose. I don't know. They tried to explain it to me, but it's gibberish."

"What are you going to do?"

"What can I do?" she asked. "Remain hopeful. Doctors have been wrong before."

"I'm sure he'll come to." He reached out and covered her hand in his, gave it a gentle squeeze. "If there's one thing I'm sure of is that he can hear you—like Lilly can hear me when I talk to her—and he's fighting to make it back to you."

"How can you be so sure?"

"Because I have to."

David felt bad for Abigail. He knew she had no family. Both her and Frank's parents were dead, she was an only child, and Frank's older sister had run off with some guy never to be seen again. And she hadn't had time to befriend any of the locals, besides him, that was. He was the closest person to her at the moment. Thankfully, the doctors hadn't put him in that position yet, so he still lived every day as if Lilly would come back to him. He could only imagine what Abigail was experiencing.

They sat in silence, a regular and the bartender quietly conversing on the other end of the bar. Soon David and Abigail had finished their drinks, ordered another round.

"I've had a lot of time to contemplate life and death, and you want to know a funny thing?" she asked. "I still don't have an answer. I can't make up my mind. What do you think, David? Is there someplace we go, or do we just… disappear?"

While he had been raised Catholic, he'd made his choice years ago to believe that once his time was up that was it. He wasn't sure that was the most comforting thing for Abigail at the moment, so instead said, "It doesn't matter what I believe. God, the universe… what matters is we live our lives the best we can while we have the time. If we affect people in a positive way the rest will be sorted out in the end."

A sad smile came to her. "I do wonder that if there is a God why then did he do this to Frank and me? What had we done that was so terrible to inflict this pain on us?"

"'God works in mysterious ways,'" David recited. "I know you probably think I believe in nothing." She opened her mouth, probably to deny his accusation, but he cut her off. "I saw the look you gave me, and trust me when I say it's a look I'm familiar with. It's not that I don't believe in nothing, I just think we are given a short time here to be the best that we can be—to help one another. Everything else… poof."

"That's sort of cynical, don't you think?"

"I prefer realistic." The conversation had gone south quickly. If he was going to be miserable he preferred to be it alone, didn't want Abigail brought down by his sullen mood. He held up his drink.

She raised her glass, tapped his with a *clink*. "Cheers," and drank.

They continued to talk into the evening, sharing stories like they'd done at the hospital. As the hours crept by a few more regulars showed up. A clock on the wall showed it was nearing 1 AM when the bartender announced last call. David gestured to Abigail's Tom Collins but she waved it off. "I think I've had more than enough," she said. She opened her purse and pulled out a couple bills.

"Put that away," David said. "My treat."

"Absolutely not." She offered him the cash but he pushed it back. "I insist."

"How about I leave the tip?"

David put enough cash on the bar to cover the drinks and a generous tip. "I've got it covered. Consider it a Christmas gift."

"David…"

"Please."

"Alright," she said, and put the bills back in her purse. They stood, he helped her with her coat, put on his own, and stepped into the chilled night. Their breath danced; the snow had slowed but not stopped. Abigail slipped, was caught by David, and let out a giggle. "I guess I had more than I thought."

"Are you alright to drive?" he asked.

"I think so, yes."

Both their cars were now covered in shimmering white. Abigail dropped her keys twice attempting to unlock her car. David picked them up and said, "Come with me."

"What?"

He escorted her to the passenger side of his car. "I'll see you home. I'd never forgive myself if I let you go off by yourself."

"Are you alright to drive?"

The world spun a little but was nowhere near where he thought he'd be. "I'm fine."

David held the door for her and she climbed in. He started the engine and dusted off the windows of snow before sliding into his seat. Abigail stared out the window, eyes unfocused.

"Abigail?"

"Hmm?" She continued to stare out.

"Are you alright?"

"Just thinking is all." Her voice was quiet, distant.

"I need your address."

"Why?"

"To drop you off."

"Oh. Oh yes. Silly me." She gave it to him, and he pulled out of the lot leaving tire tracks behind.

"Look out there," she said after a while. "What do you think is out there hiding in the shadows?"

David looked and saw the shapes of trees and nothing more. "The usual forest creatures, I suppose."

"Do you think we have shadows?"

He glanced at her—she stared at him.

"Not the kind we see out in the sun," she said. "No. Inside. Things we hide from the people around us, sometimes even from ourselves."

"I think they call that the subconscious." He felt the air blowing from the vents. It was warming, but still had a bite to it. "Are you warm enough?"

"Yes. Thank you."

The rest of the ride home was quiet. He was sure she'd fallen asleep when he pulled into her driveway. The gentle hum of the engine was making even him drowsy.

"We're here, Abigail."

"Are we?" She looked up and smiled. She ran her hand across her face, the veil that had covered her for the ride lifting. She turned to David and thanked him.

"I can swing by in the morning and give you a ride back to get your car."

"You're too kind, David. I'll take a cab though. I appreciate the offer." She opened the door and stood. "See you tomorrow at the hospital?"

"I wouldn't be anywhere else," he said.

She was almost past the car when she slipped, hand slamming onto the hood, bracing her fall. David jumped out and hurried to her. "You okay?"

"Yes," she giggled. "Ice, or these damned shoes. I'm liable to break my neck wearing these things."

"Well we don't want that." He extended his arm to her. She accepted it, and he escorted her to the door. He noted that her house wasn't that dissimilar from his own. Once the door was unlocked she reached in and turned on the hall light.

"I'd offer you a drink but I don't have anything in the house."

"That's alright, Abigail. I should be headed home anyway."

To the emptiness.

To my demons.

She reached out and hugged him. She was warm, and the smell of jasmine teased his nostrils. And then she was crying, her body shaking in dismay. David wrapped his arms around her and crooned. "It'll be okay."

"How do you know?" she sobbed.

"A feeling." He held her at arm's length and look into her eyes. "You asked me earlier what I believe. Truth be told I don't believe in God, but what I do believe in is positive thinking. If we wish, pray, believe in something hard enough then it will come true. I believe with all my heart that Lilly will wake. I believe that about Frank too."

Her eyes shimmered, the tears flowing. She reached up and stroked his cheek. Warm. So warm and soft. He closed his eyes relishing the touch.

The world spun.

The drinks. Had to be.

How I miss you, Lilly.

And then she kissed him, and he her. It felt wrong.

If felt right.

Their lips moist and wanting, needing, longing for companionship. To love and be loved.

This was wrong.

This is right.

Abigail pulled away, eyes opening, meeting his.

"Abby, I…"

She took his hand and pulled him into her home, closing the door behind him.

eight
(1958)

David got a phone call while at work—he'd better come to the hospital.

What is it? he'd asked. *Is she awake?*

Well… no. But she's talking.

Talking? Like in her sleep?

Yes.

He'd rushed to the hospital making it there in under ten minutes. Running through the hallway he'd almost fallen twice, his wet boots sliding out from under him on the tiled floor. In his wife's room was a doctor taking his wife's pulse and a nurse jotting notes in a chart.

"Mr. Rottingham," the doctor said standing up. "I'm Doctor Wilson. This is a little unusual—"

"Is she awake? Is she going to be okay?" He talked fast, practically yelling.

The doctor held up his hands. Slow down, they said. "Your wife shifted in her bed, and she did make some sort of noise."

"The person on the phone said she was talking."

"Mumbling is more accurate. Something about the number forty-six?" The doctor looked at the nurse for confirmation. She nodded. "Yes," he said, turning back to David. "Forty-six. Does that have any significant meaning?"

Forty-six? He wracked his brain but came up with nothing.

"No. None." Tears sprang to his eyes. "My wife is coming back."

The doctor gave his "slow down" hands again. "While this is a strong indication your wife is healing, we still don't yet know the damage she's suffered from being in a coma so long. It is progress, but we have to stay realistic. While it may be looking good you should still prepare for a… less than ideal outcome."

Satisfied he'd done his due diligence the doctor left, the nurse close in tow. David sat on the bed next to his wife and gently stroked her cheek. "Lilly? Honey? Can you hear me?" No response. "The doctor said you were talking. Can you do that for me now?" Nothing. "Come on, Lilly," David said. Tears of frustration sprang to his eyes. He whispered, "Come back to me. You're so close. Please."

Her head shifted. Not much, but a little. Was that his doing or had she done it herself? "Lilly?" He waited and watched, but no other movement followed—a final bow in what had transpired before his arrival. He collapsed into the chair and began to weep.

So close! He was so close to having her back!

Although he felt stupid, desperation brought him to clasp his hands, bow his head, and pray. He felt ridiculous—praying to an invisible man that probably didn't exist—but he couldn't take much more.

After what had happened with Abigail he'd lost the only person he felt he could talk to, the only person that could relate. He'd felt terrible for letting it happen, should have known better. Be it the drinks, loneliness, desperation, or all of the above, it had happened, and as a result he and Abigail had only spoken twice since. The first both clumsily apologizing to each other the next morning, both feeling they'd taken advantage of the other. The second happened while passing in the halls.

Idiot!

That was the truth. Yet as guilty as he'd felt the next day, and every day since, it had felt good. Being with someone, not thinking for a change, not wondering and worrying, just being in the moment. It had felt so good, so *right*.

But it wasn't. It never should have happened; there was no excuse. He promised himself that if—no, *when*—Lilly awoke he'd make it up to her every day.

Lilly's eyes opened, fixed on the ceiling. His mouth dropped and he grabbed for her hand.

"Lilly?" He gave a squeeze and she squeezed back, eyes darting.

"Forty-six and two," she mumbled. "Forty-six and two."

"Forty... what baby? What?"

She looked around frantically, seeing but not seeing.

She's not here, David thought. *She's not here, she's somewhere else. What is she seeing?*

A deep moan, deeper than any David had ever heard, escaped her. "Doctor! I need help!" What felt like minutes was only seconds. Lilly's movements were frantic; she clawed at the air.

Then she began to convulse, her entire body shaking, the bedsprings groaning under the movement. And, as suddenly as it began, it stopped. Her eyes closed lazily and she was still.

The wall clock ticked.

"Lil? Lilly?" David stroked her face, grabbed her shoulders, gave her a shake. "Come on, Lilly. Wake up. Wake up now!"

Doctor Wilson ran in followed by the nurse. "What happened?" he asked as he pulled a stethoscope from his pocket. He checked Lilly's heart rate, then her respiration. "Mrs. Rottingham?" he asked, pulling the stethoscope from his ears. He looked at David. "What happened?" he asked again.

"I don't know. She opened her eyes, started talking... I think she may have had a seizure." He began to cry, couldn't help it. He wiped at the tears feeling shamed.

"Well," Doctor Wilson said with a sigh, "her heart rate is escalated but it's returning to normal. How long did the seizure last?"

"A couple of seconds. It was—"

"David?" said a hoarse yet beautiful voice. Lilly was looking at them with tired eyes. "What happened? Where am I?"

"Lilly?" he whispered. "Oh my God, Lilly!" he cried and embraced her in a hug. He sobbed into her neck, months of pent up emotions flooding out.

He didn't know how long he was there, hugging and rocking his beautiful wife. His heart felt ready to burst. "I knew you'd come back to me," he whispered. "I never stopped doubting."

"Mr. Rottingham?" he heard the doctor say. He held onto Lilly a few seconds more, pulled away slowly, and gazed into her eyes.

"What's going on?" she asked him. He responded by giving her a gentle kiss on the cheek.

"I'll let your husband fill you in on the details," the doctor said. He introduced himself to her and only said she'd been in an accident. He checked her pulse, flashed a light in her eyes, did a few other tests before giving her a reassuring smile. Ten minutes later David and Lilly were alone, the door shut.

They hugged again, David still emotional but controlling his tears. When he finally felt like he could talk without breaking down, he told her about the accident and how long she'd been out. She sat sullen for a long time, not saying a word, digesting the news.

"What about the baby?" She looked up into David's eyes and he could see she knew the answer. Her face contorted, tears began to flow, and it was his turn to comfort her. He couldn't bring himself to tell her that she was now incapable of bearing children. That would have to wait.

There was one last thing he needed to tell her. It might be too much for one person to bear but she needed to know. He felt her tense as he delivered the news about her parents.

"Do they know who?" she asked.

"No. They're still investigating."

"Oh."

And that was all. It wasn't the reaction he expected, and wondered if she might have a breakdown.

With each passing day Lilly got stronger. The hospital ran their tests, the results positive. Lilly was out of bed and walking by the end of the week—carefully steered by David to avoid Frank's room—and by the end of the second week she'd been cleared to return home. By then David had told her the equally bad news, that she could no longer become pregnant. To David's surprise she didn't cry. She barely bat an eye.

"Are you alright?" he asked.

"Yes. Somehow… I just had a feeling, you know?"

He nodded.

When David arrived the morning to take her home she was packed and ready to go. She wasn't in bed but sitting in the chair looking out the window. It was sunny, the brightness accentuated by the reflective snow. She wanted to walk out on her own but they wouldn't allow it. The paperwork was signed, smiles and thanks went around between the Rottingham's, the doctors and nurses, as Lilly sat begrudgingly in the wheel chair. David grasped the handles and began to push her down the hallway, ever so happy to leave. The glass doors to the outside world never looked so beautiful. He was ecstatic and overjoyed, so focused on getting her out of the hospital that he didn't hear the quiet sobbing coming from Frank's room.

It wasn't until he saw the obituary in the paper two days later that he learned Abigail's husband had passed.

* * *

Life in River Bend returned to normal for the Rottingham's and Amberson's in 1958. The previous year had been difficult, more than difficult, but as David and Lilly were continuing their lives, the Amberson's, too, were making adjustments.

School had been rough for a while; rumors of their father spread like wildfire. The words affected Willem the hardest. He didn't have the thick skin Elliott had, and the kids Sam's age had yet to develop the cruelty of adolescence.

Willem tried to ignore the rumors and hurtful things people said to him like his older brother, but in the end he could only take so much. He absorbed the words, letting the anger at his father and those spreading the rumors fester. With no one to blame he began to resent his mother. One afternoon a fellow classmate said the wrong thing.

It was the last week of school when Bobby Stapleton came up to him with a large grin on his face, not even attempting to hide the fact of his intention. It was recess and Willem and William were sitting in the dirt baseball diamond playing marbles. After their talk at the bridge Willem had warmed to William, and while not best friends they had a mutual respect and appreciation for each other.

"How's your mom's new job going?" Bobby asked.

"Fine," Willem said with hesitation. He and William exchanged a knowing look, that Bobby was up to something.

Bobby was a little taller than both Willem and William, short blond hair, and a mouth full of crooked teeth. He covered a snicker with his hand. "You're going to have a new dad soon, eh? Which guy is she going with?"

Willem didn't know what Bobby was talking about so stayed quiet. That just added fuel to Bobby's bullying.

Bobby gasped. "Oh! You didn't know? How do you not know? It's the talk of the town!"

"What are you getting at?"

"Don't listen to him," William interjected. "He's just talking out of his ass."

Bobby looked devilish. "Oh no. All the kids know."

Ignore him, Willem told himself. *Whatever he says ignore him, just like Elliott does.*

He looked down at their game and rolled a marble. He'd been aiming for a light blue one but missed. "Go away, Bobby."

"But don't you want to know what you're mom's been up to?"

"He said 'go away'. Don't you listen?" William stared at Bobby, his eyes commanding. That got Willem curious.

"What's he talking about?" he asked his friend.

"Nothing. He doesn't know what he's saying."

"Do too," Bobby said. "Not sure why you're protecting him from his whore mother."

"My *what?*" Willem was on his feet, staring Bobby down. He felt his face grow warm, nails dug in his palms. "What did you call my mom?"

"A. Whore."

Willem was on Bobby before either boy knew it. He fell back into the dirt, a puff of dust catapulting into the air. Willem's fist came down hard smashing into Bobby's temple. The boy cried out in pain. Willem blocked Bobby's feeble attempts to hit back, batting away his fists easily. Kids saw the fight and ran over, circling them, provoking them.

"My mom is not a whore!" Willem bellowed, his fists coming down faster and more furiously. There was a solid crunch as Bobby's nose collapsed under Willem's balled fist. Blood splattered his blond hair.

"Ow! Knock it off! Stop it!" Bobby cried, kicking out, flailing about, trying to escape the furious onslaught.

"Take it back, Bobby!"

"I take it back! I take it back!"

But Willem couldn't stop. The words of dozens of kids over the past months burst free, the pent up anger escaping through one punch to the next.

"What's going on?" The voice of one of the teachers seeped into Willem's fog. Who was it? From the corner of his eye he saw Mrs. O'Flyng. "Stop it! The two of you stop it right now!"

She pushed through the crowd to the two boys and struggled to pull Willem off, finally succeeding with the help of William. Willem stopped struggling, relaxing his body, going limp. "What is wrong with the two of you?" she scolded.

"He started it!" Willem hollered, pointing at Bobby.

"I don't care if the Devil himself started it."

"But he called my mom a whore!"

A few kids gasped at the obscene word. Never had they heard one of their own use an obscenity in front of an adult.

"Sticks and stones, Willem. Sticks and stones."

Willem felt her let go of him and he immediately wanted to attack Bobby again, felt William squeeze his shoulder. *Not now*, it said. Willem held his ground, teeth clenched, eyes stabbing.

"Oh dear, Bobby. I think your nose may be broken." Bobby had his mouth and nose covered with a hand, blood oozing from between the fingers. His face was covered in dirt and blood. Mrs. O'Flyng crouched and grasped Bobby's wrists gently. "Let me see," she said.

Bobby glared at Willem through tears and slowly moved his hands away. Mrs. O'Flyng let out an audible gasp. Willem smiled, couldn't help but feel proud for knocking out two teeth from Bobby's shit eating grin. Served him right.

"Let's go. The both of you."

"Why me?" asked Willem. Bobby got what he deserved for calling his mother a whore. Why should he be punished?

"Look at poor Bobby here and tell me you don't know."

Willem wasn't sure what would happen next as Mrs. O'Flyng escorted them into the school, but he felt like an inmate making his final walk to be executed.

* * *

Willem sat at the kitchen table, Elliott across from him, while his mother paced the room furious. He hadn't seen his mother this angry since, well, ever.

"I am so disappointed in you, Willem," his mother said. "What came over you?"

"I lost my temper."

"Temper? You broke that boy's nose!"

Willem couldn't bring himself to look at his mother so stared at the fruit bowl in the center of the table.

"And where were you?" Willem rolled his eyes up and saw his mother focused on Elliott.

"Me? I was in class."

"I told you to watch out for your brothers."

"I can't watch them all hours of the day, mom. Besides, after today I don't think Willem needs protecting."

A pang of pride coursed through Willem at his eldest brother's praise. In many ways it felt as if Elliott was saying he wasn't a little boy anymore and was capable of taking care of himself.

"Doesn't need protecting? If you had done as I'd asked then he wouldn't have gotten into this mess!"

"Don't put this on me," Elliott shot back. "If that kid had kept his mouth shut and hadn't provoked him then this wouldn't have happened."

She turned back to Willem. "I don't care what this boy said. The fact remains—"

"He called you a whore," Willem interrupted. His mother recoiled as if slapped.

"He what?" she asked, the anger seeping away.

"He called you a whore."

She pulled a chair out from the table and sat between her boys. "Oh," was all she managed, letting the hurtful word sink in. "Did he say why I was a... a—"

"He said I was going to have a new dad soon and wanted to know which guy it would be."

"Oh," she said again, more quietly. She looked at Elliott. "Did you know about this?"

"Its talk, mom. You always told us to ignore that stuff."

"And this is the talk around at school?"

Elliott shrugged.

"I see," she said. She slapped the table with her hands, back and forth, *tap-tap-taptaptaptaptap*. "I have to get back to work, but we'll talk about this tonight, okay? And you," she pointed at Willem, "are going to be punished. What you did was completely unacceptable regardless of what that boy said. You understand?"

"Yes, mom."

"Good." She stood, swept her purse up on the way to the door. "No outside play," and then she was gone.

Willem looked at Elliott who stared at him with sad eyes. The muffled car engine started then disappeared as their mother drove away. From upstairs a door opened followed by creaking steps. Sammy peaked around the doorway. "Is she gone?" he asked.

Elliott waved him over. Sam ran to him and jumped onto his lap. Elliott had become the father figure missing in his life, one he didn't seem to mind playing if it made Sam happy.

"Why was mommy mad?" he asked, his big doe eyes looked between his brothers. "Was it something I did?"

"No," Elliott said. "Willem got into a fight is all."

To Willem he said, "Did you win?"

Willem smiled. "I think so."

"Good."

Wind blew through the screen door.

"Do you think there's any truth to it?" Willem asked.

"Not in the way we're hearing it, no."

"But do you think—?"

"No, Willem. I don't." Elliott was forceful in his words as he bounced Sam who was giggling. "They're rumors, not gossip. Big difference."

"What are you talking about?" asked Sam.

"Nothing," Elliott responded, ruffling his hair. "Nothing at all."

Willem stood and went to the door.

"Where are you going?" Elliott wanted to know. "Mom said to stay in."

Willem said nothing, just opened the door and walked out.

In the backyard was a tire-swing their father had put up for them years ago, and it was there he went. Inside the tire was a pool of stagnant water. He dumped it out as best he could, then crawled through, kicked, and started to swing lazily.

Elliott said the rumors weren't true, but what if they were? He suspected Elliott was protecting him and Sam by lying, much like his mother had done last year. It felt like Elliott knew more than he was letting on, something he didn't want his brothers to know about. From William's reaction it seemed that he, too, knew something more. If he couldn't get answers from Elliott maybe William would spill the details. He wasn't sure he would like what William was going to say, but he had to know. Were people spreading lies about his family, or were they simply stating facts? Next time he saw William he'd find out.

"Are you okay?" The soft voice of Sam brought him back to reality.

"Yeah. Why do you ask?"

"Seems like something is bothering you is all."

"Just stuff on my mind."

"I get stuff on my mind, too."

Willem hesitated, wondered if he should say anything. Most likely everyone at school had heard by now, so might as well be upfront with Sam.

"I got into a fight at school. Broke a kid's nose."

"Why did you do that? Was he being bad?"

"Yes. He was saying mean stuff."

"What kind of mean stuff?"

"It doesn't matter. What matters is I got angry and I shouldn't have."

"And you got in trouble?"

"Yes."

"Mom will probably ground you."

"Probably."

"It's okay if she does. I'll keep you company."

Willem smiled, his sullen mood lifting.

"Can I have a turn?"

"Sure." Willem dragged his feet in the grass until he stopped and pulled himself out. He held the tire as Sammy climbed in.

"Can you give me a push?"

Willem obliged, pushing Sammy one, two, three times, each push getting Sammy higher and higher. He laughed and giggled and kicked his feet, his smile so infectious Willem couldn't help but laugh. At first he had been terrified about coming home in the middle of the day, but now he was glad. He hadn't played with Sam like this in a while and having his baby brother so joyful eased his mind. He realized in that moment that he hadn't felt happy in a long time.

His father was gone, his mother was working, and Elliott had started doing odd jobs around town. When was the last time he'd seen Sam smile? Not since before their father had disappeared, that much was certain. He felt a pang that maybe, just maybe, things would be okay after all. He didn't know what sort of mood their mother would be in when she came home tonight, but he decided he wouldn't worry about it until then. No sense souring the day with worrisome thoughts when there was nothing to worry about at the moment.

And yet, as happy as he was, the words Bobby said lingered in the back of his mind.

Your mother is a whore.

As much as Willem tried to quiet the words, to let them bounce off him, he just couldn't do it, the anger starting to fester again. No… he didn't feel bad about breaking Bobby's nose or taking out two of his teeth. In fact, he felt pretty damn happy about it. Really, really happy.

He laughed with Sam as he pushed him even higher.

* * *

Willem and William sat on the edge of Willow Creek Bridge. Both had a fishing pole in hand, lines cast to the water below. Neither had had a bite since they started a half hour ago. Not that they cared; it was nice to be out of the house after a week of gray skies and on-and-off showers.

Willem's gaze kept drifting to the willow tree, wondering if their buried treasure would be safe. If it rained anymore there was a good chance the creek would crest and flood the surrounding area. At one point he'd even considered going to pull the box from its hiding place but had thought better of it. The creek was higher than usual, and its rapid movement had scared him from getting too close. Even sitting on the edge of the bridge made him nervous, but he didn't want to appear scared in front of William.

It had been a month since school had let out and the fight with Bobby a distant memory. He'd expected retaliation early on, but as the days crept by the on-edge feeling he'd constantly felt when out and about started to subside—the beating he'd expected never came. Now it was summer, school was out, and he rarely saw anyone from his class.

He felt safe.

A topic he'd wanted to discuss with William had been postponed several times as the time never seemed right. It was a delicate one and he wanted to make sure there were no interruptions, no way for William to change topic. He'd told himself many times that he should just let the rumors go, but the stories of his mother haunted him, and he needed to know what was being said.

"William? I have a question for you, and I want the truth."

"No I'm not secretly a fan of *Archie*. I told you—horror and supernatural only—and you will not get me to try it."

"I'm serious."

"So am I."

153

William glanced at Willem, realized his joke wasn't getting the laugh he'd hoped for, and stopped grinning. "Okay," William said reluctantly.

"You remember those rumors that got started at school? The one about my mom?"

"Yeah," he said cautiously. "What about it?"

"Was there any truth to it?"

William gave a cursory glance. "I don't know. You know how rumors are. Someone says they like potato chips, that's passed around ten times and suddenly werewolves are space aliens from Mars. Don't you remember the experiment in Mr. Miller's class?"

"Yeah, but I think a couple kids deliberately changed up the story."

"That's exactly how rumors work. People change them to make them more interesting. Whatever was said about your mother I wouldn't worry about it. They were rumors, and that is all."

Willem wished he could—had tried—but he hadn't been able shake it.

"Who started the rumor?" he asked.

"You serious? How should I know?"

"Where did you hear the rumor then?"

"I don't remember. Jesus, Willem. I feel like I'm on trial or something."

Willem had to make William understand why he needed to know, why this bothered him so much. Maybe then he'd be less reluctant to spill the beans.

"You know that itch you get under the skin, the one you can't scratch away no matter how hard you try? That rumor is sort of like that for me. I can't get rid of it, and I think the only relief will be knowing the truth."

William gave Willem a long hard look, sighed, and said, "Why don't you ask your brother? The rumors started with the older kids anyway."

"I've tried, but he won't say."

"I don't know…"

"Please."

He sounded more desperate than he intended, but this was probably the last chance he had to hear the rumor for himself.

"Fine. What exactly do you want to know?"

"What is it you heard exactly?"

"It's not a big deal, Willem. The story I heard is that someone saw your mom with someone."

"What, like talking?"

"No not like talking!" A brief pause, then: "Making out."

"Oh."

That was it? His mom was spotted kissing someone? While the image kind of grossed him out he knew that people kissed. What was the big deal?

William's mouth contorted into a sideways pinch. "A couple times."

"A couple... How many?"

Another glance from William followed by a shrug. "Two, maybe three?" He obviously was avoiding giving a definitive number. He countered William's look with one of disapproval. William sighed. "Five is what I heard."

"At the same time?"

"Eww! No! See? This is how rumors go."

While the gross factor increased he failed to see how making out translated to whore for people.

"And there was touching," William relented.

Willem reacted as if slapped. "Like what?"

William gave him the most curious look, as if to say, *Are you kidding me?* That was answer enough.

"Oh." While disheartened he was happy that someone had finally told him the truth.

"Remember this is all rumor. Who knows if it's actually true, and it could have been someone that looked like your mom. I wouldn't worry about it."

"Easy for you to say. What if our positions were reversed?"

William opened his mouth, had no comeback, and closed it.

Yes it was a rumor, but Willem knew it to be true; he felt it in his soul. The woman that had raised him, taken care of him, comforted him, she was a different person, a person he no longer knew. Willem now understood that the world was a dark and ugly place. People lied, people did unspeakable things, and for what?

"Hey, uh... did I tell you I went looking for Caroline's Cottage?" William was obviously trying to move the conversation away from Willem's mother.

"Hmm? Oh. No you didn't."

"I heard someone talking about it a few weeks ago. I spent a couple days wandering the woods but didn't find it. I did find something neat though—an abandoned road. Had a street sign and everything. There was an old bridge, too. And on the other side—and this was really cool—I found a pit. It may have been a well."

"Why do you think that?"

"You know the cemetery on 8? Across from that. Deep in the woods."

Willem found himself thinking about William's find and less so about his mother. Good. He didn't want to think about her right now. He suddenly wanted to see this place, could feel its mystery pulling at him. "Can you show me?"

"Sure. When?"

"Now."

"Can't—not enough time. Me and my folks are going to visit my cousins in a few hours. How about tomorrow?"

Willem wanted to see this place, was impatient to see it in fact, but wasn't brave enough to go trouncing in the woods by himself. He'd have to wait.

"Fine. Tomorrow."

* * *

It was Sunday, and as Willem headed out to meet William his mother had called after him, telling him to take Sammy with. She hadn't known their agenda for the day—nor did he want to tell her for fear she'd put a stop to it—so he'd begrudgingly agreed. As their house disappeared in the distance Willem finally told Sammy where they were going. He'd been enthusiastic until the sky had darkened.

"I don't know if we should do this right now," Sammy said as they rode up to William. They'd decided to meet at the entrance to the cemetery.

"What? You scared?" William teased.

"No," he scoffed. "It's just… our mom might worry if we're not home when it starts to rain."

"It's just overcast is all."

"It'll be alright, Sammy," Willem soothed. "Nothing is going to happen. I promise." He looked across the highway to the barely visible crumbling and overgrown road. "Is that it?"

"Yep."

The boys continued on, the woods seeming to darken as they went in deeper.

A crow cawed, leaves rustled.

Several times they had to stop and carry their bikes over downed trees that covered the road. It weaved from left to right, down and up—a winding twisting road to nowhere.

"What do you think this was used for?" Willem asked.

"Not sure. Maybe logging? Hasn't been used in a long time though, that's for sure."

William skidded to a halt, Willem and Sam following suit. "Why'd you stop?"

"There." William was pointing to a rusty street sign. It's where Pine and Oak crossed, though where Oak was he couldn't say. There didn't seem to be a cross street, yet this sign indicated otherwise. Maybe it had never been finished or had just been a dirt road.

A great flapping sounded above. He looked up and an eagle with the largest wingspan he'd ever seen was beating its wings, launching itself from a tree. Off to their left dead leaves rustled on the ground as something moved beneath them.

Probably a squirrel or chipmunk, Willem thought.

"We're getting close." William started to move again, Willem and Sammy matching his speed.

"How did you find this place anyway?"

"I overheard some older kids talking about this place and figured it might be it. They'd mentioned the cemetery so I just started exploring."

The road curved and was suddenly gone. "Whoops!" William said grabbing the brake, his wheels sliding to a stop. Willem and Sammy skidded next to him. "Sorry. Forgot it came up that quickly."

They were a few feet from the edge of the collapsed bridge, the ruin in the stream below, the water trickling around the white and cracked stone. Willem could imagine it had been a beautiful bridge at one point, but years of neglect must have taken its toll. He estimated the length across was no more than thirty or forty feet, the stream ten feet down. They could easily cross it as the water was only a few inches deep.

"How do we get across?" Sammy asked as thunder rumbled.

"There's a trail just over there," William said, pointing. He walked his bike to the embankment next to the bridge, and Willem watched as William made his way down. It wasn't exceptionally steep, but the leaves made it slippery.

Willem followed, taking each step cautiously.

"Watch it right there," William said.

Willem saw the skid mark of where William had slid. A rock lay half buried in leaves. If either had hit their head on that there was a good chance they'd be out for the count, bleeding, possibly dying. Willem stepped over the spot, tested the ground, and shifted his weight. A few more steps and he was down.

"Its okay, Sam. Just watch your step and take it slow."

He stood at the bottom and watched his brother slide down ever so carefully, taking ginger steps. He nearly lost his balance—let go of his bike—but managed to grab onto a tree branch. His bike rolled down and crashed into one of the bridge stones.

Sammy tested his footing, seemed satisfied, continued down.

His foot shot out from under him and he went down, arms flailing. He landed on his butt and yelped.

William laughed.

"Sam!" Willem cried. "You okay?"

Sam nodded furiously, fear showing.

"Just slide on down. You'll be fine."

Sam took it nice and slow. Once he was on level ground he stood.

"Oh my God you should have seen your face!" William tried to stifle the laugh but another came with a short snort.

"It's not funny!" Sammy cried out, tears in his eyes.

Willem scowled at William, said, "Knock it off."

Sam went to his bike, now in inches of water.

"It okay?"

Sam stood it up and inspected it. "I think so."

"You okay?"

"Yes, but can we go home now? Please?"

Willem didn't want to, but he also didn't like seeing Sam scared. He was trying to hide it but not very well. He turned to William. "Maybe we should."

"It's just up ahead, maybe five minutes."

So close. It would be a shame to turn back now. He went to Sam and crouched so he was at eye level. "Five minutes, okay? Any more and we'll turn around."

Sam was sullen. "Fine."

William led the way across the shallow water, trying to step on rocks that weren't completely submerged. The embankment on the other side wasn't as steep and they made it up without incident. Mounting their bikes they continued to ride.

A gust of cool wind hit them, and the first drops of rain hit his cheeks. The broken road darkened drop by drop.

"Shit," Willem muttered.

Thunder rolled above, a low deep rumble.

And then the road ended, blocked by two giant boulders. William guided them around the boulders to a barely visible narrow dirt road. They followed it, splashing through a puddle, then crested a hill where the boys stopped.

Below was the clearing. William was right; it looked like a foundation but not quite. More of an indentation. To the left of that was a black hole in the ground.

If it wasn't Caroline's Cottage then they'd stumbled upon some other relic of a bygone era.

"Come on," William said and led the way down the hill.

They stopped and dismounted prior to the clearing, the threshold of the property. When they crossed the temperature seemed to drop, the light darkening further.

My imagination, Willem thought. *Has to be.*

The well fascinated Willem, and he felt himself drawn to it. William mumbled, "Be careful."

A few stones lined the perimeter, but the ground was mostly eroded. The water within was milky black.

He turned and joined William at the indentation of the cabin or house or whatever it was. Sam hung back, not venturing any closer than the clearing border.

Willem noted there were no broken or rotting wood beams, remnants of walls, shingles from a roof—*anything*—lying about. If the place had been abandoned then were was all that stuff? Strange the building wasn't here. Or maybe it was all just their minds playing tricks on them.

"This is it?"

"As far as I could find," answered William.

Willem placed his foot on the other side of what he thought was the foundation, the tip of his shoe first as if testing the stability of the ground.

"What are you doing?" Sam hissed.

He looked at his brother and shrugged. "Looking around."

"Don't! Can't you feel it?"

He'd thought it had just been his mind playing a silly trick on him—letting the weather and mood of the situation get the better of him—but Sam voicing a shared experience unnerved him.

"I'll only be a second." He brought his other foot across. He turned and smiled. "See?"

Another crack of thunder rolled across the land. "Fine, but hurry up!"

Something was drawing Willem here, a tiny voice whispering unintelligible words masked by static in his mind. It was eerie yet comforting. He was nervous but felt safe.

He took another step in, then another, moving towards the center, towards the whisper. And then the voice shifted, luring him in a different direction.

At the point where he felt the voice strongest he stopped.

Here. Right here. Something…

He got on his knees and started moving the dirt around. He wasn't sure what he was looking for, but he sensed it was here.

William asked, "What are you doing?"

"Just a minute," and continued to dig.

His finger touched cold metal. He dug around it, got his fingers around it, and pulled. A heavy circular smooth ring about the size of his hand came loose and popped from its dirt prison. Willem stared at it, unsure what it was. He turned it in his hand, rubbing the grime away.

"What have you got?" William wanted to know.

But Willem didn't answer, just stared at it.

The forest lit with blue light, flickering wildly before growing darker still. This time, instead of a gentle gradual roll of thunder, it cracked.

"We should go," William called. "Think it's going to be bad." He got on his bike and joined Sammy at the edge of the clearing.

The static and voice had faded away, and with nothing to lead him he felt aimless. Whatever had drawn him had dissipated, the mystique of the place dead, yet the curiosity lingered. He definitely wanted to come back another day and explore, and when he did he'd come prepared. There was something magical about this place, something unique, he just didn't know what.

A flash of lightning brought him back to reality. He looked around and saw William and Sam at the top of the hill waving their arms.

Willem ran to his bike and slid the ring on the bike handle, then joined William and Sam. Willem glanced back once, saw the property disappear, consumed by the surrounding forest.

I'll be back, he kept telling himself. *I'll be back again.*

He increased his speed, pushing forward, the wind at his back.

nine
(1960)

He was dreaming but try as he might David couldn't wake. He was in his pajamas standing barefoot in the black woods, full moon shining through the naked fall branches. His feet carried him along the decomposing leaves, a blanket of autumnal rust. He crested a hill, and below stood a single-story wooden cabin. Golden light shown in one window.

Three ghostly figures rode past on bikes startling him. *Boys,* he thought. They were just boys, their faces masked in distortion and hollow laughter. David followed them down, and by the time he reached the clearing in the woods the boys had neared the cabin.

No! he wanted to cry. *Stay away!*

There was something in this place, something dangerous that was imprisoned—something other and mad.

Mad and bat shit crazy.

One of the boys approached the wooden porch and passed through it at shin level. The door was an ominous fixture, a maw ready to tear its prey apart. David sensed it, but the boy seemed oblivious. He wanted to run to him, to stop him, but his feet would take him no further. Instead he stood beside the youngest of the three, the one smart enough to stay away.

The ghost boy crossed the threshold, passing through the door. *Come back! You have to come back!*

The door swung open silently and a man emerged.

DeMarcus.

He had that shit-eating smile on his face, and he was looking directly at David. He was suddenly very cold, and the hair on the back of his neck stood.

DeMarcus beckoned David forward. He realized he was no longer shackled to this spot, that he could move on his own. He stood his ground and stared at the smiling man.

Again DeMarcus waved him over and said, "You're safe here."

His feet moved on their own, ushering him toward The Smiling Man.

"This is the shadow dream—what was and will be again," DeMarcus cooed.

A ghostly inhuman screech echoed around them. David jumped at the sound and looked frantically around. "What was that?"

DeMarcus' eyes never wavered. "A prisoner of nowhere, a guardian of everwhere." He stepped forward. "You must bring her to me."

A high-pitched buzzing intoned from some far off place.

"I don't understand. Who?" David asked.

"Lilly."

The buzzing grew louder.

"How do you know my wife?"

And louder still. He felt like his teeth were rattling.

"There isn't much time," DeMarcus responded. "She'll listen to you. Bring her."

"Where? What are you talking about?"

DeMarcus held up his hands and said something but the buzzing was too loud.

"What?" he yelled, trying to be heard over the now deafening sound.

DeMarcus' unnaturally wide smile grew wider still.

There was a flash of blinding blue and DeMarcus and the deafening tone was gone.

The boy reappeared through the door carrying something. David tried to clear his head, watched the figure move away. It looked like a ring in his hand, but he couldn't be sure. He tried to catch up, but the boy was too fast, unfazed by what had transpired.

And then the woods encircling the cabin darkened, the boys swallowed by the engulfing blackness, until David was alone in a void.

He blinked. The light from a late night passing car moved across the ceiling of his bedroom. Crickets chirped outside the open window, and a breeze blew the partially closed drapes. He looked at Lilly who was on her side, back to him, sleeping soundly.

He lay awake until the stars faded, chirping birds replaced the crickets, and the sky brightened to an orange hue. Sleep had evaded him, but not the dream.

* * *

After Lilly had woken from her coma David had become concerned about his wife. After the initial tears and bout of depression she had rebounded quickly—seemingly fine—as if nothing had happened. He'd watched her closely at first thinking she might be having some sort of breakdown, but after a month his concern eased. They returned to their pre-accident routine.

One evening after dinner he was sitting in his chair in the living room reading *To Kill a Mockingbird*. It had been released a few months earlier and the reviews were fantastic. Lilly's crying pulled him from the story and he'd gone to her.

She was standing at the door of what was to have been their child's room. Between ever increasing sobs she said she knew how much he'd wanted a child—they both had—and now that they couldn't she completely understood if he wanted to leave. That had taken him by surprise; such a thing had never occurred to him. He took her in his arms and together they cried, she for what she thought she was losing, he for not seeing the pain his wife had been hiding. He kept apologizing, for nothing and everything, a wave of depression he'd ignored in himself pouring out. After their emotional fire had been expunged they sat together saying nothing. More confident in each other than ever before, they pressed ahead with their lives.

David had never told Lilly about Abigail, something he continually regretted, but this far in he decided it would do more harm than good. Not that it mattered anyway; Abigail had moved that April after selling the house. With her husband dead there was nothing to keep her in River Bend. Since the possibility of an awkward encounter was remote, why upset his wife?

David and Lilly were sitting out on the back patio drinking sun tea and reading the morning paper. A squirrel hopped around the lush backyard digging for nuts, and a chickadee chirped from the edge of their roof.

They heard the truck first, a deep rumbling coming down the street, and then the compressed air brakes before the engine was killed. Curiosity got the better of David. He stood and walked to the edge of the yard where he watched as three moving men opened the back of a truck. A red Plymouth Suburban turned into the driveway and a young couple—roughly the same age as David and Lilly—got out. The man was fit, hair trimmed short, wearing khaki's and a blue polo. The woman wore a sundress and had her long brown hair pulled back in a ponytail.

"The new neighbors are here," he told Lilly, continuing to watch.

The man walked to the movers and said something, though David couldn't make out exactly what the muffled voices were saying. The woman opened the back door and futzed with something. When she stood she held a toddler in her arms, the young girl looking excitedly around, taking in her new surroundings. She had a white bonnet on her head and wore a similar patterned dress as her mother.

The picture perfect American family, David thought.

He returned to his seat. "They look like a nice couple," he said and took a sip of his drink.

"Excuse me," a voice called out. He and Lilly looked up and saw their new neighbors. "Sorry to interrupt."

"No, no. Not at all." David and Lilly stood and crossed the yard. "I'm David Rottingham, and this is my wife Lilly." They shook hands.

"I'm Frank Underhill. This is my wife, Jeanine, and... where did she go?" He looked around the yard and saw his daughter waddling towards the back of the garage. "That's Claire."

"Quite the explorer," David said with a smile. Frank beamed, a very proud father if David ever saw one. "How old?"

"She's two and a half," Jeanine said. "Gets into everything."

"I can imagine." He watched Claire waddle back to her parents and smiled at the new faces.

"Aren't you precious?" Lilly said and smiled back.

"Do you have any children?" Jeanine asked.

Two and a half, about the age their son or daughter would have been. A flash of envy crossed Lilly's face so fast that if you weren't watching for it it'd be missed. David saw it—he always saw the hurt in her eyes when a child crossed their path.

"No," Lilly said with a shake of her head.

David steered the topic to that of the house the Underhill's were moving into, saying he was happy someone had finally bought it. Too nice a house to sit abandoned. They chit chatted a few minutes more before the Underhill's excused themselves to start unpacking. "It was a long drive, and I wasn't quite ready to begin," Frank confided when Jeanine chased Claire inside. "But we best get started or it'll never get done."

"If there's anything you need just holler."

"I'm sure I'll be needing something sooner rather than later."

He nodded politely to Lilly. "Pleasure."

"Same," she responded. "I'll stop by later tonight and drop some dinner off for you."

David shook his head. "That's very kind of you, Mrs. Rottingham, but really not necessary."

She waved his objection off. "I insist. I'll tell you right now that the last thing your wife wants to do is cook after the day you've got ahead of you." There was still a slight hesitation on Frank's face, so she finished with, "I insist."

"If there's nothing I can say—"

"There isn't," she interrupted. "It will be heated and ready to go. All you'll need are a couple of plates."

"We'll graciously accept then."

"Good. Until this evening."

* * *

"What's wrong?" Lilly asked. David looked up to see her staring at him from across the table. "You've barely touched your dinner."

He gave a weak smile. It had been nearly a week since his dream of DeMarcus, and each night was a struggle to stay asleep. In the shadows of his dreams he heard that unnerving screech and saw DeMarcus' terrifying grin. "Just tired is all. I haven't been sleeping well."

You must bring her to me.

The words had rattled him. Was it possible she knew DeMarcus? If so, how?

"I know you too well, David," she said wiping at the corner of her mouth with a napkin. "Spill it—tell me what's wrong."

He saw compassion in those eyes.

"When you were in the hospital a man came to visit you. He claimed he knew you." He readied himself, waiting for some indication of recognition. "DeMarcus." She blinked, though he couldn't be certain that was a damning sign. "Do you know him?"

She shook her head. "Name isn't familiar."

"He was well dressed, wore a white suit. Grinned a lot."

Her eyes shifted, if only for a second. She shook her head again. "No... doesn't sound familiar. He came to visit me? In the hospital?"

"Yes."

She reached up and touched the pendant around her neck, sliding it back and forth. "What did he say?"

"That you were friends as children."

"Anything else?"

"No, nothing. Except... he did say he looked forward to seeing me again."

Lilly's fidgeting stopped, her breath caught. "When?"

He shrugged. *I don't know*, it said. "You do know him, don't you?"

She came to him and crouched, took his hands. "Promise me, David. Promise me that if you see him again you'll avoid him."

He'd never seen her scared before; it was unnerving. "Why?"

"Just promise me. If you see him again you will stay away and tell me."

"Isn't it me that's supposed to protect you?" he asked with nervous laugh.

"This isn't a game, David. Do you trust me?"

So DeMarcus had been telling the truth—Lilly was hiding something. The concern in her eyes, the love, David couldn't help but nod. "Of course I trust you, but now I want you to trust me. Tell me... who is DeMarcus?"

Her mouth contorted, struggling to find the words. "I..."

David grasped her hands and kissed them. "Whatever you have to say—"

"You'll think I'm crazy."

"I already think you're crazy."

They searched each other's eyes, neither blinking nor looking away. "This cannot be repeated to anyone," she said. "It's vitally important."

David nodded.

"Good," she said as she slid into the chair next to him. "It wasn't supposed to happen this way."

"What wasn't?"

She looked up, gestured around. "This. Everything. Things became more complicated than they were supposed to—but that's life in general, isn't it?"

"Lilly—"

"Let me try to explain. I'm not from here."

"I know you're not from River Bend—"

"This is going to take a long time if you keep interrupting me."

"Sorry."

"When I say I'm not from here I don't mean this town, nor do I mean this state or this country." She squeezed his hands and stared into his eyes. "There's another existence... elsewhere."

His brow furrowed. "Elsewhere?"

"I'm from a place called Turmoore."

"Turmoore? I'm not familiar with it. Where is it?"

"Not here, not Earth as you know it."

She was right; he was starting to think she was crazy. Maybe his belief that she had suffered some sort of psychosis was accurate.

"Where we are now—where *I* am now—is the Shadow. A prison. A plane we send those excommunicated."

Plane? The only thing he could imagine... "Do you mean Hell?"

She shook her head no. "That's too simple. Think of it like this: life is a path up a mountain." She hovered her hand horizontally. "Where we are at this moment is here. And Turmoore is here." She placed her other hand directly on top of the first. "We're born and as we grow we live and experience, then we die. When that happens we move up a level."

"So Heaven."

"Stop thinking religion; it's too archaic. While Turmoore is a beautiful place it's not Heaven." She sighed. "Maybe it would help if I gave you some context."

"That might help." It came out condescending. "Sorry."

She scowled at him. "Turmoore is similar to this plane. We have more advanced technology and are more in tune with nature. I guess the best way to describe it is pre your industrial revolution with organic technology. It's hard to describe.

"So anyway, the way it works with planes is that when you die on one you move up to the next like rungs on a ladder. For instance, when you die you'll move on to Turmoore, and those that die under your plane move to yours. Understand?"

"I think so. How many of these… planes… are there?"

"We don't know. So far this is the only one we've been able to access."

"Then how do you know there are others?"

"I don't know all the details, but those that have been studying this believe it to be so."

"Is your plane the last? Are you at the top?"

"Unknown but doubtful."

"Then what's next?"

"We don't know."

"You said our plane is a prison. Why?"

"Some in our government thought it would be a humane way to handle our criminals. We have very few, you see, and it seemed better to re-educate as opposed to lock up or execute. Unlike you we cherish life and won't kill as punishment. There were no wars, no conquests—we worked together to further all Turmoorians. It was harmonious and beautiful and wonderful.

"When we discovered your plane and figured out how to send…" She paused, her head bobbing back and forth. "I guess 'souls' for lack of a better word… when we figured out how to send them to it, some felt it was a fair punishment for those most guilty. Not death, but a redo. A lifetime reliving an existence in the Shadow to learn and to be educated before getting a second chance in Turmoore. And with no way to return until the life here expired there was no concern of the person coming back. Out of sight, out of mind, as you say. We sent them back and washed our hands of it. However, there was a growing unrest regarding this practice. There was a revolt and then a war."

He was trying to wrap his head around it but found it difficult. "And how does this work… this exile? Is it like reincarnation?"

"You are not reborn in the sense you are birthed. Your presence enters a host."

"So you're a prisoner in someone else's body?"

"Not really. The presences, or souls, merge creating an alternate one. A chimera. Fragment memories of Turmoore remain in the shadows of the conscience, as do certain… quirks. To the casual observer it may go unnoticed, for others…" She shrugged.

"If this is a place of exile why are you here? What crime did you commit?"

"None. For me it was a refuge. While we have a government similar to yours we also have a ruling family." She hesitated then said, "My family."

"You're royalty?" David asked.

"They didn't want to risk my life in the growing unrest. When DeMarcus became… infatuated… with me, my parents had two of their advisers bring me here. When the time came I would return to Turmoore, in whatever state it might be." She looked at him expectantly.

"If the presence from Turmoore retains only fragment memories, then how do you know so much?"

"I came by an alternate route. I didn't inhabit a body here like the others. I presume it's the same method by which DeMarcus came."

"And who is DeMarcus?"

"He led the revolt." She said it matter-of-factly, as if that explained it all.

"He loved you?"

She shrugged.

"Why?"

"Why does anyone fall in love? Though in his case I believe it more to be lust than love.

When the time came I would return to Turmoore, she'd said. "How were you to return?"

"I don't know. We were supposed to receive some sort of sign, a signal. And don't ask… I don't know what it was to be."

"If there is no way back then why would he risk following you?"

"He's insane. Does there need to be any other reason? I can only surmise he succeeded in taking over Turmoore and has come for me. But," she added, "I don't understand why he would sacrifice himself like this. Unless…"

Her eyes were distant, searching.

"Unless?" David coaxed.

She looked at him, and what he saw was fear and hope. "He found a way to return."

ten
(1961)

It was clear and sunny, with just a hint of a summer breeze. The sky was deep blue and cloudless, and the tall field grass danced and sang as Willem and Sam ran through it, both laughing at the joy of being free of the confines of their house. The day was theirs to explore.

As they ate toast and drank juice they watched the birds at the feeder. In their imaginations the birds were carrier pigeons, one of which had a message about a notorious bandit that needed to be captured. Willy "Deadeye" Wild had been on the run for weeks and there was a sizable bounty on his head Willem and Sam intended to collect.

They hollered and laughed as they ran through the fields, the grass tickling their legs. Each wore a holster around their waist, and each carried a toy revolver. The morning was pretty much what you'd expect from boys—rough housing and imagination abound.

By noon they had yet to capture Deadeye, so they decided to take a break for lunch. Elliott was at the kitchen table studying when they'd returned, the screen door slamming shut behind them.

"Watch that door, guys," he said, barely looking up.

"Sorry, Elliott," Willem responded.

Elliott finished his note and looked up. "Where have you two been all morning?"

The words spilled from Sam's mouth in glee. "Deadeye robbed a bank and murdered a bunch of people, and we were trying to catch him! He burned farmers' homes and we got into this big gun battle and we thought we had him but he got away! But we know we hit him 'cause he left a trail of blood and we tracked that to the lookout. But we lost the trail there so we think he had some help and got away. We're going to go out and look for him some more after we eat."

"Deadeye, eh? Tall guy with a black cowboy hat?" Elliott said with a smile.

"Yeah!" Sam said.

"You know, I think I know where he might be headed."

Sam's eyes grew wide. "Really? Where?"

"Well," he said, drawing out the anticipation as best he could, "I'm not positive but I'm pretty sure I heard him pass by here a while back. Headed towards town would be my guess. Something about… ice cane? Ice reams?"

"Ice cream!" Sam shouted.

"That's it! Ice cream! Here…" Elliott stood and walked to a cabinet. Inside were bowls, plates, and glasses and, on the top shelf tucked in the back, a small canister.

"You can't!" Willem hissed. "That's only for emergencies. What if mom finds out?"

"It *is* an emergency. You have to stop Deadeye, don't you? Besides, I'll put it back the next time I get paid." Elliott handed them each a quarter with a smile, then crouched so he was eye-to-eye with Sam. "I expect you to nab Deadeye and bring him to justice." Sam beamed ear-to-ear as Elliott ruffled his youngest brother's hair. "Go on now. He might not be there for long, and you don't want to miss him."

They were almost out the door when Willem remembered something. "One sec!" he shouted and ran from the room. He'd been meaning to drop something off at the willow tree, but every time he went that way he'd forget to take it with. Not today. He grabbed the brown paper bag from his desk, the key to the box from Elliott's room, then joined Sam outside.

"What's that?" Sam asked.

"I'll show you later."

When they got to Willow Creek Bridge, Willem handed Sammy the paper bag and jumped onto the ledge. Willem walked the length of the ledge with his arms outstretched for balance. He noted the concerned look on Sam's face, said, "It's alright," and hopped down. "You want to try?"

Sam looked over the edge at the shimmering water running along its rock bed. "What if I fall?"

Willem ran back and took the bag. "Boost up." Sam gingerly put his hands on the ledge and with Willem's help cautiously climbed up. Willem never let his brother go, and soon Sam was standing on shaky legs.

"This is scary." He looked down at Willem. "Promise you won't let go?"

"Promise. Just take it slow."

Sam took one slow step at a time, pebbles sliding out from under his feet. Halfway across the bridge the sound of a car's engine grew, and Sam looked toward it. A black Ford slowed, the sun glistening off the polished metal. The driver, an older man with glasses, peered through the window as he passed the boys before speeding off. Shortly thereafter Sam was across and jumped down beaming with pride. "I did it! I did it!" he cried.

Willem patted his shoulder. "Nicely done. Good job." Sam gave a toothy grin. "Come on." Willem followed the path down to the creeks edge.

"Where are we going?" Sam asked.

"Have to make a quick stop." They followed the embankment to the willow tree. When they were beneath it Willem handed Sam the brown paper bag.

The ground was soft and mossy beneath the canopy. Willem moved the rocks from the hole of their buried treasure. He glanced at Sam who watched him curiously as he pulled out the box wrapped in a dirty cloth.

"What is it?" Sam asked. Removing the cloth, Willem revealed the dented metal box.

"This," Willem said with an air of suspense, "is our buried treasure."

"Buried treasure?" Sam repeated in awe.

"Elliott showed it to me a while back." He handed it to Sam. "Go on. Open it."

Sam crept closer, knelt next to his brother, and gingerly took the box with its intricate design. "This was moms," he said matter-of-factly. "She kept her sewing stuff in it."

"Elliott found it in the trash."

"Where's the key?"

Willem pulled it from his pocket and handed it to Sam who unlocked and opened the lid. Inside was an old pocket watch, a family photo several years old, a green fishing lure, and other odds and ends. "What is all this stuff?"

"The watch was dads; he gave it to Elliott a long time ago. The lure is mine." He didn't mention that it, too, had been a gift from their father. "And that photo… do you remember it being taken?"

Sam shook his head.

Willem continued. "It was taken at Blue Gill Park. We were there having a picnic."

They all looked so happy, each with a smile on their face. An imperfection in the photo—a small lens flare or damage of some sort—hung over his head.

Sam looked at each item in-turn before focusing on several toy cars.

"And those?" he said, pointing.

"Those," Willem said with a smile, "are just some toy cars." Sam looked at him surprised. "Never hurts to have some toys lying around."

"Why are you hiding this stuff?"

"I don't know. Elliott and I just sort of started collecting stuff. It was his idea to hide it here. Can you keep it a secret, Sam?"

There was no hesitation on Sam's part. "Yes."

"Good." Willem pointed to the paper bag next to Sam. "Hand me that."

Sam picked it up and handed it to Willem. "What is it?"

"This," he said opening the bag, "is something special." He reached in and pulled out a single item, one that made Sam's eyes grow.

Willem had been holding onto it since the day they had gone with William into the woods in search of Caroline's Cottage—the metal ring. He'd stuck it in his closet and had forgotten about it until two weeks ago when he'd uncovered it. Ever since then he'd felt an urge to hide it here.

"This I found in the woods that day with William. Do you remember?"

A nod. "Why are you hiding it here?"

Willem shook his head. "I don't know. Just a feeling."

Willem put it in the box; it barely fit, taking up most of the remaining room.

"Can I put something in there?"

"Sure."

Sam dug into his pocket and pulled out a toy soldier and placed it in the box. "He'll protect the treasure."

Willem smiled. "Good idea, Sam."

He took the key from Sam and relocked the box, wrapped it back up, and returned it to its hiding place. Together they covered it with rocks trying to make it look as natural as possible. Once done, they stood and Willem led Sam away. "Let's go get that ice cream."

"And Deadeye!"

"And Deadeye," Willem agreed. They walked back to Willow Creek Bridge and continued on their way.

Willem and Sam were on Main Street and rounded the corner stopping at their destination, simply named The Soda Foundry. Not only did they sell ice cream and soda pop, they also sold comic books. To say The Soda Foundry was a popular destination for kids was an understatement.

Willem and Sam spent time flipping through the latest issues of Green Lantern, Superman, and Batman. They bumped into William who had recently earned the not-so-pleasant nickname Pube after his voice screeched in English class.

"Still DC with you? Really?" William asked not unkindly.

"Best writing out there," Willem responded. "Everything with Atlas is mutant, mutant, mutant! DC has originality."

"Originality? Please!"

"X-Men? Fantastic Four? Mutants. Spider-Man? Mutation from a radioactive spider. At least with DC you've got a man who gained his powers from the sun, a man who got a ring from a dying alien, and a rich guy who makes his own stuff and *no* special powers. Marvel? Mutants." This was a long running debate between the two friends.

"Whatever. I gotta get going anyway. To be continued," he said with a smile.

Willem and Sam walked to the back of the store where the ice cream was. "What flavor are you getting?" Sam asked as they stared through the glass display. "I'm getting chocolate!"

"You always get chocolate."

"It's because I love it!"

There were only two real flavors to choose from—he didn't consider strawberry a flavor. He could follow his brother's lead or go with vanilla. Today felt like a chocolate day, so follow Sam he did. "Two chocolate cones," he said to Mr. Taylor when the middle aged man approached. He paid and they took their cones.

They wandered the town aimlessly before ending up at Blue Gill Park. They played on the seesaws then chased some lounging mallards. One of the picnic tables caught Willem's eye, the table where the photo in the lockbox had been taken. Happier times—it seemed like so long ago.

When they approached Willow Creek Bridge Sam tugged at his brother's hand. "Can I try again?" he asked.

"Go for it. Want help?"

Sam looked at the ledge, determination in his eye. "No. I can do it all by myself."

"Alright. Just be careful."

Sam peeked over the ledge, timidness now creeping into his movements.

"You don't have to do this," Willem said even though he sensed Sam's determination.

Willem stayed close as Sam put both hands on the ledge and boosted himself up, first one knee and then the other. He got one foot under himself and tentatively stood, arms outstretched. Once at full height be began to smile. "I'm doing it!" he shouted proudly. "I'm doing it, Willem!"

"Great job, Sam! Now start across… slowly. No need to rush."

Sam put one foot in front of the other, slowly making his way across, and Willem paralleled him on the street ready to grab him if the need arise.

Willem was so focused on his brother that he didn't hear a car fast approaching. It wasn't until it was almost on top of them that he turned to look. The car swerved toward him as the driver laid on the horn. Four teenage boys hooped and hollered out the window as they flew past, well over the speed limit, forcing Willem to jump back. The car then swerved back into its lane.

"Assholes," he said as he watched after.

The brake lights lit up and the car screeched to a stop.

"Willem? What's going on?"

The cars reversed.

"I don't know," Willem said keeping his eyes on the car. Bobby jumped out of the back seat.

"Well look who we have here," Bobby said as he strode to Willem. Behind him three older boys got out. Bobby stopped a foot from Willem, eyed him up, and snorted. "I knew I'd finally get a go at you if I waited." He looked around, arms outstretched. "Here we are and not a soul around! You ready for payback?"

Willem was nervous. "Payback? It's been three years, Bobby. You still sore over that?"

Bobby pointed to his crooked nose. "See this? And this?" He opened his mouth showing the hole where two teeth had been. "Yeah… I'm still sore."

He could feel a dampness under his arms, his face growing warm. Could Bobby really have held a grudge for this long? "Are you serious? We were kids!"

"There are always consequences for our actions; my dad says that all the time. Today you finally get yours."

"Come on, Bobby. I've got my brother here…"

Bobby glanced at Sam for only a second.

"Can we do this another day?" Willem asked. He looked at the older boys who had moved closer. "Just you and me."

He tried to duck but was too slow. He hadn't expected Bobby to throw the first punch without warning. His teeth rattled and his jaw throbbed, pain shooting through his legs as his knees slammed onto the concrete.

"Willem!" his brother screamed.

He tried to stand, but before he could Bobby's foot connected with his gut. Wind exploded from his lungs—he wanted to puke. A punch to a kidney.

"Leave him alone!" he heard a tiny voice scream through the ringing in his ears.

Another kick, then a third punch to the side of his face as he tried to look up. Gravel bit into his palms and face.

He lay there, curled up in a ball, waiting. What was Bobby waiting for? Was it over?

He heard tires peel out, an engine disappearing into the distance. Willem tried to push himself up but couldn't. He hurt. So fast! The fight couldn't have been more than twenty seconds yet he felt like he'd been beaten for hours.

Why wasn't Sam trying to help him? "Ugh…" he grunted, looked up, vision unfocused. "Sam?"

Couldn't see him. Had the boys taken him? His baby brother had nothing to with this. Why would they take him? Made no sense.

Willem struggled and managed to push himself up, took in his surroundings. "Sammy?"

The wind and birds and creek his only companions.

Standing he hobbled in the direction the car had sped off in when he heard a tiny sob. He looked around again, saw nothing. "Sam?"

Then a terrible thought came to him, and he lunged to the ledge of Willow Creek Bridge and peered over. There, lying in a heap, water trickling by, was Sam.

"Sam!" cried Willem.

He almost lost balance on his way down the embankment. Pain coursed through his body but he didn't care. He grabbed his baby brother. "Sam!" he cried out again, tears of heartache and terror streaming down his cheeks. Sam whimpered, eyes unfocused. "Sammy!" And then they closed and his whimpering stopped. "Please wake up!" Willem began to sob. "Please!" He ran a hand through his brother's wet hair as if trying to comfort him. He felt a gash on the back of Sam's head. He pulled his hand back and looked at it.

Blood. A lot of it.

"No-no-no-no-no!" he kept crying, shaking his brother, trying whatever he could to wake him up.

Willem hobbled up the slope to the road and looked in both directions. No cars! What was he going to do? He could either stay here, go for home, or go for town. What would be best for Sam? He felt dizzy, unsure of himself. What to do? *Think!* There was a doctor in town. And his mother.

Elliott was at home, but what would he be able to do?

Decision made, he ran back towards town.

* * *

The death of Sam Amberson—and the boys responsible—made the front page of the River Bend Times. It wasn't often something as tragic as a child's death rocked the small community, but what made it even harder to digest was the fact it was done at the hands of another boy. No one thought Bobby had done it intentionally—more a case of "boys being boys", a little spat if you will—that had ended in tragedy. David and Lilly both felt bad for the family; they knew the loss all too well.

David's dreams had subsided for a while but never completely stopped. Now, though, they were back with a vengeance, DeMarcus in them all. *Stay away from him*, Lilly had begged him, but he knew no matter how hard he might try to keep that promise it was futile. DeMarcus would find him; of that he was certain. He would toss and turn, sleep evading him, until he would leave the comfort of his bed so as not to disturb Lilly.

Tonight he'd ended up sitting in the backyard with a cup of tea enjoying the cool breeze, the familiar smell of autumn swirling around. The seasons were changing fast this year, and the leaves had begun to darken from lush green to an assortment of reds, yellows, and oranges.

His mind wandered to Claire. Such a beautiful little girl, and he often wondered what their child would have been like had they not lost it. They'd talked of adoption, but neither seemed ready to pursue it.

Over the months they'd learned more about the Underhill's. It wasn't that they were bad people, but the happy-go-lucky perfect American family exterior they radiated was a façade. It's just that Frank was rarely home and stuck at the base, always coming in late. Jeanine and Claire, at least as far as David could tell, rarely saw him. While it wasn't obvious to the casual observer, David and Lilly knew Frank and Jeanine were having problems because, on too many occasions, they'd asked them to watch Claire. They were happy to do so because it gave them the opportunity to plug a hole in their lives—to play parents. At first it was infrequent then became something they did several times a week. And while it wasn't their place to say anything, both David and Lilly suspected Jeanine was having an affair.

That family is going to break one day, Lilly said matter-of-fact one night. *Mark my words*. David didn't doubt it.

The buzzing started gradually, and it brought back his dream. The dark dream. The backyard flashed a blue strobe light as the buzzing increased to a near deafening volume. And suddenly it was silent, so silent David imagined it must be what death sounded like. He sensed a presence, turned, and sitting in a second chair was DeMarcus.

His head was turned toward David, that everlasting smile on his face. His hands grasped the armrests of the chair. He looked comfortable, lounging. "You didn't bring her to me, David." DeMarcus looked around the yard in an unnatural and damn unsettling head turn. "I'm disappointed."

"Why?"

"What transpires from this moment on will resonate throughout everything." DeMarcus turned back. "You have a choice to make," he said and tapped his temple. "There is a girl that needs your help."

The buzzing increased, the blue strobe flickered. David looked around and caught a glimpse of his reflection in the window, yet much older and frail.

Is that me? he wondered.

"We're all reflections of each other." DeMarcus' eyes focused elsewhere. "She's going down the up staircase."

"Who?"

DeMarcus' smile widened. "She sees the girl in the photograph." He looked again to David. "Now she's screaming. They're both screaming."

The buzz turned to screams, and then the world came crashing back. The night sounds, the autumn breeze.

At first he thought he had been dreaming, had fallen asleep in his chair, but then he heard Jeanine screaming next-door, panicked.

David leapt up just as the light in the bedroom he shared with Lilly turned on. He rushed across the dew-covered grass to the Underhill's back door and banged on it.

"Mrs. Underhill? Mrs. Underhill! It's David! Are you alright?" He banged on the glass again.

Lilly came out the back door in her robe. "David! What is it? What's wrong?"

"I don't know," he said with a shake of his head. He knocked again, ready to throw his shoulder against the door, when Jeanine opened it.

"Claire's gone!"

David said, "Wh—what? Where's Frank?"

"Still at work, I think!"

"Call the police," he instructed and ran past.

He assumed Claire's room was upstairs, took the steps two at a time. When he reached the top he spotted it and burst through. A few toys were scattered about but most were put away all nice and neat. Claire's bed was empty. He looked under it and in the closet. Nothing. The window was open, went to it and looked out. The screen window was intact and it was unlikely it had been tampered

180

with. He searched the rest of the upstairs with quick glances calling out Claire's name.

He nearly collided with Jeanine at the bottom of the stairs. "What happened?" he asked.

"I don't know!" she screamed. "I thought I heard something and went to check on her and she was gone!"

Lilly asked, "Is it possible she got out on her own?"

"I don't think so. She's only three!"

"Were the doors locked?"

"Yes!"

She's going down the up staircase. DeMarcus' words echoed in his ear, and he suddenly knew who took her, but where?

Lilly.

Sirens in the distance.

Why would he take Claire?

To ensure you come, he told himself.

The police were at the door a minute later, and David and Lilly stepped away so they could do their job.

"The poor girl," Lilly said. "Do you think it was Frank?"

He shook his head. "DeMarcus."

Lilly looked at him, shocked.

"He came to me again."

"David… you promised me you'd stay away from him."

"It's kind of hard when he just appears." Her brow furrowed, so he told her what happened earlier. "We just need to find him."

"I'll go," she said.

"Where? You're not going anywhere by yourself."

"He wants me."

"But…"

"He's using you, David. Don't you see that? He can't get to me directly so he's using you and now Claire to get to me."

"If true then more reason for me to go."

"While I appreciate your chivalry we don't have time for it. Claire's life is very much in danger."

"Then tell me where he went."

He stared her down, and her lips pursed. "I have to show you. You'll never find it alone." He opened his mouth to argue and she gave him a look so fierce he shut it.

They slipped out the back while the police talked to Jeanine. They changed for the cool night, jumped in their car, and headed out.

"So where are we headed?" asked David.

"South on Highway 49."

They drove in silence, the gloomy darkness trying to seep in. A comment Lilly made earlier came to him. "What did you mean when you said he can't get to you directly"?

"I think he's projecting himself. That's how he can seemingly appear and vanish to you. His physical body is trapped and he's unable to enter this plane, though whether by choice or not I don't know."

"But why me?"

"Because I'd reject him; he wouldn't be able to influence me. Coming through you is the next best thing. Just keep going until I tell you," Lilly instructed.

The urgency was suffocatingly muggy. David felt sweat on his brow. Lilly kept her focus out the window, eyes whipping around, taking in everything. Finally, she piped up. "Turn left up ahead. There's a road and it comes up quick."

He saw the drive and turned down it. The road wound around going deep into the woods.

David asked, "How far?"

"I don't remember. A ways."

"To what?"

"The cabin you saw."

David glanced at his wife who stared out the window. He wished he knew what she was thinking and feeling, but her expression was blank.

Something caught his eye—a reflection—and David stopped the car. He looked where he thought he saw it. A rusted street sign stood in the shadows: Pine and Oak. Pine seemed to have been a street at one point, the concrete cracked and long forgotten, while Oak crossed it. Unless you knew what you were looking for Oak would be easy to miss. A pair of boulders blocked the old road. He drove on.

They rounded a hill then went up another. David hit the brakes and slid to a stop. Down in the valley a blue glow pulsed, similar to the one he'd experienced in his yard. They stepped out, and Lilly led the way down the hill, determination in her stride.

The blue light looked like TV static, and in it the shimmering image of a cabin. The buzz David had heard when DeMarcus visited was present.

"What is this?" David mumbled.

"This is the entrance. Some call it the waiting room, others the room with a view, yet they are one and the same. A pocket between. The thing is you shouldn't be able to see it; it's supposed to be hidden."

"Well I see it, and if I'm being honest it's scaring the hell out of me."

Lilly turned to him. Was that fear in her eyes? "I should do this alone. There's no telling what DeMarcus will do."

David shook his head. "No. I'm not leaving your side, not for a minute. So how do we do this? Just… walk in?"

"No," said Lilly.

She took a step towards the blue static, closed her eyes, and spread her arms. After a time David thought nothing would happen, but then a deep bass echoed as a halo exploded outward erasing the deafening buzz, and the world was suddenly silent. The light dissipated, and the cabin stood there as if it had always been. Lilly relaxed and opened her eyes. "Ready?"

"Yes," David said, and approached the cabin.

* * *

It was a single square wooden room, one Lilly had never seen before. A worn couch was pushed against one faded and chipped lime-green wall. In the center was a wooden straight-backed chair and sitting on it was DeMarcus. A teary-eyed Claire was on his lap, and she held a ragged hand crafted doll missing a button eye. Off to the side stood another man, this one in a red cap.

DeMarcus' stared at Lilly, love and lust in his eye. The strangest thing though, the thing that gave her chills, is that he looked the same as when she'd last seen him. She'd aged over fifteen years since her arrival, yet here he was, looking exactly as she remembered him.

"Who's that?" Lilly asked, pointing to the strange man.

"An associate friend. I'm so happy you recovered my love," he said smoothly.

"Why are you here?" she asked.

"For you." That's what she expected. "I've claimed the empire and have come to bring you back."

Her parents had never signaled her or given her any indication it was possible to return, so as far as she knew it wasn't possible. "Impossible. If there was a way I'd know."

"Do you really think your parents would have sent you here without a way to retrieve you?"

Her foster parents may have known, but if they had that information they took it to the grave with them. She figured she was here until it was her time to pass on.

"How?" Lilly fought the tremor in her voice, hoped only she could hear it. She didn't want DeMarcus to know he scared her. Fear was his strength, and he was a master of it.

"They gave you something, something to help you return. They must have."

"If they did then I don't know what it is."

His jaw pulsed as he clenched his teeth. "We'll find it together then."

"Why come for me? That little girl you once knew is no more. It's been years—"

"Months, actually. It may have been years for you, but in Turmoore only three months have passed. Your kingdom fell, princess. Quite quickly I might add."

"Princess?" she heard David mutter.

She ignored him. "What of my parents?"

"Dead." He said it without compassion or remorse. "To hear their tortured screams…" He closed his eyes and tilted his head up. "Music. It was the most beautiful thing I've ever heard."

"Impossible. My parents, the government, was stronger than you. There's no way you could have defeated them."

"Come with me and find out."

Yet she knew what he said was true; she could sense it in his eyes. "You tortured them?" she asked.

He looked back to her. "I did."

"You were their friend. An adviser. Why would you do that?"

"You can't have a revolution without making an example of those that were in power. If they had lived they would have instilled hope, and that would have slowed progress. I did what needed to be done to bring order to the new regime as quickly as possible."

She fought back the tears; there'd be time to grieve later. "I don't believe you would have risked becoming trapped here. You fought too hard to take control, so why are you really here? I can't imagine it was for me. With all that power you could marry whomever you liked."

His trademark smile faltered, and he stroked Claire's hair. She shied away.

"Such a beautiful child. The innocence… The hope." He chuckled. "You need to return with me to save our future."

She said nothing, unsure of where this was leading.

"Either your parents knew and gambled with our way of life to save you, or they were too stupid to care," he said. "Because if you don't return with me life as we know it will cease to exist. You see, our plane is eroding."

"Eroding?" she said with a quiver.

"Rather quickly I might add."

"You lie."

The man in the red cap moved from his position, circling behind them. She kept an ever watchful eye on him.

"Never. It's rotting away. The working hypothesis is that the planes were never meant to be crossed."

"But Turmoorians have been crossing for decades—"

"Their minds, yes, but not their physical bodies."

Could he be telling the truth? She couldn't believe her parents would have risked Turmoore to save her. But it would explain why DeMarcus came himself to find her; he didn't trust anyone else to do it right. Could she trust him to be telling the truth? If he was she couldn't let her people die.

"How do I know you're telling the truth?" she asked.

"You don't, but I assure you it's true."

"How long?"

"At the current pace they're predicting everything will cease to exist in three years."

Lilly looked at her husband. As the months had turned into years she'd accepted the fact she probably wouldn't be returning to Turmoore. And as her love for David grew she expected to live the rest of her life with him. But if her people needed her, if they were in fact dying, didn't she owe it to them to return? If her mother was gone then she was to be queen.

Her mind set she turned to DeMarcus. "You'll let her go? David too?"

"I have no use for them. I give you my word."

"No, Lilly!" David grabbed her shoulders and turned her. "You can't do this! He's lying! Has to be!"

"I can't take that chance. If what he says is true then I need to return and save my world."

"You can't leave me!" He began to cry.

"I'm sorry, David. It would be selfish of me to stay." She looked at DeMarcus. "Do we have a deal?"

DeMarcus stood and approached Lilly, handed her Claire. "Give her to your husband then come with me."

She turned to David, heaviness in her heart. "I'm sorry," she said, and handed Claire over. Lilly leaned up and kissed him tenderly on the lips, lingered a moment, pulled back, and stared into his pleading eyes. "But I have to do this."

"But how? He himself admitted he doesn't know how to return."

He had a point. How did DeMarcus plan for them to return to Turmoore? She turned to him slowly, realization dawning. "You know how to return."

DeMarcus nodded.

"Then why all the preamble?"

"I needed your word."

"Then… how?"

DeMarcus stepped to her, nearly chest-to-chest. He tenderly cupped her cheek, ran his finger along her jaw and chin, down her neck, clutched the pendant, and tore it from the necklace.

"Open your hand," he instructed. She did and he placed the pendant in her palm. "Now close it. Picture a key."

"Any key?"

"Yes. It will appear as it should."

She closed her fingers, felt the metal beneath. Lilly grasped at the first image of a key and held onto it. She felt the pendant in her hand transform. When she opened it the pendant had been replaced by a key. He took it from her, a twinkle in his eye.

She felt a hand grasp hers—David's hand—and she turned back to him. "Will I see you again?" he asked. "When I move up to Turmoore… will we be together?"

"Yes," she lied. She hated it, but what other choice did she have? If she didn't then he might try to stop her, and she knew DeMarcus would not let that happen. If David went up against DeMarcus he'd surely lose. While she had some power, DeMarcus was far more advanced than she. "I promise you we'll be together again."

David backed away hugging Claire tightly. He cooed to her, comforted her.

He would have made a great father, she thought. *Perhaps he'll have another opportunity.*

"I love you," he said.

"I love you too." She turned away and walked to a nondescript wooden door. As they approached she asked, "What about the *gormock?*"

"I'll deal with them if they become a problem."

She didn't know how he planned that. The *gormock* were terrible creatures that hid within the *belere*. They existed to stop any being from traveling between the realms, part of the reason they sent minds back. The *gormock* couldn't stop something that had no physical form.

DeMarcus inserted it into the lock, grinning as he turned it.

* * *

No! David screamed. He couldn't lose her, couldn't just let her go. He took a step. The associate's hands grabbed his biceps and held him in place, squeezing. Claire dropped to the ground and ran to a corner, cowering in terror, whimpering.

"Let him go," Lilly demanded.

"This is an insurance. Once we leave this place he'll be returned home." DeMarcus regarded David like a disgusting thing. "I don't know what she sees in you, a sniveling thing such as yourself."

"You got what you wanted. Let's be done with it."

"Indeed." He regarded David one last time. "I know you care for her as I do, so I give you my word she will be safe." His attention then shifted to the man in the red cap. "Once he's returned you're free to follow us." DeMarcus turned and opened the door. An industrial wind sang. He guided her to the threshold.

A sniveling coward…

The words stung. He'd fought for Lilly from the beginning, then through the miscarriages and the accident… no way would he allow this man take his wife away. Not without a fight.

He jabbed his head back catching the man in the mouth and heard him grunt. It was enough for the man to loosen his grip. David whirled and slammed his palm into the man's nose. He felt it crumple and blood squirted.

DeMarcus' associate wound back and punched, smacking David in the temple. He dropped to the ground, his vision blurred. The man approached, a river of crimson running down his face.

"I'm going to kill you for that," he said, reaching for David.

David kicked out and got the man in the knee. His leg buckled and he fell back, howling. David stood, regarded the man for only a second before kicking him across the face. DeMarcus' associate was out.

He lunged at DeMarcus, his full weight propelling them through the door.

The first thing he noticed was the deafening sound, a combination of screeching metal and wind. The second was the pungent odor of decay.

He looked back at the door twenty feet away. Even with his full weight they couldn't have gone that far. He needed to get out and shut the door, lock the bastard in. Whatever this place was—the *belere*—and whatever lived here, DeMarcus could face alone.

David ran towards the door. Fifteen feet. Ten. He pumped his arms and legs, his lungs burning, the smell infecting his senses.

DeMarcus smashed into him and together they collapsed on the ground.

A screech louder than the others. He flipped over and kicked DeMarcus in the face, his nose compressing. DeMarcus fell back and screamed in pain. David rushed for the door.

And then he was through and back in the room. He turned, ready to slam the door, when half a dozen black tendrils lashed out and grabbed him.

"No!" It was Lilly but she sounded distant. His feet slid across the floor as he was dragged back towards nothing and everything, pain and love, fear and joy. He grabbed onto the door frame, fighting.

And then he was engulfed in a light so pure and white it burned his eyes. The screech came again but higher pitched—the sound of pain. The black tendrils loosened their grip.

David caught a glimpse of a *gormock*. His mind couldn't comprehend what he saw and broke.

As his consciousness faded he heard the echo of a door slamming shut.

* * *

When David came to he wasn't sure how much time had passed, but he guessed not long. Lilly was comforting Claire in the corner embracing her in a motherly hug, and DeMarcus' associate was still unconscious.

"Oh thank God," he heard Lilly say. He met her eyes, a soft smile on her lips. "Are you alright?"

"I think so, yes."

"Are you able to walk?"

He pushed himself up. His legs felt like jelly, but with considerable concentration he felt he could stand. "Yes."

Lilly said something to Claire—he couldn't make out the words—and the girl gave a small nod. She looked to David, said, "It's okay. It's over."

Lilly carried Claire and lead the way out. When they got to the car Lilly sat in the back with the girl and David took his place behind the wheel. As they drove away he made cursory glances out the rearview mirror, the cabin cast in the red glow of the taillights.

"What if someone finds this place?" he asked.

Lilly shrugged. "It's just a cabin, David." She held up the key. "Without this, it's only a cabin."

His face grew warm. "Just a cabin? Lilly... but someone could find—"

"It's just a cabin," she said again, this time sternly.

"But what about... Turmoore?"

She sat quietly a moment. "If he was telling the truth, and I think he was, I've been here fifteen years yet he claimed only three months had gone by in Turmoore. If I live out my life here and die an old lady in fifty years less than a year will have passed in my world. That still gives me two years to fix whatever is wrong."

"Assuming you can."

"Assuming I can," she agreed.

"If you still have the key then why not go back?"

"The *gormock*. I have no idea how to avoid it or fight it. There's a very real possibility I'd be killed. Then how would I help my people?"

"But if you were killed you'd transcend, wouldn't you?"

She shook her head. "I don't know. Transcendence is from one plane to the next. If you're between then you're lost. We discovered that early on."

As they entered River Bend Lilly asked Claire, "Would you like to see a magic trick?" The girl nodded solemnly. Lilly held up the key and broken necklace. "I'm going to have to fix this," she said more to herself as she placed both in her hand then closed it. When she pulled out the necklace the key had transformed into a pendant. A smile of awe came to Claire and she reached for it.

"You know," Lilly said with a hint of mystery. "Do you know what's better than one necklace?" She hid the necklace in her hand a few seconds, then opened it. Her necklace now had a duplicate. She put the first around her neck then reached to Claire and put the second one around hers. "This necklace is very special to me. Wear it always and it will protect you." Claire looked at the pendant, lunged at Lilly, wrapping her tiny arms around her.

They pulled up to the Underhill's house. Lilly carried Claire to the front door, David bringing up the rear. Claire touched the young girl's face and whispered something. Frank threw open the door and ran to them, sweeping Claire into his arms. Jeanine ran out crying, hugging both her husband and daughter.

The police took a statement and David gave them DeMarcus' description. *Let them chase a ghost,* he thought. With Claire safely back at home, the police through with their questions, David and Lilly returned to their house.

"So it's all over?" he asked, brewing a cup of tea. "DeMarcus is really gone?"

"Yes." Lilly leaned up, touched his face, kissed him, and whispered in his ear.

interlude

Lilly pulled back and let the connection tendrils slip away. She'd shared what needed to be shared and now it was up to them. Hopefully they understood and they could bring it all full circle.

She was powerless to do anything more. All she could do was wait and hope.

III
present

eleven

Stavic swam toward blurred light. He blinked away the clouded darkness, the world coming back into focus. His mind was foggy, trying to remember where he was, what had happened.

He sat up and groaned as stabbing pain shot through his side, looked around. He was in a hospital room, tubes and wires connected to him. He felt like throwing up.

The previous night came back to him. He'd confronted DeMarcus, and when he was ready to take him in DeMarcus' goon had come up from behind. They never spoke, not until they were deep in the woods. Stavic was sure he was going to die.

When The Thirsty Whale was but a pinprick of light through the trees, Stavic's face was smashed into a tree trunk. He dropped to the ground and was kicked in the gut, punched in the face. He was ready to black out and then the attack stopped. He heard the teens cry out somewhere; he couldn't see them.

DeMarcus crouched into Stavic's vision, cocked his head. "Now you will talk." Stavic coughed blood, could feel his eye swelling. "If you don't my friend here will be happy to… encourage you."

"I'm investigating… murders. Thought you might know something."

195

"As I'd gathered by your poor interrogation at the Underground. The question is why me?"

"Description," he slurred.

"Do you know who I am?"

"DeMarcus."

DeMarcus' eyes ran over him as if searching, brow furrowed. "No. I was mistaken." He rose, said, "It's a terrible thing, living in fear."

For the first time in his life Stavic was afraid. Even in Chicago, when he'd almost been killed during the drug bust, he hadn't been afraid. He'd been exhilarated. But now? He was fucking terrified, and he suddenly knew that all those years of not caring if he lived or died were false. He wanted to live. For the first time in his life he cared about what happened to him.

He nodded.

"I'm not a murderer, Mr. Detective. I'm a savior. Your death serves no purpose. You will not seek me out again."

A fist connected with his brow. As consciousness faded he watched DeMarcus turn to the two girls.

As the world faded he heard DeMarcus say, "Bring her."

"The others?" The words becoming hollow echoes.

"Leave them."

"They won't talk?"

A long pause. "No."

Then there was the dream with Willem and Claire and the old man. David. In it he was his father, but that couldn't be true. His mother had told him he'd died from a work injury before he was born. That was the truth, had to be. Whatever he thought he'd seen was a delusion, a fabrication in his brain rattled head.

No.

His real father was alive. He'd even talked to him by Willow Creek.

Just a dream.

Not a dream.

He shook it off. What was important is that he'd found the killer.

Stavic gingerly stood, grasping his side. The pain was excruciating; his entire body ached. One step and he realized he wasn't going after DeMarcus in his current state. He was more determined now to catch the son of a bitch, if not for the murder then for making him feel weak and fearful.

Payback was going to be a bitch.

* * *

Willem opened his eyes to blinding white. A hospital room.
How did he get here? Was he still dreaming?

The past few hours swam back to him. He had been in the
Underground, taken something, and after that some memories of
Elliott and Sam had come back. He'd remembered past events as if
they were yesterday, and the box.

The box! He'd had it!

He sat up too quickly. His head pounded.

In whatever lethargic ethos the drugs had caused, the memory
of the letter and key came back. He had thrown the letter out, yes,
but he'd put the key in the most logical place imaginable: the kitchen
junk drawer. Why hadn't he thought to look there?

He'd left the Underground in a hurry. Justin was focused on the
dancers on stage, didn't seem to care he left. Willem didn't care
either. He'd somehow managed to get home, find the key, then
headed for the bridge. He'd parked on the shoulder and gone to the
long forgotten buried treasure of his youth. He half expected the box
would be gone—by now surely someone would have found it—so
when he reached into the hole and touched the protective cloth he'd
cried out. It took him two tries to unlock the box his hands were
shaking so much. He opened it and found their treasure as they'd left
it. Saw the green toy soldier Sammy had put in it to protect it. He
smiled and kissed it. "Thank you."

He sorted through the contents, memories of the objects hidden
away for years. One of the contents pulled at him, demanding his
attention. He touched the smooth metallic ring.

The cabin.

This was paramount, but for what he didn't know.

Willem put the contents back into the box and closed it.

He'd been making his way up the embankment when he'd lost
his footing and slipped. He remembered rolling down the side—that
was it—until waking up just now.

All he wanted was to go home, take some aspirin or ibuprofen
or whatever the hell you took for a headache the size of North
Dakota, and crawl into his warm bed.

Willem touched his forehead, felt gauze.

197

The other visions—dreams—crept back. A woman and her daughter, a cop, an old man, DeMarcus and... his father? Whatever drugs Justin had given him had truly fucked with his mind if he was seeing him.

He closed his eyes longing for his comforter at home. Then he was thinking about his childhood quilt, a brown one with teddy bears on it. It was extra soft, and one he shared with Sam many times on cold winter nights. Their mother would stoke the fire, and the two of them would lay side-by-side under it reading comic books by firelight. It was warm, it was soothing, it was safe.

Willem began to cry.

* * *

Claire awoke in a brightly lit room. Sunlight streamed through a small part in the tan drapes directly into her eyes. *What a nightmare,* she thought, the dream being beaten away by a pulse pounding headache. Something about people and places, a hospital room and Emily...

It was gone, the dream beaten back. She snuggled deeper into the bed hoping the headache would ease enough so she could go back to sleep. Only one way to get rid of a headache like this and that was rest.

She was on the precipice of sleep when the dream returned to her. A car accident... she swerved off the road. No. That wasn't right. She was driven from the road, a red car pushing her into the ditch. She'd barely been aware of the crunching gravel as the other driver approached when a phone rang. She struggled for consciousness, heard a debate about leaving her.

Emily.

What was it about her daughter? Something teetered on the edge of remembrance. Something...

Emily's in danger!

Claire's eyes shot open. She was in a small hospital room connected to several monitors. It was quiet and warm.

She tried to stand but pain rocked her back. She looked down, saw the bruises on her arms, gingerly touched her chest, felt the one left courtesy of her seatbelt. The accident had been real? And if that had been, then the hospital too...

She struggled for the phone, dialed Emily's number. Her heart sank as she heard Emily's sweet voice. Voice mail. *Shit!* Was she too late? No. Couldn't be. Probably sleeping, or had it on silent, or just wasn't picking up. Not unlike her.

Claire heard the tone. "Emily, honey? It's mom. Stay home. If you're not home go there now. I'll explain when I get back." She was about to hang up, reconsidered and said, "I love you, Emily." She hung up.

How was she going to get out of here? There's no way they'd discharge her, not without a doctor consulting her first.

Shit! Shit! Shit!

Hospital policies be damned. She yanked the wires from her body and stood, the pain dulled by determination. Looking around she realized her clothes were missing, though her purse sat on a chair. She dug in it, searching for her keys but they were missing. Car was either at the junkyard or impounded anyway. She had her wallet though—could call a cab. But with nothing but a hospital gown what driver would take her home? Might be a liability. The hospital was across town from her house, maybe a forty-five minute walk. But it was fall, too cold to be out in the thin fabric she was wearing, and if someone spotted her they'd most likely call the police.

Did she have anyone she could call? She didn't really have any friends. Maybe her boss would be sympathetic enough to cart her back home.

She grabbed her purse and peeked out the door. The hallway empty, she crept out.

* * *

"What happened to you, Nick?" the doctor asked as he entered the room.

Doctor Johnson was one of two people who ever called him by his first name. The other had been his mother. He was trim with silver hair and black rimmed glasses. Unlike a lot of family men in their fifties he'd never let himself go. His only vice was a drug he couldn't get legally. For that he needed Stavic. He'd always made sure the doc was a happy customer because you never knew when you might need to call in a favor.

Stavic looked as Doctor Johnson said, "What happened to you?"

"Would you believe me if I said I fell down the stairs?"

"Not in the least."

The doctor pulled out a pen light and shined it into Stavic's good eye, the light blinding it. Satisfied he moved onto the next, working to open the swollen lids. Stavic could suddenly see out of it albeit blurry. Again the light, again a satisfied nod. "Shirt off and arm up please."

Stavic did as instructed, lifting his right arm as far as he could before the pain in his side prevented him. "You got some nice bruising, that's for sure." Stavic felt fingers gently prod the area, each caused a stabbing sensation, each making him wince. "How bad?"

"It doesn't feel good."

Doctor Johnson wiggled the stethoscope into his ears and placed the opposite end to Stavic's chest. "Deep breath."

Stavic obeyed, only moderate pain with the inhale. He felt the stethoscope move.

"Again."

Stavic let the doctor do his thing without complaint.

"I don't think anything is broken," Doctor Johnson said as he pulled the stethoscope from his ears. "I assume this needs to be kept off the record?"

"You'd assume right."

"Well," the doctor sighed, "in that case I can give you a prescription for some painkillers. It should help a little."

"All I needed to know was if something was broken."

"I can't say with one hundred percent certainty, but no, I don't think so."

"That's all I need then."

"Fine," the doctor said. He stood, walked to the door. "You know the way out."

As Stavic put on his shirt he thought of David. "You got an unconscious old man here? Maybe in a coma?"

"This is a hospital, Detective." His title. Doc must be annoyed if he was going the professional route.

"He would have been brought in the last day or two."

"I can't give you that information."

"I understand of course."

Doctor Johnson was almost out the door when Stavic continued. "By the way, I'm not sure I'll be able to fill your next order." That stopped him. "Supply is getting harder and harder to come by. Government crackdown from what I hear."

Doctor Johnson was back in the room, door closed. "Y—you can't. You wouldn't. It's for my wife for gods sake!"

"I don't know what to tell you."

"Please!"

A few years ago Maggie Johnson was diagnosed with Lesch-Nyhan Syndrome. "What you provide… it helps calm her. You can't take that away from her!" Over the counter medications could only do so much, so the good doc had sought out Stavic for something more helpful that he couldn't get on his own.

"I'm sorry."

Stavic stayed quiet as he watched Doctor Johnson wrestle with his dilemma. "Fine," Johnson conceded. "What's his name?"

"David Rottingham. Elderly man, eighties, thin… he was probably admitted within the last couple days. Not sure if he's a John Doe."

The doctor loaded up the computer in the room, typed something on the keyboard, and scrolled down a list. "Room 217. Coma. No immediate family."

"What happened?" Stavic asked instead.

"Don't know. He was found in his hotel room. You know him?"

Stavic stood, grunted, hobbled to the door. "I'm going to go find out right now."

* * *

Willem had decided he couldn't stay in the hospital. What if it got out a paramedic had been hopped up on drugs? Not only would his reputation be in jeopardy but so would the company he worked for.

With no way home he picked up the phone and dialed a number. There was a *click*. "Hello?"

"Justin? It's me."

"Willem? Where did you go? I was worried as fuck, man! You say you're going to take a leak and then just up and disappear? Not cool."

Willem made up an excuse, apologized, and asked for a ride. Justin was happy to help. Probably felt somewhat responsible, Willem thought.

He collected his things, making sure everything was still in the box, and left the room. He felt naked wandering the halls in just a gown, but what choice did he have? Who knew how long they'd try to keep him here, and at this point he just wanted to go home, nurse his wounds, and try to get back to some sort of normality. Maybe he was losing his mind, and if he was he preferred to do it away from the confines of doctors and nurses.

He wound through the corridors trying valiantly to find the way out. He followed the glowing exit signs but still managed to get turned around twice. Several times he'd almost gotten caught by a nurse or doctor. Hard to look like he belonged dressed as he was, and he knew one look and they'd know he wasn't where he was supposed to be.

Willem passed a stairwell then saw the elevators. Pausing, he wondered what the safer bet was. Less likely to bump into someone in the stairwell. He headed back and opened the door a crack, waited. Relieved by the silence on the other side, he pushed through and closed the door. He headed down the single flight of stairs to another door and peered out. When he didn't see anyone he stepped out.

"Oh!" a woman gasped.

He turned and was shocked to see the woman from his dream.

"My God, it's you! What are you doing here?" she asked.

"Y—you're real?" He sized her up, noticed she was in a hospital gown as well.

"Of course I'm real."

Willem shook his head and headed toward the entrance.

Claire followed after. "Where are you going?"

"Home."

"But my daughter… I think us bumping into each other… it must be a sign."

"I don't believe in signs. Right now I just want to go home." Willem walked faster wanting to be rid of Claire. He didn't want to be rude, but he also didn't want to get sucked into helping her. He hoped she'd take the hint.

"But something unusual is happening."

"No doubt."

"Emily—"

"Is not my problem. Besides, you have no proof she's in any danger—"

"I know."

"Mother's intuition?" he asked with disdain.

She frowned. "I know the same way I know about that box you're carrying. The toy soldier within. I know just like I do the reason you left River Bend in the first place, the feeling of abandonment." She stepped closer. "I know because I've been there.

Just like I know all that, I know my daughter is in danger, so if you want to call it mother's intuition that's fine, but I believe it's something more."

"Why did *you* come back here?"

She shrugged. "I'm not sure. I felt something pulling at me. When my husband and I came here for vacation it felt like home."

It had been the same for him in many ways. When he'd left River Bend he'd felt aloof, and it wasn't until he'd returned, no matter the pain, he'd still felt at home. He knew then that this was where he belonged.

Still, he had his own past—his own demons—that he needed closure on, and didn't want to get involved in someone else's.

"The best I can do is get you home," he asked. "If you need a ride, that is."

Claire deflated a little, but nodded. "A lift would be good."

Together they made their way to the exit.

* * *

Room 217 had good lighting from the beautiful day filtering in through the open window, and while the fluorescent lights were on they weren't necessary. The morning news was on the television, its volume barely audible. White noise is what Stavic figured. Probably using it to keep the old man company.

Stavic wondered if he should be feeling something. A vision within a dream was a far cry from fact.

"Father," he mumbled, the word sounded foreign. He looked down at the frail old man. He'd met him only briefly but knew more of his past than he should thanks to… what? A psychic connection? What was it they'd experienced? If it hadn't been a dream and was in fact real then there was a good chance that woman's daughter was in trouble.

He sat in the chair next to the bed, stared at David. Everything he'd recently experienced screamed insanity. It made no logical sense. How could he share memories with complete strangers? So odd, too, that they had a connection. He hated enigmas.

You're a cop. Figure it out.

Assuming everything they'd experienced was true—and he had no reason to doubt it—then it wasn't much of a stretch to assume they'd all been pulled into some web that revolved around David's wife. She seemed to be the catalyst. What was her name?

Lilly.

Then there was her husband, a man she'd met as a teenager. They fell in love and got married; nothing unusual there. DeMarcus pursued her from this other place—Turmoore. Why hadn't DeMarcus aged? He should be as old as the frail man before him. Unless that place—the cabin—stopped aging. Either there was something about that place or DeMarcus himself. Since Lilly had aged his assumption was it was that place.

Stavic ran a hand across his face, massaged his eyes. This was all maddeningly confusing. No matter... he wasn't going to accomplish anything feeling the way he did at the moment. He needed to go home, shower, take some of his non-prescription drugs, and figure out his next move. Maybe work in a couple hours of sleep too.

Time's ticking.

He decided it could tick a little while longer.

* * *

"Emily?" Claire called out. She knew she wasn't here; the house felt empty. She ran up the stairs, the footfalls echoing through the stillness.

Claire pushed opened Emily's bedroom door. The bed was made, room tidy. Nothing amiss.

She made her bed before heading out this morning is all. Claire knew it was a lie the moment the thought popped into her head. The room had an unslept in feel. No... Emily hadn't been here since she'd left last night.

She'd tried repeatedly on her trip home to get through to Emily, and each time it rolled over to voice-mail.

Claire beat back the panic. How was she supposed to track her down?

Stavic. Maybe she could appeal to his to serve and protect instinct. Maybe he could do something if she could get through to him. She ran downstairs, pulled out the phone book and looked up the police department's number.

"River Bend Police Department. How may I direct your call?"

"Detective Stavic please."

"Please hold."

Soft music floated through the ear piece. She knew it was meant to keep her calm but she was anything but. There was a click and the music cut out.

"I'm sorry, but he's not in today. Is there something I can help you with?"

Not unless you're willing to give me his address. "No thank you."

"Would you like his voice-mail?"

"Please."

"One moment."

There was another click as the connection transferred. She was greeted by a robotic female voice until Stavic said his name. Weird going from robot girl to Stavic. A final tone sounded alerting her to start. "Hi. This is Claire." How to word it? "You may not know me, but I really need to talk to you… it's about Emily. I came home and she's gone. I could really use your help. Please call me back." She gave him her number and hung up.

Claire's next call was to Emily's two closest friends. The first didn't answer, and the second said she hadn't heard from her in a couple of days. Claire thanked her and hung up.

What else could she do? If Stavic was out for the day he probably wouldn't check his voice-mail until he went back in. She opened the phone book and flipped to 'S'. A quick scan revealed one Stavic, N. in River Bend. She dialed the number and waited. A recorded message answered, and it was the same voice. Hanging up, she tore the page out of the book. Since her car was gone, either at the impound or junkyard, she needed a ride. Claire flipped to the yellow pages and looked for a cab company and called one. She was told one would be there in fifteen minutes—plenty of time to throw on a fresh pair of clothes.

She ran to her room and changed in two minutes flat. In her hurry her leg knocked over the box with **DEVON** on it, the contents spilling out.

"Shit," she said, kneeled, and threw everything in haphazardly. As she tossed in the manila envelope the divorce papers flew out. "God dammit!" she screamed. Why was it when you were in a rush everything seemed to try and slow you down? She picked up the papers and was about to toss them in the box when two words at the top of the page caught her eye.

Death Certificate.

What? She shuffled the papers, flipped them over. This had to be a joke! Devon wasn't dead! An asshole, maybe, but not dead!

Claire looked over the page again and saw his name. The date of death was… No. It couldn't be.

She searched her memory. But… he abandoned them after the accident. But according to this he died around the same time. She couldn't remember the exact date but knew it was around what was printed on the certificate.

He left you. You divorced him.

But he was dead.

Has to be a joke.

Yet she knew it wasn't. It felt right. All this time she'd hated him for leaving her and Emily but he hadn't. And suddenly it was as if a veil dropped and the painful memories of what had transpired returned.

She had become increasingly paranoid he was having an affair, and she had confronted him in the car about it. The paranoia was from her own insecurities, the feeling she wasn't beautiful or sexy enough, that he would find someone else on his business trips. The poisonous thoughts contaminated her the nights she lie awake alone in their bed, wondering…

She'd started to drink to curb the fear, and that night at the party it escalated. She'd yelled at him in the car, then slapped him, then attacked him. But that was where her memory changed. He hadn't just disappeared and run off like she thought, but had been thrown from the car. She saw it now, his body slamming into the steering wheel, blood exploding from his mouth.

Oh God. It was her fault. His death… it was on her.

How had she forgotten? *Why?*

Tears flowed down her cheeks, fifteen years of emotional buildup pouring out.

Her husband hadn't cheated on her or abandoned her like she thought. Her husband was dead.

Outside she heard the faint sound of a car horn, then her doorbell, but she needed time to process this, needed time to understand, to accept.

Claire needed time to wake.

* * *

After dropping Claire off Justin took Willem to the auto pound where he got his car. Justin wanted to follow Willem home, but he wouldn't have it. After he promised to call Justin later that night, Justin begrudgingly drove off.

Now Willem was home and try as he might Willem could not fall asleep. His head was spinning. His mother, his brothers, the old man…

David Rottingham.

He turned on his back, stared at the ceiling.

Sleep unobtainable, Willem sat up and pulled out the box. He was still kicking himself for not thinking to look in the junk drawer when he'd gotten back from visiting Elliott. Where else did you put shit you didn't know what to do with? Idiot.

He didn't know where the key was now—probably washed away when he fell—but, thankfully, he hadn't relocked the box after he'd rediscovered it. Willem opened it and stared at the contents.

He lifted the metal ring out of the box wondering what had made him keep it. Just a piece of a missing cabin, yet when he'd found it he'd felt something in it, felt it now in fact. A warmth. He set it to the side.

There was the flask Elliott had added. He ran his thumb across the engraving: *Amor Meus*. He never had learned its meaning. He twisted the cap off, sniffed the opening. While it was empty he still smelled a hint of fifty-year-old booze.

The lure was still there, exactly as he remembered it. The watch Elliott had stored here was gone, then he remembered Beth placing it in Elliott's pocket at the funeral. He wondered when Elliott had come back.

Next he picked up the photo of all of them smiling at the park. He remembered the day being warm and sunny. Their mother had packed a picnic lunch—blanket and all—and brought their new Polaroid camera. Their father had driven them to Blue Gill Park, a grassy area with a playground next to the river. He'd asked a passerby to take a photo who'd obliged.

Happy. This is how his family should have been, what he'd longed to return to, if not for his father.

A flicker of remembrance emerged and Willem grasped at it. Something about the picnic. His father… It was around that time his father changed. He stared at the photo. It had faded considerably over the years, the colors bleeding to orange and yellow. What looked like a tiny pin-sized lens flare hovered over his head. He'd forgotten about that, and how he'd found it oddly surreal.

What had happened during the picnic, or shortly thereafter, that caused his father to start hating him? What had changed?

Anyone that may have been able to tell him—his mother, his father, Elliott—were dead. He was the last of his family and had no answer.

Sometimes you just have to let it go, Willem.

Maybe Elliott was right. He'd hung onto this for so long it had infected him, allowed the anger and hate and all the emotional baggage to dictate his life. Well, no more.

His eye wandered back to the ring, picked it up. His finger traced its smoothness.

DeMarcus. A man who hadn't aged. He'd only seen him from a distance and that had been when he'd been drunk and stoned. Even then that grin had made him uneasy, and he could only imagine what his presence was like sober. Definitely something off with him, something dangerous.

He thought about David and Lilly's confrontation with DeMarcus and his associate. If Emily had gotten involved with him she was definitely out of her element.

Demarcus' associate. There was something about him…

And then he suddenly knew where his father disappeared to all those years ago. Somehow he'd become involved with DeMarcus.

He stared down at the ring, his finger tracing.

And then suddenly he knew where he could find them. All of them. It was so obvious.

* * *

Stavic was tying his shoe when he heard a knock. Who the hell? He wasn't expecting anyone. He went to the door and opened it. Claire looked like hell, her nervous eyes bloodshot.

"Why am I not surprised?" he said.

"What?"

After the things he'd seen, the least of which was discovering his father was still alive, seeing Claire was not surprising. And if Claire existed that meant Willem did too. He was sure it was only a matter of time before their paths crossed.

"Nothing. Come in," Stavic said and stood to the side.

"What happened to you?" she asked as she entered his apartment. She tried to hide her shock and failed. It sounded false even to her.

"Doesn't matter. What can I do for you Claire?"

"My daughter's gone." She wanted to cry, to shake him, to make him understand. "She's not answering her phone, she's not at home, and none of her friends know where she is."

"Emily, right?" He sighed. "What makes you think I can help?"

"The cabin. That's where DeMarcus is, and you know where it is."

He scowled at her.

"Please!" she begged.

He ran a hand through his damp hair. Daylight was burning, and he wanted to get out of here. But first he needed something. Coke was off the table—he wouldn't do that with someone in his home—but he could have some liquid courage. He went to the fridge and pulled out a beer. When he'd collected his thoughts after a long drink, he said, "Everything that's happening revolves around David, Lilly, and DeMarcus. DeMarcus was holed up at the cabin in the past, and I've no doubt that's where he is now. It's just…"

"What?"

"I was there a few days ago, and the place was deserted. No one had been there in decades." Not a complete lie, he just didn't want to talk about the body.

"You were going to go there. Before I showed up that's where you were headed."

"Yes."

Claire perked up. "I'm coming with you then."

"Nuh-uh. No way. Too dangerous. Look at my face for Christ sake! DeMarcus did this to me."

"And he's got my daughter."

Stavic considered debating her but realized it was futile.

"Fine," he said begrudgingly. "Let's get going."

* * *

Willem was stopped at a light. Coming from the opposite direction was a Ford Explorer and, behind the wheel, Stavic. Claire sat next to him in the passenger seat. He flashed his lights at them, got their attention, and pointed to the Dale's Supermarket lot. They parked next to each other, and Willem rolled down the window.

"Hey, hey, the gangs all here," Stavic said with mild amusement. His eyes flicked up. "What happened to you?"

"I could ask you the same thing. Where you headed?"

"On our way to find Emily. Hop in."

Willem killed the engine, grabbed the metal ring on the passenger seat, and got out. He didn't bother to lock the doors; River Bend was still small and friendly enough that people trusted each other not to mess with someone else's stuff.

"Where were you headed?" Stavic asked as Willem slid into the backseat.

"Mr. Rottingham's place."

Stavic turned and looked back. "Really? Why?"

Willem smiled. "Forty-six and two. 462. It's his address."

"Jesus. A fucking *address*? And what's there?"

"Lilly's necklace." Stavic gave him a look, so he continued. "The necklace was the key to unlocking the passageway to Turmoore."

"What makes you so sure?" Claire wanted to know.

"We all saw what happened in the past. When I went there with William the cabin was missing. A few years later Lilly and David and their friend went there to save you." He nodded toward Claire. "Lilly did... something... and the place materialized. Right? I don't know how it was hidden before or why it's not now, but that cabin is the doorway."

"I've been to the cabin. There's nothing there; no door, no lock, no nothing."

"That's why we need the necklace."

Claire cut in. "I still don't understand what all this has to do with Emily. Why does DeMarcus want her?"

"She obviously has some part to play," Willem said. "Let's just hope we're not too late."

twelve

There was a gloominess when they pulled up to the old Rottingham house. Gray clouds were moving in blanketing what was a fantastic blue autumn sky in dreariness. The yard was unkempt, and the once immaculate home faded. Stavic felt uneasy, as if something was moving in to intercept them.

"Dear Lord," Claire mumbled as she took it in. "I haven't been back here in years. It used to be so cared for; my father was always jealous of it." She glanced to the house next door. "That's where I grew up," she said, pointing.

"Do you feel it?" Willem asked as he stared out the window.

Stavic waited a full three seconds before glancing over his shoulder. "What?"

"It's like a... presence."

Stavic figured Willem was just having a heebie-jeebies moment until Claire chimed in. "I feel it too."

He looked back at the home, stared at it. The way the shadows fell on the windows made it look like the house had eyes, the door its mouth. It was unsettling, as if the house was warning them away. But a presence? No... must be their imaginations. "Like it or not one of us has to go," he said. "If you two want to stay here that's fine. I'll

211

go. You said this necklace was in the basement? Anything more specific than that?"

Willem shook his head. "No, but we should all go."

"Stay behind me," Stavic said as he took the lead. He unholstered his weapon and walked up the front door. It came as no surprise it was locked. "Around back."

They made their way around the side of the building. At each window he peered in and only saw abandonment.

The backyard was worse off than the front. Not only was the grass long and unruly, the maple tree's leaves had begun to blanket the ground. A gust of wind caused a wave-like movement.

The back door opened easily, and Stavic gave Willem and Claire a nonchalant shrug.

"Do you feel like we're walking on eggshells?" Willem asked. "I mean… whatever is in here… it doesn't sense us—not yet—but if we make one false move…"

"Yes," she whispered. "That's exactly what it's like."

"You two are just being paranoid." While Stavic wasn't in on whatever it was they were feeling, their mood was infectious. If he wasn't careful it would begin to cloud his judgment.

The warmth that must once have dominated this house was no more, replaced by a rot that permeated throughout. A wisp of decayed breath coursed through the cold under belly, as if the house were now a living breathing creature.

Stavic looked in the empty pantry, tiny mouse turds littering the corners. He moved to another door, this one open an inch, though what lay beyond was shrouded in darkness. Stavic aimed his gun, finger alongside the trigger, and opened the door with his foot. It creaked, the sound deafening in the stillness. The room dimmed as the sun fell behind a cloud. "Perfect," Stavic mumbled.

"Downstairs," Willem said, pointing. "That's where we have to go."

Through the doorway stairs descended, the basement barely lit. Just inside the stairwell was a light switch, though flipping it yielded no results. Stavic pulled a small flashlight from his pocket, pressed the ON button, and a thin stream of light illuminated the stairs. He started down, Willem and Claire following.

With each step a wooden stair groaned. He felt he was moving towards the entrance of an immense labyrinth of unseeable evil. The hair on his arms stood up, sensitive to the barest touch of the fabric of his shirt, almost painful. He wondered if this is what Willem and

Claire were talking about. It didn't feel like a presence, but his flight instincts were up to the max.

Stavic reached the bottom and moved the light across the room. Half windows near the ceiling allowed a fraction of light in. A wooden door was set in the wall ahead, and to the right was an open entryway that went deeper into the bowels of the house. He hoped they didn't have to go that way; a stench waft from that direction.

"Ideas?" Stavic whispered. "I don't want to be down here any longer than needed."

There was a moment of silence before Willem responded. "It should be just through that door."

"How can you be sure?"

"No, but I'm getting a definite vibe and it's not the bad kind."

He reached for the door handle and the knob turned easily. The light from his flashlight was swallowed by the inkiness.

"Where?" Stavic hissed.

"Just ahead."

Stavic crept forward, passing the beam across wooden shelves. "You sure? There's nothing here."

Willem was at his side, pointed. "Right there."

"I don't see anything."

Willem pointed to a hole in the wall. "In there."

Perfect. The last thing he wanted was to stick his hand in the wall. He'd seen movies, and he knew what usually happened. "You sure?"

"Yes."

He reached toward the hole and stopped, hand quivering. "How do you know?"

"Same way I know something is here."

Stavic reached into the hole and felt only coarse brick and dust. He shined the light in the hole, saw no necklace. "You sure this is right? There's nothing there."

"Impossible!" Willem slid next to Stavic and peered in. He was sweating, a tiny droplet dangling from the tip of his nose. "But... this isn't right. It's supposed to be here." Willem reached into the hole and felt around. His shoulders slumped as he slowly pulled back, hand covered in dust. "Where is it?" he hissed.

Claire asked from behind, "How long has it been buried? Could someone else have found it?"

"If it was gone I don't think I'd be sensing it. No... it's here somewhere."

Willem grabbed the light from Stavic and waved the light across the floor, going in circles, careening it every which way. A piece of dirty red cloth caught his attention. He grabbed it, shook it. No necklace.

"Fuck!"

"Slow down! You could be missing it," Claire offered.

Either Willem didn't hear her or didn't care. "Willem… slow *down*," said Stavic as he grabbed for the light and missed.

"It has to be here somewhere!"

Claire's slender hand wrapped around his arm. "The door!" she hissed. He couldn't see her face, but the grip said it all. He strained his eyes and, in the strobe-like light from Willem's frantic movements, he saw a small silhouette.

"Stop Willem." The authoritative command got through, and Willem turned and pointed the light towards them.

"What?" he asked, annoyed.

"The door."

In his peripheral vision he saw a figure standing in the doorway, but when he pointed the beam towards it the figure vanished.

"What the hell?" Stavic said.

The room's presence was suddenly gone, as if they were now in a vacuum.

"Oh hell," Willem said. He looked at Stavic, terror in his eyes. "It knows we're here."

* * *

The feeling was sudden. One minute he felt as if they were sneaking behind some unseen giant, the next it was focused on them. "We have to hurry!" he said, swiveling back to where the necklace should have been. God! Where was it? He could sense it right here, right in front of him, yet it wasn't there!

Ever since he'd touched the metal ring again he felt as if he were awakening to an unseen world around him. He could feel the tug of the necklace before he knew what it was, knew it was necessary. It was a feeling, something he could see, a golden pulse of light. That had all disappeared when they'd gotten into the basement, the darkness consuming that magical light like a black hole. He could sense the necklace, just not see it.

From the shadows he began to hear whispers, distant but growing louder. They didn't have much time.

"Keep an eye out! It has to be here somewhere!"

Willem dropped to his knees, shined the light under the shelves. Nothing! Where the hell was it? It's supposed to be right here! He felt sweat streaking down his face.

Whatever was coming was almost here.

Claire, panicked, said, "We have to go, Willem!"

"Not yet! If we don't find it we won't get another chance!"

"And if we don't leave we're dead!"

"We need that necklace!"

Stavic dropped next to him. "Where is it? Come on, Willem, if we're going to do this it has to be now. Where!"

Willem aimed the light and saw it. "Yes!" Willem shouted. It had fallen into a crack in the floor. He grabbed it.

"Guys," Claire urged, the whispers now unintelligible talk.

Willem and Stavic stood and turned, pointing the light toward the door. Shadowed figures evaporated in the light, screeching, and behind them a maggot covered dog stood. It growled.

"Let's get out of here," Claire whispered.

The dog barked as Willem pocketed the necklace. Stavic raised his gun and fired. The bullet went through the dog and ricocheted off the stone wall. It howled, the shadows reaching toward them. Stavic swiveled the light across the room burning away the shadows and the approaching creatures. They hissed and shrieked. Huddled as a collective, Stavic, Willem, and Claire shuffled toward the door, the flashlight their only salvation.

"Don't forget behind us!" Claire urged.

Stavic pointed the light behind them, shimmering teeth in oily maws twinkled. "What is this place?"

Willem said, "A trap of some kind? Set by DeMarcus maybe?" As soon as he said it he knew it to be wrong. No… this was something else.

They were almost at the door, another ten feet and they'd be out. Willem could see the natural gray light in the next room. It was dimming, but if these things didn't like light then maybe it was enough to keep them at bay until they could get out.

"Keep moving," Stavic said. "Do not stop for any—"

Something crashed into them.

* * *

Claire pushed herself up to a sitting position. Stavic had knocked her back into the shelves, one of the boards smashing her kidney. Pain shot through her side and she fell to the ground. Good thing, too, considering the gun went off seconds later. She was less likely to be hit by a stray bullet while hugging the cold concrete floor. That's what she told herself at least.

Her ears rang as she tried in vain to focus. The light from the adjacent room filtered in through the open door. The beam from the flashlight extended across the floor, pointed away, from where it had clattered to the ground.

"No. Oh God, no!" Willem cried out.

The gun fired again, the muzzle flashed to her left. Something inhuman screeched and snarled.

The voices continued to mumble their unintelligible chatter. She crept along the floor towards the small flashlight. Something scraped across the floor.

Claire stopped. "Stavic? That you?" She held her breath, waiting.

"Yeah," came his response, a little raspy. "Something took a chunk out of my leg. You okay?"

She exhaled. "Fine." Claire crawled the few feet needed to grab the flashlight and pointed it in Stavic's direction. He was holding his leg, blood oozing from between his fingers. She guided the light in front of him and saw what looked to be a decaying dog. It whimper-howled as the light stayed fixed on it, its chest rising and falling rapidly in distress. It gurgled, a guttural sound escaping its maw, then its chest was still.

A few feet from Stavic, Willem was sprawled on the floor. He held the gun loosely in one hand. Claire swung the light around. The creatures seemed to have backed away, at least for the moment. Willem mumbled something, she looked back. "What?"

"On the precipice of *belere*—the in-between realm." He looked into her eyes. "I'm starting to remember." A creature cried out, the whispering again returning. Willem looked around as if coming to then stood. "Let's get out of here."

With the help of Willem and Claire, Stavic stood. She shined the light on Stavic's leg, the jeans stained red, blood oozing from puncture wounds. "We're going to need to stop this bleeding."

"I've got some rags in the car," Stavic grunted.

Stavic put an arm over each of their shoulders and they hobbled to the next room. The shadows seemed to have taken on a life of their own; they moved across the windows shrouding the basement in a blanket of gloom. They were at the foot of the stairs when the sound of cracking wood and exploding concrete echoed through the basement.

They looked back. A big mistake, Claire realized. The walls were pulsating, transforming into arms of splintered wood and rusty nails. The door to the fruit cellar exploded knocking them to the ground. Squarish holes appeared in the wall.

Claire's eyes went wide. They were looking at a manifestation of a creature, the wall transforming into a crooked face. It howled and reached for them.

"Jesus Fucking Christ!" Stavic bellowed.

Claire screamed and was on her feet, propelling Stavic up the stairs.

Willem screamed. They looked back and saw him being dragged away, arms flailing about, a colossal stone hand clamped around his foot. Below him on the floor was the gun.

"Shit!" Stavic tried to push himself up but dropped, grabbing his leg. "Wait!" he yelled as Claire hurled herself down the stairs.

Willem squirmed, helpless to break free, inching closure to the splintering mouth. "Help me!"

Claire jumped the last three stairs, collapsed to her knee, and picked up the gun. She aimed it at the creature and fired. The bullet penetrated the wood but did no damage. She aimed for the eye, pulled the trigger. This time the bullet disappeared into the hole. Willem was almost at its mouth.

"Look out!" Stavic shouted. She looked to her left and saw the giant wooden arm reaching toward her. She swiveled, aimed, fired. The shot went wide and smashed through the window. Light cascaded in washing away some of the shadows. She shot out a second window, the daylight landing on the wooden arm. The creature cried out in pain. She shot out the remaining window.

Light streaked across the back wall blinding the protruding face. It pulled back, dropping Willem. He grunted as he landed on his shoulder and rolled. Without hesitation he bolted for her. She guided him past and followed. Halfway up there was an explosion and the staircase vibrated. She looked back, the creature pulling it's fist away from the destroyed bottom stairs. She went faster, almost at the top now. Then suddenly the stairs were gone and she was falling.

She managed to catch herself, struggling. Willem and Stavic grabbed her arms and pulled, wood biting into her flesh. Both men's eyes went wide and pulled harder. She looked back, a closed fist rearing back. She kicked helplessly, ignoring the pain in her abdomen.

Her knees bumped the edge of the stairs, her shins, then she was standing again. She pushed into the two men, all three falling. The remaining stairs exploded seconds later, and a howl echoed up from the basement.

The creature reached for them. She sat up, grabbed the doorknob, and yanked it open. They were jettisoned from the basement and landed in a heap in the kitchen.

"Move!" Stavic bellowed as the claw reached through the doorway. They staggered to the back door, were almost through, when they were propelled out, and hit the ground hard.

As the ringing in her ears died down she realized it sounded like any other day in a rural town. Birds chirped and the wind blew; a lawn mower idled in the distance. Claire looked through the broken door, and saw the basement was as they'd initially entered it. She stood on shaky legs and helped the other two up.

"What was that thing?" she asked.

"That was a *gormock*," Willem said. "They're the guardians of *belere*."

"Guardians? For what purpose?"

"Our realm and that of Turmoore—all realms, in fact—are not intended to intersect. The *gormock* are there to prevent people from passing between."

Claire saw the expression on Stavic's face, one of bewilderment. "Where are you getting this shit anyway?" he asked.

"Like I said, my memory is coming back. Let's get to the car, and I'll explain what I know on the way."

thirteen

The storm had swung north, dumping whatever torrential downpour it had planned elsewhere. That was fine. Stavic didn't much care for the idea of going to an unfamiliar and hostile environment in the dark let alone in the rain. It made things much more difficult. And after what they'd experienced in Rottingham's house he'd rather this take place on a sunny beach. Nothing bad ever happened on a sunny beach.

Stavic lay in the backseat, Willem tending to the laceration, while Claire drove. His leg burned with infection—no telling what crap that dog had in its saliva—and he kept pressure on it.

My memory is coming back, Willem had said. Memory of what? Five minutes into the drive he'd said nothing, just stared out the windshield.

"Mind telling us what the hell that was back there? What did you call it… a *gormock?*"

"Yes," Willem said quietly. "A guardian of the *belere*."

"Gormock? Belere? Come on Willem… you gotta give us something here. Your memory—"

"It's coming back."

"So you said. Memory of what?"

Willem glanced at Claire who kept her eyes on the road. "Everything."

Stavic closed his eyes and rubbed his forehead. "You better start making some sense, or I'm likely to push you out the fucking door. Just tell us in layman."

Willem sighed, "Alright. I'll do what I can." Willem dug into his pocket and pulled out a folded scrap. He opened it, gave it to Stavic. It was a faded family photo. The people didn't looked familiar except maybe... He looked more closely at the middle child, looked at Stavic. "This you?"

"Yes. Notice anything else?"

Stavic examined the picture, scanning it for any anomalies. He shook his head. "No. Nothing."

"Above me."

"That white dot?"

A nod.

"What of it?"

"That's me. Or, more precisely, a part of me."

He could feel his temperature rise, his face turning red. "What did I tell you—"

Willem waved down his objection. "I know. Bear with me. You know some of the details already from David, his and Lilly's encounter with DeMarcus. Turmoore is another plane in layers of existences, our plane below theirs."

"I have to admit none of that made a whole lot of sense to me."

"Layman terms," Willem mumbled. He said, "Okay. Let's use religion as an example. Heaven and hell and all that. That doesn't need to be explained, does it?"

Stavic shook his head no.

"While not heaven, for our explanation let's pretend that's Turmoore. We die here on earth and depending on if we were good or bad we ascend to heaven. Right? Same thing with hell. If we're bad we're cast down to be tormented for all eternity. Now imagine there are infinite heavens and hells."

"Planes?" Stavic asked.

"Exactly. If we were on the heaven plane then we would be in Turmoore's hell, and whatever was above them would be heaven. Each plane has its own heaven and hell."

"But religion is all about faith. There's no proof."

"True, but all religions share a common thread, and all religions are ways of interpreting what we see and experience around us.

Maybe in the shadows of our subconscious we have some innate knowledge of this because, if we have been moving up on some cosmic lift for eons, then why couldn't some of those details travel with us? Almost like a computer hard drive… you can format it, overwrite files, but fragments remain.

"We know that people from Turmoore are cast down to our plane and that their conscience is absorbed here." Willem nodded to the photo. "I think that's what happened to me, because it was shortly after that picture was taken my father started treating me differently."

Stavic looked at the photo again, the pinpoint of light. It was a good story, but it was hardly proof. He handed it back, said, "You said your memory is coming back. Why did you forget?"

"It wasn't really forgetting. Remember Lilly told David that consciousness of those cast down resides in the hosts. But Lilly knew all about Turmoore, and she speculated her parents had ensured that. Don't ask me how she pulled that off—I don't know—but I do know we're not supposed to remember. While the brain is a fantastic thing it is still fragile, and it struggles if it perceives competing existences. I don't really remember Turmoore as a place but as a concept.

"Now, I don't know if what David showed us is true—that DeMarcus overthrew Turmoore—but I do know there are doorways between Turmoore and here, probably doorways between here and the plane below. They're supposed to be hidden, but we managed to harness its power. While we never found a way for a two-way path between plains, that doesn't necessarily mean it couldn't happen. I suspect that if DeMarcus did come after Lilly then he was pretty damn sure he could get back, because I seriously doubt that if he did overthrow Turmoore he would have left knowing he couldn't return.

"So now you know as much as I do."

Claire had been silent the entire time, but now piped up. "Not everything." The men looked at Claire who kept her gaze straight ahead. "What does he want with my daughter? Why am I involved in this?"

Willem shook his head. "I wish I could tell you. We know why you were involved initially, but now? I have no idea."

Just ahead Stavic saw the curve in the road with its accompanying yellow traffic sign. "Slow down," he instructed. "Right after the sign it's on your left."

Claire slowed the truck as she approached. Even though he knew where the road was it still came up quick, the underbrush hiding it well. As soon as he saw it he pointed. "Right there."

"I see it." Claire slowed further and turned onto the road. "How far in is it?"

"Not far. Road goes right up to it. Can't miss it."

As the truck moved in deeper the forest pressed in on them, branches whipping the sides of the truck. It grew gloomy as the leaves blanketed them from the overcast sky. They passed the remnants of the fallen tree, went down and around, came back up. Claire slowed, the brakes squeaking them to a stop.

Below sat the cabin.

And parked next to the cabin was a red car.

"That's the car that ran me off the road," Claire mumbled. "I'm sure of it."

Tentatively, she pressed the accelerator, and they descended into the valley.

* * *

Willem supported Stavic as they made their way toward the cabin. Willem had tried to convince Stavic to stay put, that he'd only slow them down, but he'd refused to let them go on alone without him. Something about wanting to see this through to the end.

When they reached the porch Stavic said, "Wait." The wind had stopped and save for a single cawing crow off some distance, the forest was silent. Stavic stepped away from Willem, hobbled onto the single step leading to the porch, his boot clomping on the old wood. He pulled his gun and raised it, letting it lead. He tried the knob and pushed it open, the door swinging inward with a long steady creak. He stepped in and disappeared into the shadows.

Seconds ticked by, adrenaline coursing through Willem. He was ready to rush in to aid Stavic if he needed help. His tension eased when Stavic called out the place was clear.

"Is she here?" Claire asked hopefully as they entered.

"Empty," Stavic said. "There's nothing here."

Willem patted his jacket pocket, felt the metal ring within. Of course! Where had he found it?

He thought back to his childhood, stepped back to the entrance. "When I was a boy," he said slowly as he retraced his footsteps, "I felt something pulling at me. It guided me around…" He was talking more to himself, trying to visualize his movements as a boy, trying to remember where he'd found the ring. The floor was in remarkably good shape considering this place had been subjected to the elements for decades. He turned, walked towards a couch. It had been right about—

"Here!" The excitement he felt was palpable. He patted the couch. "Under here! We have to move it!"

"I told you we went over everything in this place. There's nothing here."

"Did you move it?"

Willem grunted as he pulled and pushed the couch. He felt his back straining. Finally, when the couch was pulled away from the wall, he looked over the back.

Nothing!

"But… it was right here."

Willem reached into his pocket and thought back. This is where it was; he was sure of it. Maybe he was wrong? Maybe there was no hatch after all, or maybe the ring had been dropped or…

His fingers grazed the necklace in his pocket and he felt a spark. Curious, he pulled it out, stared at it. Nothing special about it except… The pendant dangled at an awkward angle defying gravity. What the hell? He let the necklace guide him, taking a few steps to the side until it pointed down properly and crouched. The pendant tapped the wood, the chain curling up around it.

A square section of the floor cast a dim hallow glow, the hatch becoming visible.

"I knew it!" Willem beamed.

"Well I'll be a son of a gun. Blends in well, I'll give you that."

The indentation of where the handle was supposed to be was caked in dirt. He leaned down, cleared it out.

"Do you have a crowbar in the car?" asked Claire. "I'm not sure we'll get this open otherwise."

"I have something better." Willem reached into his pocket and pulled out the ring. "I took this when I was a boy. Never knew why."

He placed the ring in the indentation, and there was a tiny *clink*. Willem pulled on the ring and, as if by magic, it was connected to the hatch. He pulled and the hatch opened silently. He peered in, a ladder descending into blackness toward a pixel of light far below. Stavic aimed the beam from his flashlight into the hole, the light swallowed.

"I don't remember anything like this from what David showed us. What is this?"

"We don't have Lilly. Maybe she had a means to bypass this." Willem sat, dangled his legs over the side. "Come on. Let's start climbing."

"Whoa, whoa, whoa. Are you nuts? You have no idea what's down there." Stavic glared at him.

"It's not like we have a choice."

Stavic, obviously torn, conceded. "Fine. But I'm going first. Move."

"Now wait a minute—"

"No discussion."

Willem knew it was a futile debate so slid out of the way. Stavic grabbed the necklace and held it up. "Think we'll need it?"

"Can't hurt to take it."

Stavic pocketed it and climbed down.

Willem looked at Claire. "You next. I'll bring up the rear."

She didn't fight him, simply slid her legs into the hole, and followed Stavic down the ladder.

As soon as he knew there was ample spacing Willem followed, the darkness consuming him.

* * *

It was a long climb. Stavic wasn't sure how much time had passed, but they never seemed to make any headway toward the light. He began to wonder less about what was at the bottom of the abyss and more about how far a drop it was.

"How you doing up there?" Stavic asked.

"Doing alright." Willem's wheezing said otherwise.

"Claire?"

"Is now a bad time to tell you I'm afraid of heights?"

He stopped, looked up. "Serious?"

"Just keep moving." There was a quiver in her voice.

The three continued to climb. For Stavic, past memories began to creep back. His life in Chicago, working undercover, Jennifer, his mother... memories buried in cocaine and booze. He shook it off, not wanting to relive them. Ancient history, better left buried.

The next time he looked at the light it seemed it was closer, and something was materializing from the dark. "I think we're almost there."

"What do you see?" Claire asked.

It was a white rectangle, maybe three-feet-by-four, and the ladder disappeared into it. "Not sure yet."

He climbed the remaining distance silently praying to nothing in particular that if he did die that it would be quick and painless. His feet were on the last rung before they disappeared.

Willem asked, "What do you suppose it is?"

Stavic shook his head. "Only one way to find out."

He reached down with the tip of his boot and tried to tap, but his foot went through, disappearing into the light. Stavic closed his eyes, breathed to calm his nerves, and reached down farther.

While he didn't feel anything to stand on, he could feel gravity pulling his leg down, and there was a slight pins and needles sensation. He let it go and his foot bumped a surface. "I feel something, not sure what though. Wish me luck." He put his other leg through and climbed down, his arms straining.

And then the strain disappeared and his legs took the weight and he was standing. Stavic pulled himself through the rest of the way.

At first he couldn't believe what he was seeing, and he blinked away the flash of brightness that stabbed his brain. Then that, too, washed away, and Stavic was standing in a white room. David lie unconscious in a bed, and DeMarcus sat in a chair grinning. Next to him was a man in a red cap. Behind them was a strange photo of an empty wooden room, a dark window set in the wall.

Stavic turned back and looked at his own reflection and realized that that is where he'd come from, that he'd climbed out of a goddamn mirror.

"Stop! Don't come down!" he screamed and tried reaching into the mirror. Instead his fingers touched its smooth cool surface. He pounded on it with his fist trying to let Willem and Claire know not to come through. Stavic knew it was futile when Claire's legs came through. He hit them, trying desperately to stop her, to warn her of the trap. Claire pulled herself through.

"What the hell?" she said. "Where's Emily?"

Willem dropped out next, staggered, and Stavic helped balance him.

"So predictable," DeMarcus said and laughed.

* * *

225

Willem was having trouble keeping focus. He felt like vomiting. "Dad?" he managed say.

The man in the red cap regarded him.

"No longer I'm afraid," DeMarcus said.

Willem ignored him and addressed his father. "It's really you. But... how? Why?"

Yet his father only stared at him and said nothing. But... was that a glimmer of recognition?

"Where's my daughter?" Claire asked.

That cool head movement and DeMarcus focused on Claire. "She's here."

"Where?" she asked.

DeMarcus breathed deeply as if enjoying the scent of a flowering garden. "What do you think this place is?" He passed his hand through the air.

"The doorway to Turmoore," Willem offered.

"That it is." DeMarcus nodded with approval. A discomforting notion, Willem thought. "Well, more a bubble, I suppose, between Turmoore and your... place." The final word seeped of disdain. "It's a watchtower, a moat, a blockade. It's all these things and more, all for a single purpose: to stop the re-entry to perfection. Do you know why?" No one responded. "Because those cast down are sullied and unworthy of living in it."

"I just want my daughter back." Claire's voice quivered ever so slightly.

DeMarcus stood in one fluid movement and, for the first time, his expression faltered. "That's not an option. You see, I need her to return home. Her and one other."

"Wh... why?" Claire stammered.

"Turmoore is better than your place. It's above, not below. Layer upon layer upon layer. In the grand scheme of things I know not where we lay, only that they exist."

"We know all this," Willem interrupted. "David told us." He continued to watch his father trying to understand why he was in league with a madman.

"David?" he asked with a glance at the old unconscious man. "Oh. I see." He turned back, seemingly displeased. "So you understand the two never connect as was its design. The synergy held in tandem by some invisible force. Co-existing but never influencing directly, only indirectly. You die you move up to the next floor.

Good, bad, it doesn't matter. It's the same on all levels. A constant for all."

"Like our Heaven and Hell," Stavic offered, sounding proud of himself.

At least he'd been listening, Willem thought.

"Please!" scoffed DeMarcus. "Would you believe in a talking lamb? No… that's too archaic. A human construct to understand a complex realization you are not yet ready for. We were that way too, for a long time, but then we found…" He inhaled, the air whistling through his lips. "There is no word to describe it. But then we found you, and we watched you like you might a colony of ants. We began to understand where we came from and where we were going to. The knowledge there was life before drove us to explore life after. We had tasted the past, now we longed for what came after.

"You see, while we come from your level we don't remember it, much like you don't remember what came before you. We were curious, and in our curiosity we broke down the barrier to understand. But the expeditions we sent never came back, and we learned that there was a failsafe in place that prevented it. But, anything that is a failsafe has a probability of failing itself.

"While we looked for a way to bring our people back, others came up with the idea of using your plane as a sort of prison—a place to send the exiled. The other thing we learned is that the flesh is destroyed, that their memories are wiped out, competing souls in a single body. Usually it all balances out becoming harmonious, but on occasion conflict emerges. And on the rarest of the rare—and it's only been documented a handful of times—a person doesn't forget about Turmoore at all." His smile grew. "Being exiled here…" He shook his head gravely.

Willem wondered if there was a way to reach his father, to have him help. He couldn't believe his father would allow his own son to be killed at the hands of DeMarcus. But if he'd been corrupted maybe he wouldn't think twice?

What was it Lilly had told David? That when a Turmoorian presence descended and entered a host that the casual observer wouldn't notice. But sometimes some people *did.* His father must have been one of them; he must have sensed something had changed in Willem.

"How is it you haven't aged?" Stavic asked.

"You assume time is as you perceive it; it's not. In here, time does not exist." He paused, eyed each one. "I assume David told you of me? What did he say?"

"That you led a revolution. That you wanted to marry Lilly."

DeMarcus nodded, said, "Everything was ruined when they went into hiding. When we found her parents Lilly was gone, and it took considerable effort to learn where she'd been taken. They robbed me of her, so I came looking, damning myself to your existence.

"When I got here I didn't know where she was, though I could sense her." He cocked his head, eyes danced. "I stepped onto your plane once. I felt dirty, violated, and I dreaded having to further contaminate myself in your filth. I was lucky to have found a shell to traverse your plane, and I used him to track Lilly down. Her foster parents were strong, but they cracked as I knew they would, just like Lilly's parents."

"So it was you," Stavic mumbled. "You killed the Shaw's. Back in '57, it was you."

DeMarcus shrugged. "Indirectly. The pain they suffered is nothing to what I endured. Not only did I learn of her accident, that she lay dying in your archaic hospital, but that she also married him. She was almost lost until I stepped in." A slight head tilt to David. "Ironic now that he is as she was."

"Why didn't you just kill him too?"

"I'm not a monster. Had I done that then there'd be no way of convincing her to return to me, to honor our agreement. No… I needed to find another way. I knew if I just bided my time then maybe I could change her mind.

"After she returned home I paid her a visit to try and convince her to come back with me, but it was futile. She refused, and I was powerless to force her."

"I was lost. I didn't know what to do. I couldn't go on nor could I go back, and as much as Lilly was lost to me I was lost to myself." He paused, looked at each in turn. "So here I was stuck in your world, and a world I'd conquered left crumbling. And then it hit me. I knew the affection she had toward a young neighbor girl, the daughter she'd never had." DeMarcus looked at Claire. "I knew then I had what I needed to convince her.

"Unfortunately it didn't go according to plan. Lilly betrayed me a second time and I ended up imprisoned in there." He gestured to an old wooden door. "She probably didn't expect me to survive but, well…" He looked at Willem. "I have your father to thank for that."

"He released you?" Willem asked.

"I didn't have a way of unlocking the door between *belere* and this place like Lilly did. He stumbled in here seeking refuge and opened the door allowing me to pass through. For that I released him of his pain and confusion and promised he could return to Turmoore with me. He was also there when David and Lilly came and was knocked unconscious but, thankfully, came to and released me again. I am forever in debt to him."

"If Lilly is gone," Claire said, "then why are you after my daughter? What has Emily got to do with this?"

"Because she's not gone." His lips curled. "It confused me to say the least. First I found David and then you. Her presence in two places. How surprised I was to find that little neighbor girl Lilly adored. But it wasn't you she was a part of but your daughter; somehow she managed to transfer herself to her. And to him," he said, acknowledging David with a glance.

"I don't know where she is, but I'll never let you get your hands on her," Claire said.

"It's unfortunate you say that. You see I already have her."

"Where!" Claire roared.

"She's safe, and I will give her the most wonderful gift imaginable. Not only will she help me return to Turmoore, she will also be at my side. And, with the ability to move between planes, we will be gods. We will learn all there is to know, who created the realms and orchestrated our existence, and join them."

"No!" Claire screamed and charged DeMarcus.

Then she stood frozen, unmoving. Willem tried to go to her but was unable. All he could do was stand motionless, eyes ahead, watching the grinning DeMarcus.

"The necklace… who has it?" His eyes darted between the three of them before landing on Stavic. "Bring it to me."

Stavic glided toward DeMarcus. Willem was sure Stavic was fighting DeMarcus' control but was powerless to stop it. He came to a standstill in front of DeMarcus and reached into his pocket and pulled out the necklace.

"Beautiful. Just beautiful," cooed DeMarcus.

A scream erupted from within the picture. High pitched, terrified. It echoed through the room. DeMarcus joined in, screaming a deep baritone. Together the screams faded out as the air left their lungs. Emily emerged in the frame, looking around aimlessly, scared. She looked right at them—*through* them—yet did not see.

DeMarcus grasped the necklace, and the world began to darken and burn like newspaper in a fire. Pieces broke free and floated away, orange embers burning out high above. The white room dissolved around them leaving the underlying cabin.

And then Emily appeared, opaque at first, then solid, DeMarcus' red capped man behind her.

Dad! Willem wanted to shout. All this time he thought his father had run off or died, but here he was working with DeMarcus. He looked the same he did the last time he saw him all those years ago, the day he'd walked out after saying those terrible things.

She looked around. "Mom!" she screamed, pulling herself free from Willem's father's grasp. DeMarcus signaled to Willem's father to stay as Emily ran to Claire and threw her arms around her. Yet Claire didn't move.

Must be killing her not being able to embrace her daughter.

"Come out, come out Lilly. I know you're here," DeMarcus sing-songed, his eyes searching the room. "I can't believe you're going to stay hidden away like this. Are you truly going to sacrifice these people?"

"Why are you doing this? What did you do to her?" Emily screamed.

"I don't have time for your petty games. If you need convincing then I best start with the man you love."

Stavic approached David, pulled out his gun, and aimed it.

* * *

It was the strangest sensation. She could feel but couldn't move. When she heard the screaming she knew instantly who it was. She wanted to cry out, run for her daughter, protect her. Then when she saw Emily in that picture her heart sank. She felt powerless. Then, when she appeared right in front of her, ran to her and hugged her, she felt even more so. She couldn't even wrap her arms around her.

Claire watched as Stavic moved to the side of David's bed, pulled out his gun, and pointed it at his face.

No! Don't do it! she wanted to scream.

She felt Emily stiffen and pull back, saw a glimmer in her eye. Her demeanor hardened. This wasn't her daughter; these eyes were that of aged experience. Emily's jaw set.

Not Emily. Lilly.

"Wait," Lilly said, the word commanding and unflinching. She turned from Claire, faced down DeMarcus. "Enough."

"That's a neat trick you pulled," DeMarcus said, "entering Claire and then Emily as you have. Though I have to admit I'm perplexed how you achieved it."

"As am I regarding how you escaped *belere*."

DeMarcus stepped towards Lilly, eyed her up. "I have to admit that you choose well. You're even more stunning now."

"And you're a lecher."

A shrug. "I have good taste." Another step; Lilly held her ground. "So, Lilly, will you deny our original agreement?"

"After killing my parents? I think the agreement is void."

"That was only because they hid you from me."

"Can you blame them?"

"I can blame them for a great many things."

"You *think* you can, but—really—it boils down to madness."

DeMarcus' grin dropped ever so slightly. Must have hit a nerve. Claire wanted to know what Willem and Stavic were thinking.

"I'm not mad."

"You waged a war."

"A revolution."

"Call it what you will. You attacked us. You attacked the people. Turmoore hadn't seen such blight in over a millennium."

DeMarcus chuckled. "I see what you're trying to do. You're trying to convince me that I was wrong." Another step. In a mocking tone, he said, "Please take me back and put me away. You were right!" For the first time his smile dropped, eyes hardened. It caused a shiver to run through Claire.

"You could have ruled, could have run Turmoore as you saw fit. No one would have stopped you."

"You would have."

She nodded. "I would have tried. Out of curiosity, why didn't you go back to Turmoore? Surely you could have."

"It requires the two of us. You and me. Of this I'm sure." He stepped closer. "Why did you stay? Your father, before I cut out his tongue, told me you were supposed to return when you were twenty."

Her eyes flicked to David lying helpless in his bed. DeMarcus did not miss it.

"Are you kidding me? You stayed for him? Is that why you didn't transcend when your body gave out?"

"You wouldn't understand," Lilly said with a hint of sadness.

DeMarcus exploded, spit flying. "I came here for you! Don't you dare claim I don't understand!" And as suddenly as his anger flared, he regained his composure, eyeing her. "Do you have any idea what your staying here has cost Turmoore? Death. A plague across the entire plane that is wiping out all."

Lilly's brows furrowed. "You lie."

"Did your parents never tell you who you really were? Why you were supposed to return at twenty?"

What was that? The sensation of pins and needles in her extremities. Claire tried to wiggle her fingers, thought she saw one move ever so slightly, but not again. Shit!

DeMarcus chuckled, and then it turned into a hearty laugh. Claire wasn't sure if he actually thought it was funny, or was provoking her, trying to get under her skin. Once the laugher died away, he said, "You are the embodiment of Turmoore, the physical representation of all existence on our plane. When you stayed here, the realm perished."

"You lie," Lilly said again, a tremor in her voice.

"Believe me, don't believe me, I care not. When you return you'll see for yourself."

She couldn't tell if he was lying—the desperate ramblings of a madman—or if he was telling the truth. One thing had to be said, he was convincing. She could almost appreciate his plight.

Almost.

Lilly glanced at Claire. "Release her."

"You'll come with me?"

Lilly looked at DeMarcus. "Release them all." Her voice was firm and commanding, a degree of defiance she'd never heard in her daughter's voice.

And without warning Claire could move.

* * *

David was having an out of body experience. He could see and hear what was happening, not from his frail shell, but instead as a specter. He could move about the room freely. His heart hurt seeing Lilly superimposed over Emily.

"I will go with you so long as you let them leave," Lilly said.

"Done," DeMarcus responded with a shrug. "I have no need for them anyway. They can go about their insignificant lives as far as I'm concerned."

"So… that's it?" DeMarcus and Emily turned to Claire, her eyes wide. "What about Emily?"

"She is host to Lilly." He said it matter-of-fact, as if that should be answer enough.

"She… she has to go with you?" She looked at Emily. "What will happen to her once you leave?"

Lilly said nothing; Emily's eyes said it all.

"No!" Claire screamed, making a grab for her. DeMarcus raised his hand and Claire flew across the room, crashing to the floor. She picked herself up, sobbing. "You can't take her! She's all I have left!"

"A pity," DeMarcus cooed.

"Please! You can't! She's still a child!"

"I need Lilly to return to Turmoore, Lilly is in Emily. I'm sure you understand the position I'm in."

Claire stood on shaky legs. "I won't let you."

"Won't?"

With a flick of his hand, DeMarcus sent Claire sailing through the air again. This time the wind was knocked from her.

"Stop it," Lilly said. "What you're doing… it's unnecessary."

DeMarcus ignored her as he watched Claire get on her hands and knees. "Stay down, Claire. There's no need for this."

"You will not take my daughter." She stared him down, fury in her eyes.

DeMarcus raised his hand, Claire's body stiffening. She looked as if she were preparing for a punch to the gut.

A deafening gunshot rang out. DeMarcus flinched and looked around wildly. He stood stoic and unmoving, stared down Stavic.

"Your weapon will not work on me."

"You will leave her alone. Both of them. Claire and Emily are staying."

"That's not possible. We have to return to save our people."

"Bullshit. I don't buy it."

"Whether you buy it or not is irrelevant. I will not be stuck in here or on your plane indefinitely. My time is at an end and Lilly is my key."

Willem glanced at his father, cut in. "Why are you convinced you need her?"

"Her parents would not have sent her here unless they had a way to bring her back. No parent would do that."

"Our history is full of parents that have done that, parents that would stop at nothing to ensure their children survive, even if it meant never seeing them again."

"They told me—"

"What you needed to hear. You were cutting out their tongues for god sake. People will say anything under duress."

DeMarcus considered it. "No they would not have lied. Not to me." He grabbed Emily's arm. "You will not break another agreement. I spare them and you come with me. If not for me, then for our people."

He marched her to the door, Claire howling behind. She lunged but was caught by Willem, who struggled to hold her back.

"Do you want to get yourself killed?" he asked.

"But Emily—"

"We'll find a way."

On the opposite end of the room DeMarcus pushed Emily to the door, Willem's father falling into step behind. DeMarcus glanced back. "Where are you going?"

"With you."

DeMarcus chuckled, shook his head. "No."

"You promised. After I saved you, you said I'd go with you."

"I say a lot of things," he said and cocked his head.

Willem's father was thrown back, smashing into a wall. He crumpled to the ground, unmoving.

"Open it," DeMarcus screamed, shaking her. "Open it now!"

She scowled at him, said slowly, "Let. Me. Go."

He did and took a step back.

Stavic moved next to Willem and Claire all the while keeping his gun trained on DeMarcus.

DeMarcus slammed his fist against the door, screaming, "Open it!"

Emily gave one sad look back and made eye contact with Claire. "I'll protect her."

"No!" Claire cried, tears streaming down her cheeks. She fought Willem, but the man held her back. "Let me go with you! Let me come!"

"I'm sorry, Claire, but it doesn't work that way." There was a brief flash in her eye, then, "Goodbye, mother," and she looked away.

Emily removed the necklace from around her neck and palmed the pendant, wrapping her fingers around it.

David watched sadly. It wasn't supposed to have been like this, and he felt like an abject failure. All he'd planned to do was return to River Bend and warn Claire and Emily away from DeMarcus. That's what Lilly had wanted him to do, that's what he believed she'd been telling him. He'd almost done it too but DeMarcus had stopped him. Here he was, witness to an event he'd been trying to stop, powerless to do anything about it.

Emily opened her hand, the key sitting in it.

DeMarcus' lips curled. "Excellent," he said. "Open it."

She slid the key into the lock and twisted it. There was a *click* and the door opened an inch, the industrial sound David remembered reverberated through the room. Emily pulled the key out of the lock, and DeMarcus grasped the door. He pulled it open and was greeted by blackness on the other side.

DeMarcus, in a very gentlemanly way, offered Emily to take the lead by extending his arm out. She moved into the doorway.

"No!" roared Claire. Willem tried to hold on but lost his grip and Claire swiveled to Stavic. "Shoot him!" she cried and grabbed for the gun in one last frantic move. The gun went off and there was a sharp squeal. Emily dropped to the floor.

The gun blast faded, and all eyes were on Emily as a pool of blood formed beneath her.

Lilly!

"Emily!" called out Claire, sobbing.

How…? Why…? David couldn't wrap his mind around what he saw. He'd seen Lilly nearly die once, then pass away twenty years ago. Was he really going to be subjected to her death a second time?

"What have you done?" DeMarcus said, monotone. He looked from the struggling girl at his feet to Stavic and Claire, eyes wide and on fire. He gritted his teeth, raised his arms and pointed at them. Both went flying across the room, the gun dropping. DeMarcus slammed them from one wall to the next, bouncing them like a ball in a pinball machine.

Willem ran toward DeMarcus. His body froze and crumpled to the floor.

"You killed her!" DeMarcus bellowed as he took a step forward, continuing to slam Stavic and Claire against the walls.

What can I do? How do I stop this? Yet all David could do was stand there and watch helplessly.

And then he saw movement. Emily lifted her head and skimmed the floor, her eyes locking on the key. She stretched for it, grimacing in pain, snatched it up, and looked directly at David.

If he was breathing it surely would have caught. *Does she see me?* Emily smiled.

From the other side of the door came the terrifying screech he remembered from oh so long ago, and in the blackness he saw movement. Through the doorway a four clawed lizard-like foot slammed into DeMarcus, knocking him to the ground. His concentration broken, Stavic and Claire fell to the ground, and Willem began to move.

DeMarcus stood and glared at the trio, eyes blazing. "When I'm through with you, you'll be begging for death." He moved toward them, raising his hand.

Willem's father crashed into DeMarcus taking him down. They grunted and landed in a heap, the wind knocked from their lungs.

An ear piercing screech projected through the room, and DeMarcus looked back, a mix of anger and surprise on his face. Then that melted to horror as a giant raptor-like eye peeked through the door. There was another screech and DeMarcus flipped over, hands and feet slipping as he tried to scramble back.

The clawed foot jetted through the door and slammed into DeMarcus. He screamed in pain as one claw pierced his shoulder and was dragged to the door. He kicked and fought, pounding on the foot.

He lifted his other hand, took aim at the creature. The things eye exploded and it howled in pain. It shook its talon until DeMarcus slid off.

"You're dead! You're all dead!"

Before he could say another word the *gormock* grabbed him again. "No!" he screamed, fighting to keep his footing. He was almost to the door, the creature on the other side screeching angrily.

DeMarcus reached out his hands, grabbed the edge of the door and the door frame, holding on, pulling. The *gormock* began to lose its grip, DeMarcus slipping through its talons.

And then he was standing, the creature's hold gone. The world slowed, and DeMarcus started to close the door, his trademark grin forming.

If he closes that then all is lost.

Before anyone could react Willem's father slammed his shoulder into DeMarcus, wrapped an arm around his body, and propelled him through.

"Dad!" Willem screamed, watching the *gormock* moving toward the two men.

Then the door closed and all was silent.

* * *

Lilly picked herself up off the floor and leaned against the door, the pain in Emily's abdomen intense. She pulled her blood covered hand away and looked down at the wound. Got her good. She felt woozy, probably wouldn't last long unless this was taken care of.

DeMarcus' words came back to her. Could her staying have caused the death of those in Turmoore? She couldn't see how that was possible, and DeMarcus was known to embellish and lie to further his cause. It stood to reason he was saying whatever he could to get her to go back. After all, he was misguided about her returning at twenty. She and her foster parents were supposed to continue monitoring the doorway for signs when a return trip was possible, but nothing ever came of it. Then she fell in love and got married and forgot about the door.

By the time of their initial confrontation, she'd become too invested in her life here with David, and decided to stick with the fall back plan—live her life until dying of old age and then transcend back to Turmoore. But first she needed to protect herself, so she'd given a part of herself to Claire. Once she was sure DeMarcus was gone, that he wasn't going to pursue her again, she'd take it back.

The problem was Claire's parents moved without a goodbye, and that part of Lilly was lost to her. She could always sense it, but pinpointing it was too difficult. So when her frail body began to give out she had no choice but to give the other part of herself to David in the hopes her two halves would find each other at a later date.

As the cancer in David grew she knew her time was running out, and that either she needed to find her other half or transport herself to a new host. But then something strange happened—a flare up—and she could clearly see where her other half was.

Emily.

She could only assume the flare-up happened when it transferred from Claire to Emily. Why that happened she didn't know, but she was thankful. How surprised she'd been to find Claire had returned to River Bend. She wasn't strong enough to take control but she saw a clear path, so she sent David images, praying he got the message.

She felt the universe was working against her. She was so close to Emily, so close to being whole, when DeMarcus put her poor David in a coma. She was stuck and powerless to do anything. What happened when David died and only half of her transcended? That was an unknown, and it terrified her.

How interesting that fate had a way of working itself out.

When DeMarcus released her from her prison and she had appeared next to David she began the process of merging. DeMarcus must have sensed it, because that's when he called her out.

Stavic and Claire stood groggily, bruised and battered. Whatever Claire was feeling must have disappeared because she ran over and enveloped her in a big hug. The pain was excruciating, but Lilly couldn't help but feel love.

"Oh baby! Oh my God! Are you alright?" Claire looked at the wound, pressed her hand to it.

Willem crouched, pulled Claire's blood covered hands away, and rolled up Emily's shirt. "I might be able to slow it, but it's deep. We need to get to a hospital."

She couldn't return to Turmoore like DeMarcus suspected, so she had only two options: stay in Emily and return with Claire letting the natural order of things work its magic, or stay here and let Emily die. It all hinged on whether or not DeMarcus was telling the truth. If she let Emily live and DeMarcus was right then Turmoore would most certainly perish, possibly all of existence. If she let Emily die she might still have a chance to save everyone.

The choice was a no brainer: the survival of countless lives for the sacrifice of one.

"I can't," she groaned. "I have to go back. DeMarcus is a liar, yes, but if by some chance he was telling the truth I have to try to stop it."

"But my daughter—"

"Will be safe."

"No," Claire moaned. "No, you can't."

"There's no other way. I don't have the ability to return like DeMarcus thought. The path is one way."

Claire wrapped Emily's in her arms and sobbed into the crook of her neck, whispered, "Please don't do this."

"I have no choice. I wish there was another way…" She let the words trail off. Standing over them were Stavic and Willem, both looking on with sad eyes. "Why don't you three go. You don't need to be here for this."

Claire shook her head. "No. I'm not leaving." She pulled back and asked, "Can I speak to her? Can I at least say good bye?"

She nodded. "Of course."

She could sense the girl wince as the pain hit her. "Mom?"

Fresh tears sprang to Claire's eyes. "Emily! Oh Emily!" She wrapped her arms around her, nearly crushing her, in a bear hug.

Emily began to cry too. "I'm so sorry, mom."

"Me too, sweetie." Claire stroked Emily's hair. "I let things get out of hand."

"I was just… I don't know what I was thinking."

"You don't need to explain. I know."

Emily shook her head. "No. You don't. I let you down, mom. I let you down."

"Don't say that. I'm the one who should be apologizing. The last couple years… none of that should have been on your shoulders. It was supposed to be me taking care of you, not the other way around. I am so proud of you. And I love you so very much."

"I'm scared," Emily whispered.

"It's alright to be. But Lilly… she's a good person, and she'll protect you."

"I don't want to go."

"I don't think we have much of a choice."

Claire gave her a sad yet reassuring smile, and kissed her on the cheek.

Emily took a deep breath and said, "I'm ready then."

Lilly moved forward taking control again. The look in Claire's eyes was heartbreaking. "I'll stay in control so she doesn't feel anything. We'll fade together and wake up in Turmoore," Lilly said.

"What will it be like?"

"I don't really know. This is uncharted territory."

They sat in silence, enjoying each other's final company. At some point Lilly realized Stavic and Willem had moved to the opposite end of the room giving Claire and Emily their privacy. Not much time left, maybe thirty minutes. She knew because exhaustion was setting in.

Lilly knew it was unfair to Claire and Emily, but there was no other choice. None. She'd spent a lifetime and more trying to understand the intricacies of the planes. It made sense but it didn't, convoluted yet simple. Maybe she should just close her eyes and let it happen.

"Wait," said a haggard old voice.

Lilly looked in the direction it had come from.

Her husband was awake.

* * *

He couldn't let it go down like this. Claire and Emily shouldn't have to suffer for something they were thrown into. Watching them, replaying his life and all he knew, there had to be something that could be done. And then it dawned on him.

Me.

Lilly could transfer herself into others. She'd done it once with Claire, and again with him. Why not again?

He glided to his body and stared down at himself. How old and frail he'd become. If he could re-enter himself would he be able to wake? How was he to do this?

He reached out and his hand passed through his body. That wouldn't work. What else? Maybe if he just focused on himself…

The lights around him began to dim. A quick glance at the others confirmed it was he who was seeing this, not them; they had no reaction. He focused, the room growing dark. His limbs started to tingle, he could feel his heart beating. It was slow and struggling, but there. And then all light went out. He felt air in his lungs, the soft cloth of the bedding, the pillow beneath his head.

It was a struggle, but he managed to open his eyes, the room burning his retinas. He squinted, blinked away the fog, and saw.

"Wait," he croaked. There was startled movement from everyone as they turned to him. Claire, Willem, and Stavic were shocked, Emily joyous. The love he saw was exuberant. With the help of Claire she stood and came to him.

"David!" Lilly said.

"It's been so long," his voice rasped softly.

"It has," she agreed warmly.

"You… you don't have much time…"

"No."

"You don't have to take her. Me. Use me."

There was a moment of confusion, and then her face brightened.

"I don't… I don't understand." Claire looked between the two.

Lilly explained, "Why didn't I think of it? I'll transfer to David."

"I've lived my life. Emily… she's not ready for this. Not yet."

Claire broke down again, this time in joy. She cupped her hands over her mouth.

"What do you need me to do?" he asked.

"Nothing. But we must hurry. Neither you nor Emily has much time." She addressed Stavic and Willem. "You'll have to get her to the hospital. As soon as I vacate her body get her out of here."

They nodded. She turned back to David.

"Are you ready?" He nodded. "Alright."

She leaned in and kissed him on the lips. It was warm and soft, strange yet familiar. She kissed him again on the cheek, and a final one on his brow. She pulled back, smiled.

"Was that necessary?" he croaked.

She responded with a smile and closed her eyes.

Then she was in him, sharing his failing body. Emily's eyes fluttered, Claire helping stabilize her.

What of the cabin? he asked.

It is now just a vacant cabin.

Will they be okay?

I think so.

Will we?

Yes.

He stood next to his expiring body, turned and saw Lilly. She was as he remembered her: stunning, perfect, flawless. And for the first time in over twenty years they embraced, waiting for the inevitable.

epilogue

Claire watched the priest conduct the service. More people had turned up than she had expected, braving the cold weather and all. She'd been hoping it would be a clear day, but the weather hadn't cooperated. There was nothing worse than gray skies and a brisk wind to sour an already dreary event. She felt fingers entwine with hers and looked over.

"You okay, mom?" Emily whispered.

"Yes. Just thinking."

"About...?"

Claire gave her a smile and hugged her. "Nothing important."

Emily turned back to the priest who was saying his final words about David Rottingham.

They had almost lost Emily; the trip back had taken longer than they had anticipated. While they'd been in the room the storm had come back with a vengeance, turning the dirt road into slippery mud. They'd almost gotten stuck twice, but Willem had managed to maneuver the car enough to keep it going. When they were almost into town Stavic had called a doctor friend of his letting him know the situation. When they'd pulled up to the hospital Emily was unconscious, but the staff was prepared. The surgery had been quick, and she'd made a speedy recovery. Doctor Johnson hadn't wanted her to leave the hospital for the funeral, but Emily had insisted, promising to return immediately after for a few more nights of observation.

"Where is he? Dad."

Claire had told Emily what really happened with Devon. Emily was surprised to say the least, thought her mother had kept it a secret all these years, but she must have sensed Claire's adamants and softened to the news. She'd brought the box to the hospital let her sift through the items. Emily seemed happy.

Claire pointed to a section of the cemetery. "Over there. Once we're done here we'll pay him a visit."

Emily nodded, a soft smile forming.

Claire looked across and met Willem's eyes.

* * *

Claire looked so happy, so content. She should be—she'd saved her daughter.

Willem was full of mixed emotions. All these years he'd hated his father and wanted to know what had become of him. Now he knew and he didn't feel any better. Piecing together the chain of events he could only assume that after the accident his father had come across the property where the cabin was. Drunk and scared, he must have been easy to manipulate, taking on a roll DeMarcus needed. Who knows what promises and lies DeMarcus had fed him.

At least he had some closure, something his mother or brothers never had.

After all the events that had transpired Willem decided it was time to retire. He had put his two weeks in the other day and was looking forward to it. All these years he'd focused on everyone else but himself, did nothing for himself, letting his past consume him. Enough was enough; it was time to move forward.

He wasn't sure what he was going to do, but he was going to start by visiting Beth and Gregory and Margaret and their kids. It was time to rekindle a relationship with his family.

Sometimes you just have to let it go, Willem, Elliott had said. *Sometimes there just isn't an answer to be had.*

A partial answer was better than no answer.

The world was a big place, that much was certain. There was a lot to see and a lot to do. Why not follow in David's footsteps and live a little?

* * *

Stavic stood at the back of the crowd as the priest spoke the final prayer. He'd had a few days to digest events and felt no closer to closure. He wasn't angry or sad, simply… he didn't know.

When they lived each other's lives he caught a glimpse, and it awakened an urge to learn more about his real father. He seemed like a good man who lived a tragic life. He wanted to learn more. There seemed to be a lot of old timers, people that knew either his father or his wife. Maybe he'd start talking to them and learn more.

He found it interesting how all their lives entwined one rainy night when Willem's father had gotten into an accident with David and Lilly. If not for that how different their lives may have been.

He may not have even been born. There was an amusing thought. And if he hadn't been born what of all the people he'd influenced throughout the years? Would Jennifer still be alive, or would she have OD'd alone in a gutter? At least he'd been able to be by her side.

Influences. He wondered if they were all influenced by the planes above and below somehow, that maybe all their actions here were the result of some cosmic force, a magnetism or gravitational tug-of-war between two others.

His head hurt and he wanted a line, but he'd sworn it off. He also let Charles know he better stop selling or he'd come down on him and hard.

You wouldn't, he'd said. *I've got too much dirt on you.*

True, but that dirt had less power if he'd fess up to his superior which he'd done this morning. Sheriff Kinney wasn't happy with the news and after a short mulling had suspended him without pay. He hadn't been all that surprised and hoped, within time, that he could prove to Kinney he was clean. He aimed to try.

He watched Claire put an arm around Emily. She didn't object.

The priest finished his prayer, and David's casket was lowered into the ground.

Now that you've finished *The Lost Door*
please review it!

http://amzn.com/069241892X

Marc Buhmann initially focused on filmmaking and has worked as a writer, director, and producer on several award winning short films. His 2006 feature film, *Dead in the Water*, has been licensed for distribution in seven countries.

In recent years he has focused his energy on fiction. Marc also has a deep rooted passion for astronomy and, because of that, loves science fiction.

Marc lives near Chicago, Illinois with his wife and two sons.

Connect with Me:

Facebook: facebook.com/marcbbuhmann
Twitter: twitter.com/MarcBuhmann
Tumblr: marcbuhmann.tumblr.com

marcbuhmann.com

www.ingramcontent.com/pod-product-compliance
Lightning Source LLC
Chambersburg PA
CBHW070911180626
46817CB00003B/1017